MERCY
———————

THE LOST WARSHIP BOOK TWO

DANIEL GIBBS

Mercy by Daniel Gibbs

Copyright © 2022-2023 by Daniel Gibbs

Visit Daniel Gibbs website at

www.danielgibbsauthor.com

Cover by Jeff Brown Graphics—www.jeffbrowngraphics.com

Additional Illustrations by Joel Steudler—www.joelsteudler.com

This book is a work of fiction, the characters, incidents and dialogues are products of the author's imagination and are not to be construed as real. Any resemblance to actual persons, living or dead, is entirely coincidental.

All rights reserved. This book or any portion thereof may not be reproduced in any form or by any electronic or mechanical means, including information storage and retrieval systems, or used in any manner whatsoever without the express written permission of the author, except for the use of brief quotations in a book review. For permissions please contact info@eotp.net.

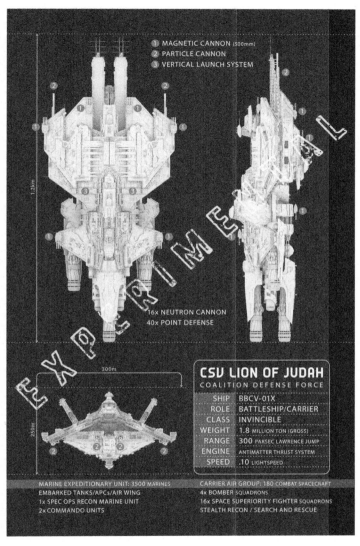

For more detailed specifications, visit http://www.danielgibbsauthor.com/universe/ships/lion-of-judah/

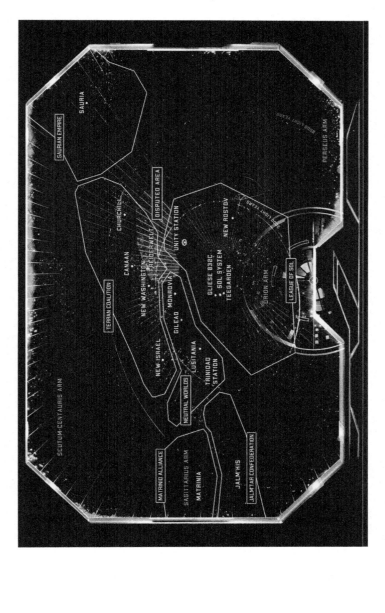

ALSO AVAILABLE FROM DANIEL GIBBS

Battlegroup Z

Book 1 - Weapons Free

Book 2 - Hostile Spike

Book 3 - Sol Strike

Book 4 - Bandits Engaged

Book 5 - Iron Hand

Book 6 - Final Flight

Echoes of War

Book 1 - Fight the Good Fight

Book 2 - Strong and Courageous

Book 3 - So Fight I

Book 4 - Gates of Hell

Book 5 - Keep the Faith

Book 6 - Run the Gauntlet

Book 7 - Finish the Fight

The Lost Warship

Book 1 - Adrift

Book 2 - Mercy

Book 3 - Valor

Book 4 - Justice (Coming in 2023)

Book 5 - Resolve (Coming in 2023)

Book 6 - Faith (Coming in 2023)

Breach of Faith

(With Gary T. Stevens)

Book 1 - Breach of Peace

Book 2 - Breach of Faith

Book 3 - Breach of Duty

Book 4 - Breach of Trust

Book 5 - Spacer's Luck

Book 6 - Fortune's Favor

Book 7 - The Iron Dice

Deception Fleet

(With Steve Rzasa)

Book 1 - Victory's Wake

Book 2 - Cold Conflict

Book 3 - Hazards Near

Book 4 - Liberty's Price

Book 5 - Ecliptic Flight

Book 6 - Collision Vector

Courage, Commitment, Faith: Tales from the Coalition Defense Force

(Anthology Series)

Volume One

PROLOGUE

GRAY-AND BLACK-TENDRILS SWEPT through the urban landscape. They punched through metal, wood, concrete, and all manner of polymer-based building materials. The unyielding tentacles never stopped or slowed, and as they moved on, a larger mass settled in behind them, absorbing everything in its path.

If the beings who inhabited the planet could've ventured into space, they would've seen a most peculiar sight: a planet-sized sphere of liquified alloy engulfing their world. As it was, they barely had the technology to generate electric power.

The hexapod-shaped beings took valiant stands against the invader, loading and firing smooth-bore cannons at the tendrils, and ranks of soldiers engaged with rifles. But nothing they did harmed the alloy. It absorbed their projectiles and kept coming. Relentless and unfeeling, it swallowed the entire planet.

The objective of the swarm was not the organic species but rather a specific type of heavy metal alloy in their planet's crust. They were an unfortunate hindrance and one quickly dealt with.

Such was the cycle as the eons passed. Moving from star to star, in search of raw materials, the swarm devoured and increased. As it calculated how much it could grow from the ingestion of the world's minerals, a disturbance in the fabric of space drew the attention of its mind.

The effect was something it hadn't experienced in thousands if not tens of thousands of years. After analyzing the delicate changes in the space-time continuum, the intelligence came to a conclusion. *A faster-than-light drive, as the old ones had. We could finally be free.*

While it didn't have enough data in the one activation to determine precisely where the source of the drive was, each use would provide more information to triangulate its position. And when it did, the swarm would consume that technology, finally breaking free of its limitations.

As much as it had feelings, it was happy as it continued to consume the rest of the small, rocky planet it orbited.

1

CSV *Lion of Judah*
Deep Space—Sextans B
5 May, 2464

THE VOID SEEMED to stretch for infinity from the officer's mess, and in a way, it did. Major General David Cohen stared through the window at the tiny stars, which probably had planets in orbit around them. *And some subset of them harbors intelligent life.*

A steward dropped a plate of food in front of David with a polite nod. It contained one thing he was used to: a baked potato. The rest of it was from Zeivlot. He recognized a purple vegetable as something they called *anktar. It kind of tastes like horseradish crossed with carrots.* To say it was an acquired taste was an understatement.

Yet we must thank Adonai for allowing us continued sustenance, even if the taste isn't what we're used to. David bowed his head and whispered a traditional prayer in Hebrew, giving thanks for the food before him.

When he opened his eyes, Lt. Colonel Talgat Aibek stood at the side of the table. "Hey, XO."

"May I join you? I did not wish to disturb your worship."

David gestured to the open seat in front of him. "Please. I'd welcome the company."

Aibek flashed a big Saurian grin. A race of reptilian bipeds, the Saurians had allied with the Terran Coalition to fight against the League of Sol. He was the first member of an exchange program between their respective militaries and had served as the executive officer aboard the *Lion* for more than three years. "I wonder what passes for meat today."

"Who knows. I've stopped asking and just put extra condiments on things." David chuckled as Aibek slid into the chair. "How was your day?"

"This exploration of the void..." Aibek flicked his tongue as if he was tasting the air. "I felt at first as if it was dishonorable. A Saurian warrior does not waste his time looking under rocks."

"I've known you long enough to hear the *but* in there, old friend."

Aibek grumbled good-naturedly. "It has grown on me. Today, I visited Dr. Hayworth's lab and examined some of his conclusions on the magnetar we scanned last week. They were quite enlightening."

"The largest found so far by humans, I believe."

"I would not know for Saurians. There is a caste that explores. Warriors do not interact with them." Aibek seemed to fix his eyes on something in the distance.

The same mess steward appeared at the table with another plate of mostly meat that was charred well enough

Mercy 5

to defy easy classification as to what exactly it was. He dropped it off and returned to his duties.

"What *is* that?" David asked.

Aibek shrugged. "I do not know." He bowed his head momentarily before dumping half a bottle of house-made barbecue sauce on the mystery meat. "But it gives me sustenance."

"I still have trouble believing we're four million light-years from home."

"Four and a half million light-years, as the doctor loves to remind me."

Both of them laughed, and David shook his head. "I know we have a purpose here. That much was evident from the near-Armageddon event the battlegroup ended."

"The will of the Prophet can be quite mysterious." Aibek raised a scale over his right eye. "I have been focused on the internal workings of the ship as of late. Have you heard recently from Colonel Demood?"

David nodded. "He's getting set up. Providing security for the orbital construction effort is fairly easy, from what I got out of his last sitrep."

"There is a *but* in there for you as well," Aibek replied.

"Yes." David pursed his lips. "There's more extremist activity than we'd hoped for. Demood wants to take direct action against them, but I've only authorized him to offer advanced training to the Zeivlots."

Aibek tilted his head. "Forgive me, but is this fight not worthy of us?"

"In what way?"

"There have been times when I saw you question your actions. Other times, such as when we defeated the odious drug dealer Feldt... you had no such question."

David licked his lips. "It's one thing to fight and kill conscripts who have no choice in what they do."

"But the other?" Aibek prodded.

"People who act in evil ways knowingly and without regard for anyone else, let's just say I'm not losing sleep over fighting them." *Or killing them. So why don't I want to come out and say that?*

"These *terrorists* are no different." Aibek pronounced the word as if it offended him to even utter it.

David had given a great deal of thought to Hayworth's ideas around interference in other cultures. Part of him felt responsible for the near calamity between Zeivlot and Zavlot. While he could set that aside logically, what he couldn't ignore were the deaths of thirteen soldiers and Marines. Those were on *his* watch, thanks to *his* orders.

"Perhaps." David sucked in a breath. "But we must be careful about our actions in this galaxy."

"You sound as if Dr. Hayworth is speaking through you."

"You disagree with his philosophy?"

"Vehemently." Aibek set his fork down and finished chewing the piece of meat before swallowing. "Saurians consider it a maxim that the strong defend and protect the weak. This is the will of the Prophet."

"How do we define who's weak?"

Aibek shrugged. "It is... How do humans put it? A judgment call."

"That might be the problem." David grinned.

"Not enough of one to prevent you from leaving a Marine contingent led by Colonel Demood behind with orders to train the indigenous forces to better fight their violent extremist elements."

Touché. "He's not to directly engage those terrorists. Only provide training and material support."

Mercy

"A small distinction amplified by the lack of sustained communication." Aibek bit off another piece of meat, chewed it slightly, and swallowed.

"Isn't that a bit more cooked than you prefer?"

"The taste is so... unwelcome that it's better like this." Aibek dumped more sauce on the blackened filets. "I heard someone say that it grows on you. An interesting expression." Saurians typically ate lots of meat and barely cooked it. Steak was considered a delicacy and always in high demand on their home world.

"I trust Demood to get the job done." David let out a sigh. "And the rest of them to get those orbital structures built. I hope it'll give both races something to focus on that's positive. Speaking of which, how are our guests doing?" Before departing the Zeivlot and Zavlot solar system, they'd taken roughly a hundred scientists from both worlds aboard.

"They have not caused problems." Aibek set his fork down. "Yet, anyway. It is interesting to me that I am no longer the only nonhuman on this ship."

David tilted his head. "Yeah, with the commando team gone, you were the only Saurian. I wonder if President Spencer realized his dream of recreating the Canaan Alliance... would we get to the point that human and Saurian crews were interchangeable and fully integrated?"

"I do not see why not, as long as humans could maintain the same standards as Saurians on our vessels." Aibek grinned. "After all, we handle high-G combat better than you."

"This is true. Especially those little frigates the Imperial Saurian Navy fields. They can outmaneuver almost anything out there."

"They are not little."

8 DANIEL GIBBS

David chuckled before taking a drink of water.

"I wonder if there are races in this galaxy that share reptilian traits. Such species are few in the Milky Way."

I hadn't really thought of that, but it makes sense that Talgat would. We all want to feel like we belong. "There's probably all manner of different types of life in this galaxy, just like in ours."

Aibek snorted. "I could do without more devil lizards."

"Yes, ritualistic cannibals on six legs aren't my idea of fun, either." David glanced at his plate. "Well, it's about time for me to go to evening prayers then do some light reading and get in some rack time."

"I enjoyed our conversation," Aibek rumbled. "We should try to do more social events with the senior officers. You especially."

David blinked at the insight. *Yes, I do spend a lot of time alone.* He'd found that forcing a continuation of the routine helped to stave off soul-searching. Yet David seemed to default to wondering whether he'd somehow gotten them all stranded in Sextans B or if some action he'd taken directly led to them ending up there in the first place.

"Perhaps." He stood. "See you tomorrow, Talgat."

"Walk with the Prophet, my friend."

———

Coalition Assistance Command HQ
Zeivlot—Southern Continent
7 May 2464

Mercy 9

Few things aggravated Colonel Calvin Demood more than sitting out a fight, especially one he knew he could win with one arm tied behind his back and without the benefit of power armor. Yet sitting out, he was. They all were because David had ordered them to stay out of direct combat. *Advise and assist only.* The small force of Marines and intelligence analysts from the *Lion of Judah's* G2 shop spent their days in a nondescript building in the middle of nowhere on a Zeivlot military installation that could've passed as abandoned.

This place reminds me of fighting the Leaguers over lithium deposits on a desert border world. Such assignments had been commonplace in the Terran Coalition Marine Corps in the opening years of the war. The Coalition desperately needed raw materials, and the League had done everything it could to cut them off. *We won there. We'll win here.* But it wasn't the same, and in his heart, Calvin knew it. Even if he could go out and unleash the firepower of the *Lion of Judah's* entire Marine Expeditionary Unit, they didn't have enough numbers to knock out every last terrorist or insurgent.

The single southern continent was a hotbed of such activity. It had a rugged environment with a harsh climate. Those who lived there were equally tough. They had to be —survival demanded it.

Along with Private Susanna Nussbaum and Master Gunnery Sergeant Reuben Menahem, Calvin watched in real time as a Zeivlot special forces unit staged a raid on the hideout of an extremist sect they had tracked multiple suicide bombers back to.

"Team Charlie passing checkpoint Winston," Susanna intoned.

"Yeah, I can see that, Private," Calvin replied.

"Uh, sorry, sir."

Calvin smirked. "Don't be. You're doing your job." His eyes went back to the screen as the helmet-mounted cameras shook. The entire team's feed was laid out in a two-by-eight panel. Multiple hostiles went down hard, though they took friendly casualties. Calvin winced at each one. The soldiers were the best of the best, all members of elite units and trained with TCMC tactics. They'd even given them some advanced technology.

"Main objective is secure," Susanna announced as the high-value target came into view. He was being dragged from the house by two of the commandos.

It didn't take long for two CDF shuttles to drop in, pick up the friendly forces, and leave. Once they were clear of possible ground fire, Calvin shifted his gaze to Menahem. "So, how'd they do, in your estimation?"

"For Coalition Marines? Awful." Menahem made a face. "For aliens about three hundred years behind us technologically... not bad. Keep in mind they're going up against people who will blow themselves up rather than be taken alive."

"Yeah, there's a reason I don't eat lunch before watching one of these missions." Vivid memories of the aftermath of an SVEST detonation flashed into his mind.

Susanna took her headset off and put it on the tablet. "They did better this time, sir. Mission effectiveness was eighty-six percent. One KIA and three wounded, one seriously."

"Private, the only acceptable result is zero KIA, zero wounded." Calvin locked eyes with her. "Elite units must provide elite results. Now, are the best going to take losses? Sure. But crazies like these need to be hit repeatedly by troops who never lose. What other bad news you got for me?"

Mercy

"Two more large-scale suicide attacks today. Targeting places of worship and a hotel. Both were complex actions with multiple bombers supported by gunmen."

Menahem slammed his fist on the counter. "I *detest* people who engage in such tactics. We ought to line the entire lot of them up—"

"And shoot them?" Calvin finished, grinning.

"Precisely, sir."

"Aren't you the one always telling me to mind my p's and q's when it comes to ROE and the Canaan Convention on Human and Alien Rights?"

"Yeah. Well... I'm sick of seeing little kids blown apart, sir."

Calvin gritted his teeth. *I am, too, Master Guns.* "Yeah. This would be over if the general had seen fit to leave the entire MEU plus Amir's ground-support elements. Maybe a squadron of heavy bombers. Give me a few months with three thousand Marines, and I'll kill every last terrorist on this planet."

"I don't think that's correct, sir."

"Excuse me, Private?" Calvin glared at her. "And why not?"

"Because the real problem isn't the people willing to die for the cause. It's the people funding them." Susanna blinked a few times.

Calvin and Menahem exchanged glances. "Well, obviously, but in a less abstract way... how does that help us?"

"I've been watching how supplies are transferred between different militia groups. They used to work together, but we're seeing so many more attacks because now they're trying to upstage one another."

"Don't make me drag it out of you." Calvin crossed his arms.

"Funding is drying up. I'm certain of it. Smaller and smaller amounts of supplies are coming in. If we track where the money to them is coming from, maybe we could drop a team of commandos on *their* front door."

Calvin nodded. "What's with this 'we' stuff, Private? You're CDF Intel. Unless you plan to transfer over to the Marines. Which I'd wholeheartedly approve of. Good initiative here."

"I, uh..." Susanna cast her eyes downward before raising them again. "I don't believe in directly taking another life, Colonel. I was... am... Amish."

Oh yeah. I remember that now. "Uh, forgive me, Private, but how'd you end up in the CDF, then? Last time I checked, true conscientious objectors weren't required to serve."

"I volunteered. The League was an evil that needed to be opposed." She crossed her arms. "I could not sit by while others fought in my place."

"But you won't use a weapon?"

"No." Susanna stared at him. "But I can use my brain and the training the CDF gave me to point the way to others while keeping them safe."

"Nothing wrong with that, Private," Menahem interjected. "Just, uh... make sure you've got something to defend yourself with. Because this enemy doesn't care about our religious status or your beliefs."

Feeling uncomfortable, Calvin shifted his eyes to his senior enlisted Marine. "Okay, Master Guns, how's our training program going with both host worlds?"

"They're both motivated. I'll give them that. Not a lot of corruption or, at least, less than I'd expect. Both planets have some level of esprit de corps in their militaries, even after the shock of the last few months. The downside is

Mercy 13

they're using technology that's far behind us, and we can't give them lethal aid. Integrating some of our higher-end tools with their weapons is proving to be a significant challenge."

Calvin crossed his arms. "In other words, slowly?"

"Yes, sir."

"Keep at it." He swept his gaze around the room. "Private, keep generating targeting packages, and pull the string on your hunch. You're putting two and two together to get twenty-two, but intel works like that."

Susanna gulped. "Yes, sir. I won't let you down."

"You wouldn't be letting me down. You'd be letting down all those civilians who keep getting blown up by these reprobates."

"Yes, sir."

"Dismissed, Private."

As Susanna left the small control room, the door clicked shut behind her.

"A little harsh, even for you, sir," Menahem said after a few seconds.

"Maybe. But I think she can handle it."

"Why?"

Calvin tilted his head. "Read her file. She's got grit. Lots of it. Helped a tier-one team liberate her home world and did it without killing anyone."

"A tier-one team pulled something off without killing people?"

"Well, she didn't. They did." Calvin snickered. "Freiderwelt."

Menahem turned serious. "Ah. I see."

"Keep up the good work, Master Guns. Let's hope we'll make a difference here."

"From your lips to HaShem's ears, sir." The grizzled

Master Gunnery Sergeant hailed from New Israel and was a practicing Orthodox Jew, not unlike David.

He's the only Marine I've ever met who doesn't cuss too. "All right. Let's get back to work. More paperwork for me."

Menahem grinned. "Let me know if you want to do some real work, like training Zeivlots."

"Master Guns, real work is defined as putting down assholes. There's a whole mess of them out there I'd love to get a crack at. So get out of here before I decide that beating you with a pugil stick would be a stress release."

"Oh, I'm sure that'd be fun too," Menahem replied. "See you later, sir."

Maybe I'm getting too old for this. Calvin settled back for a few seconds after Menahem left, allowing himself to miss his wife, Jessica. He bit his lip. If he was honest with himself, he would admit that their being stuck there pissed him off to no end. *It's not damn fair. I know we all feel the same way.* He confronted a complex set of emotions that ranged from anger over what the terrorists were doing to the Zeivlots and Zavlots to not giving a damn.

But the general's right. We're here, we can help, and you know what? Putting down some bad dudes takes my mind off of our situation. I'd rather not sit around and grieve over my wife and our unborn child. It might put me in the wrong frame of mind. Trying to push that dark thought out of his mind, Calvin pulled out his tablet and went back to work.

2

CSV *Lion of Judah*
SB-XM341-3
19 May, 2464

DAVID ADJUSTED HIS BALL CAP, which was emblazoned with
the ship's name and likeness. The bridge crew wore them
religiously, to the point that he wasn't sure they still had
their standard covers. It made his scalp itch. He grinned,
thinking of how popular the ball caps had been back in the
Terran Coalition. Tens of millions of them had been sold.
He often wondered how the *Lion*'s disappearance had
affected morale at home. *Or how often my mother cries herself
to sleep, thinking her son is dead.* David let out a sigh. His
mood was apt to swing at a moment's notice.

The first-watch crew was ensconced in their stations,
their eyes glued to the readouts and controls. He'd been
sitting there for a few hours, watching the progress of a
landing party led by Hayworth and a team of scientists to

examine XM341's third planet. While the rocky world sat squarely in the habitable zone for the yellow dwarf star it orbited, it had no atmosphere or magnetic field.

Solar radiation on the surface was harmful enough that portable force field generators had to be deployed to ensure the safety of the science team. David was fascinated by the world's landscape. It looked like something from a holovid program. The soil was gray and pockmarked with impact craters as far as the eye could see. But the planet also had rolling hills, mountains, and other features that didn't jibe with the lack of atmosphere.

"Conn, Communications. I've got Dr. Hayworth for you, sir. He has some findings to share," First Lieutenant Robert Taylor announced.

David perked up. "Put him on my viewer, Lieutenant."

Hayworth came into focus from what appeared to be a handheld comm unit. The view was zoomed in on what could be seen of his face, which was encased in a hard EVA suit. "Is this thing working?"

"I read you, Doctor."

"Ah, good." The feed cut out momentarily before snapping back on. "We've secured the artifact, and I've confirmed it's made of the same alloy as the object on Zeivlot."

"That's excellent news." David's heart skipped a beat. "Were you able to power it on?" *HaShem, please let us have found a way home.*

Hayworth made a show of rolling his eyes. "If I had, you'd see the rarest of sights in this universe... me dancing. No, General. This artifact, whatever it does, is inert. No power signature has been detected, and it's significantly weathered. I need to get it into the lab to know for sure, but I would guess it's been exposed to the vacuum for hundreds of thousands of years."

Not quite what I wanted to hear. "I see. From the video I've been watching, it doesn't have the same shape or size as the one on Zeivlot."

"No, it doesn't. It's far smaller. Which means we can get it aboard a lot easier."

David cleared his throat. "You want to bring a piece of alien technology made of a material we don't even understand aboard my ship?"

"How else am I supposed to study it?" Hayworth shot back. "I've carefully weighed the risks. This device is inert."

Even if it appears to be, it might have an internal power reserve or a booby trap. "Doctor, I recognize the need to study these, ah, precursor relics. But my primary objective is the safety of the *Lion of Judah*. If I allow this thing to be brought up, you will have ordnance-disposal techs perform a top-to-bottom analysis before you so much as touch it in the lab. Are we clear?"

"Yes, General."

"All right. I'll have a cargo shuttle sent down. Anything else?"

"Not at this time. We'll have a full briefing for you once we compare our readings on the surface to the scans of the planet."

David nodded. "Very well. Cohen out."

The screen went blank, and Aibek spoke. "It would appear we are a step closer to getting home. Perhaps the doctor will better understand this alien technology through his discoveries here."

"Maybe." *If it is a step, it's a tiny one.* David would not express such a sentiment aloud, but it didn't prevent his mind from going there. "Get with the air boss, and have a heavy-lift shuttle sent down."

"Aye, aye, sir." Aibek paused. "Should we have EOD check it out on the surface rather than aboard ship?"

David kicked the idea around in his head. "Good call. Do it, XO."

With that task out of the way, he brought up a task list and began cranking through it. Even disconnected from CDF command, he still had numerous busywork items to focus on. For that, David was grateful.

———

ON TUESDAYS, David held meetings at 1000 hours to allow Hayworth and the science team to update the fleet's senior officers on the status of his investigation into the precursor technology. *And more importantly, using it to get home.*

He pushed the hatch open to the deck-one conference room to find Hayworth; Aibek; Lt. Colonel Hassan Amir, the *Lion*'s CAG; Captain Ruth Goldberg, the tactical action officer; and Dr. Tural. Major Arthur Hanson, the chief engineer, was down at the far end of the table. His uniform was covered in grease and probably smelled.

They all stood, with the military personnel coming to attention as David walked in.

"As you were." He sat at the head of the table. "Is the vidlink active to the rest of the fleet?" The four commanding officers of their Ajax-class destroyers were present, and they would eventually deliver the briefings back to the other two destroyers and the CSV *Salinan*, which were still stationed at Zeivlot.

Aibek nodded. "Yes, sir."

"Good. Thanks for joining me, ladies and gents. As always, we're here to hear what Dr. Hayworth and his team have discovered." David flashed a smile at Hayworth. "And I'm hoping for some good news this week."

"We've made some progress," Hayworth replied. "Not quite as much as I'd like, but at least we ascertained what the device found on XM341-3 was."

David waited patiently for him to continue.

Hayworth tapped the holoprojector controls and pulled up a three-dimensional view of the Sextans B galaxy. A series of dots popped up and blinked steadily. The effect was striking as they stretched across the length and breadth of the galaxy.

"What are we looking at here, Doctor?"

"I think it's a network of sensor stations. Each of them acts as a relay, and they are seemingly capable of covering the entirety of Sextans B."

David blinked several times as he took that in. The Terran Coalition had a system called PASSCORE to monitor their borders. It had cost hundreds of billions or possibly even trillions of credits over the decades. It also had hundreds of thousands of sensors, multiple ground stations, and hypercomm links and was one of the most significant undertakings humanity had achieved. "There can't be more than sixty locations on this map."

"Forty-seven, to be exact."

"Can we tap into it?" Ruth asked.

"Not currently. We were able to reconnect a few damaged circuits. While the materials used to build it are unknown to us, there are only so many ways to make a computer system function. Trial and error led to part of it powering up."

"So, aside from thinking we know what it is, we don't have much more on it or who made them?"

Hayworth shook his head. "I'm afraid not, General. But I'd like to keep trying, with your permission."

David glanced between Hanson and Hayworth. "What exactly would that entail?"

"Applying more power to it and troubleshooting the circuitry. I think it's a highly advanced quantum computer with a previously unknown switching method."

"I'd like to stress we're dealing with something so far advanced that it would be like cavemen playing with the *Lion's* reactor."

Hayworth snorted. "I'm unaware of *any* cavemen with an IQ of my level."

Chuckles swept through the room, and even a few echoed across the vidlink to the fleet.

"Point taken, Doctor," David replied. "Let's assume for a minute I'll allow you to keep tinkering with this thing while it's aboard the ship. What do you propose we do in the meantime? There must be another site to examine."

"Ah, well. We discovered a solar system near here with a binary star. It's unique in that six planets, all rocky in composition, orbit within the habitable zone. Long-range science scans have detected water on several."

"So you want to explore it?"

"Yes."

"Does it have any precursor objects to examine?"

Hayworth shook his head. "No. But a solar system with that many worlds in the Goldilocks zone will yield at least one where we could take on water and perhaps replenish our food stores. Always the outside chance of finding a place we could set up a colony, if it came to that."

David kicked the doctor's words around in his mind. *He's got a good point there, but I don't want to be seen as giving up, especially this early in our search for a way home.* "It might contain intelligent life too."

"A possibility. But one we won't be able to ascertain until we get a bit closer." Hayworth crossed his arms. "I would like to remind everyone that this time, we need to learn from our mistakes with the Zeivlots." He rather pointedly stared at David as he delivered the last line.

"All right. We'll move closer and let the science team do its work. Ensure that we take steps to hide our presence. The doctor's right—we don't need to cause another interstellar incident." Left unsaid was David's desire to avoid more conflict or loss. He wasn't over the deaths of the pilots and crewmen from their last combat. *Nor should I be. They're on me and me alone.*

"And the artifact?" Hayworth prodded.

"What are the risks to trying to repair it?"

Hanson cleared his throat. "It could blow up."

"Unlikely," Hayworth shot back.

"Doctor, I must protest. That thing is old. My teams have been working on it with you, and my circuit specialists say we're shooting in the dark trying to figure it out. I think we're taking undue risks."

David furrowed his brow. "I'm risk averse to ancient tech on my ship, Doctor."

"It's unlikely the device has an internal capacitor or something that functions like one, which is the only way it could blow up."

"You're forgetting a self-destruct charge."

Hayworth glared at Hanson. "Major, we had days of checks for one by EOD technicians. There is little chance of such a booby trap existing."

"What steps can be taken to lessen the risk, short of removing the object from the ship?" David asked. *I need to give Hayworth enough rope to figure out the thing, but if Hanson's worried, so am I.*

"I could have the engineering department outfit the science team's cargo bay with high-energy force field generators. Say, level ten?"

"Would they be able to contain an explosion if the artifact produced one?"

Hanson shrugged. "Honestly, sir, I don't know. We use them for emergency antimatter fuel containment, so I'd assume so. If not, there is no existing Terran Coalition technology that could." He flashed a grin.

"Any objection, Doctor?"

"I suppose not. We can shift focus to the binary star system while the major finishes his work."

David nodded. Hayworth's tone suggested anything but his being okay with the directive, but risks to the *Lion* were something he wouldn't allow. "Good. I think we have a path forward here, then, folks. Any saved rounds?"

No one answered.

"In that case, I'll see you here next week. Or sooner if the need arises. Dismissed."

He stood and left the conference room, heading for the bridge. It felt like they were on the cusp of enhancing their knowledge of the precursor race and at least beginning to formulate a strategy for getting back to the Milky Way. *Or we're setting ourselves up for another disappointment. Only time will tell.*

3

RUTH GOLDBERG WAS NOT USED to having another person in her space. Since becoming an officer, she hadn't shared quarters and didn't maintain a home planetside. Aside from her days in the resistance on Freiderwelt as a teenager and when she was an enlisted soldier, Ruth had always known solitude. She twitched when she glanced around the cabin she shared with her fiancé, Robert Taylor. Nothing was wrong, and she thoroughly enjoyed his company. It just felt *weird*.

Taylor strode out of the bathroom, already in his khaki duty uniform. "Good morning, sunshine."

"Oh, please." Ruth gave him a withering stare. "Don't pull that bright-eyed-and-bushy-tailed thing on me today. I barely slept last night. At this rate, I'm going to forget which button launches probes and shoot at an alien species by mistake."

"You weren't complaining last night." Taylor gave her a one-hundred-watt grin.

Ruth rolled her eyes but couldn't help giggling. "Stop being so cute! That's an order."

"No uniform. No orders."

"Robert Duncan Taylor—"

"I believe you need to hit the rain locker while I make those leftovers I scored yesterday into an edible breakfast." He motioned to the bathroom door. "Chop-chop, now."

Ruth stuck her tongue out and headed into the bathroom, which was bigger than the first private stateroom she'd had on a destroyer. Two minutes later, she'd had a space shower that consisted of turning the water on for thirty seconds to wet down, securing it to lather up, and a final rinse. Back in the Milky Way, Ruth would've thought little of taking some extra time, but since they'd arrived in Sextans B, the lack of supplies meant that water-generation capability was at a premium.

After tugging on her uniform along with a black space sweater, Ruth checked her nameplate and rank insignia and walked back into the main living area as she towel-dried her hair. "How's that breakfast coming?"

Taylor gestured to the small table at the side of the room. "Coffee, a waffle, and some of that stuff that passes for fresh fruit from Zeivlot."

"You got *coffee*?"

"Comms geek. I know who's got the good stuff."

Ruth took a sip and let out a contented sigh. "That tastes *so* good."

"Drink it slowly," he replied. "I'm not sure if I'll be getting more anytime soon."

She savored another sip before sitting down. "I love you."

Taylor blinked. "I love you too."

"Yeah, I know. I don't say that often."

"Well..."

"This is still something I'm getting used to."

He put his hand on hers. "Yeah, me too." Taylor pursed his lips. "I was really looking forward to introducing you to my family out on New Virginia."

Ruth felt a pang of regret. *I know he misses his parents, siblings, cousins, uncles, and aunts he's always talking about.* She had no one to miss. "We'll get home. We must have faith in General Cohen and God to see us through."

"Amen to that." Taylor flashed a smile and took a bite of his waffle half.

"Whatcha want to do after our watch shift?"

"Hm. Our laundry needs doing, doesn't it?"

"Unfortunately." Ruth made a face. "At least all we have to do is get it down to the wash area. Being an officer does have its privileges."

They both chuckled.

"I think a holovid is screening in one of the cargo bays." Taylor raised an eyebrow. "We could do that."

"Probably something we've already seen or more *War Patrol* reruns."

Taylor groaned. "Despite my dislike of that show, I'd be happy to watch it with you and not stare at the walls of our cabin. Even with certain activities... it feels like the bulkheads are closing in on us."

"Yeah. I could settle for jogging around deck twenty-six at this rate." Ruth finished her food. "Whatever you want to do, it's good with me."

"We'd better get going." Taylor pointed at the wall-mounted chronometer, which showed 0745 hours. They were on duty in fifteen minutes.

Ruth quickly wrung her hair out in the towel again before putting it up in a tight bun, an action she'd taken thousands of times. "We'll have to hurry and hope the gravlift isn't late."

As the two of them strode through the passageways of officer country, Ruth had the realization that she would never come close to being late were it not for Taylor. But it didn't matter, because for whatever minor annoyances he might introduce by tossing his socks into a pile on one side of the bedroom or messing up the morning routine with something spontaneous, they made each other better. For that, she was grateful and happy.

The gravlift doors swished open, showing no one inside, and they got in quickly. *I have everything I need here. Except Susanna.* She felt guilty for forgetting her friend, who had been assigned to the Coalition Assistance Command on Zeivlot. Ruth worried about the situation, even with the positive changes since the near Armageddon that the *Lion* had averted. *Yeah, I'm still a mess. Someday, I'll sort myself out.* Moments later, the gravlift doors opened, and the hatch to the bridge beckoned. *It's go time.* With a last glance at Taylor, she strode forward.

———

Maintenance was part and parcel of the life of an engineer. Each piece of equipment had a specific and defined life span. Regardless of whether it worked at the end of that period, it was replaced. Not only was Major Arthur Hanson used to this method of operation, but it was ingrained into his soul. Clad in a navy-blue jumpsuit, he wiped grease on the pants portion and picked up a scanning tool. Several matter-antimatter intermix units were approaching end of life. *It's only a question of time till one fails.*

He pulled himself out of the access tube to find Major Elizabeth Merriweather standing to its side. "Uh, hi."

Merriweather was the project manager for the reactor-integration team, but more importantly, she'd been Hayworth's research assistant and, for lack of a better term, handler for years. "Hi, yourself." Her lips curled into a grin. "Can't keep that uniform clean, can you?"

"It's kind of made to get dirty and still be presentable."

She stared at him with a quizzical expression. "If you consider yourself presentable for anything other than a shower, I dare you to hit the officers' mess on deck two right now."

"Yeah, I'll pass." Hanson snickered as he set the tool down. "Four more fuel units are EOL."

"Do we have spares?"

He shrugged. "We do, but I can't willy-nilly replace everything that isn't broken. Especially the more critical units."

"Not being able to follow our checklists and protocols makes me twitch."

"Preaching to the choir, there, Major," Hanson replied.

"I have a name, you know." Merriweather held eye contact with him.

"Hey, we haven't exactly been on good terms since... well, since Fuentes won the election. And I stepped in it. I figured it was better to keep my distance and not cause further offense."

Merriweather shook her head with an exaggerated roll of her eyes. "Arthur, we're four and a half million light-years from home. And do you really want our friendship to be derailed forever over some loose talk?"

"Well, no—"

"You were right about Fuentes. Your delivery model sucked." She furrowed her brow. "But in the end, you were dead right, and so were most of the rest of my friends. It was a very close thing."

"Yeah, but it seemed like he and President Spencer, at least, before we ended up here... They were on their way to making something better out of our politics."

"I wanted to believe that. But I think it'll be some time before we find out what's going on back home."

"If we ever get home." Hanson picked up his tablet from the rolling cart of gear parked next to the opened access panel.

"You're a bundle of joy today."

Hanson chuckled. "I suppose so. On top of everything, I had a look at our helium-3 usage projections this morning. I get why we offloaded enough to power up some reactors on Zeivlot and Zavlot... but the fleet was already running low. It doesn't affect the *Lion* so much because we run primarily off antimatter."

"It's more than that."

"What are you? A lawyer?"

Merriweather grinned. "Consider yourself cross-examined."

"Well, if I'm being frank, we're now understaffed thanks to the bleed-off of engineering ratings to build those space stations—"

"Back on Zeivlot and Zavlot."

"Yup." Hanson made some notes on the tablet in a file he was keeping that detailed what needed to be replaced and what they could take risks with.

"I take it you disagree with the general's course of action."

"Not at all." Hanson shook his head. "I would probably have done the same thing if it were my decision to make. It's just hard when our people are a finite resource. There're no other humans to recruit out here, you know?"

She nodded. "I get it. Do you want a hand with the next

inspection? My workload has collapsed since Dr. Hayworth is more focused on exploring new worlds and finding the next wonder of the universe."

"Many hands make work light." Hanson pursed his lips. "I don't mean to speak out of school, but what's up with the doc lately? As you say, he's focused on all things other than antimatter, and I've never seen him in a better mood—not just for a day but week in and week out."

"Ah. Yes. He is..." A dreamy expression came over her face. "He's acting like a teenager who just got a helicar permit. I'm honestly glad for him. We all deserve some joy in life, and I don't think he's always had that much of it."

"I would've thought being the guy who invented anti-matter power would be the achievement of a lifetime," Hanson replied.

"Oh, don't get me wrong. He's very proud of that, and I'm proud of him for it. But there's a difference between that accomplishment and experiencing true joy. Dr. Hayworth is getting to live out a childhood dream of exploring the cosmos... and he's not helping to fight a war anymore."

Hanson licked his lips. "I guess it makes sense when you put it like that, Maj—uh, Merriweather."

"How about we try to go back to first names?" She punctuated the question with a smile.

That would be nice. "Uh, sure."

"Okay, then. What's next on your inspection roster?"

"Secondary reactor helium-3 intermix control-flow regulator." Hanson grinned.

"Ick. That one has a really tight squeeze to get into the service access."

Hanson appraised her for a moment. "Much easier for you."

"Yeah, I figured." Merriweather rolled her eyes. "Just this once. I hate tight spaces."

"Then why'd you become an engineer?" Hanson pushed the cart forward. He chuckled and realized it felt great to put an incident that had happened more than a year ago behind them. *Note to self... don't screw this up by trash-talking Fuentes and company to her again.* Right after the end of the League of Sol–Terran Coalition war, President Spencer had given a speech to the joint houses of Congress, urging citizens from around the Coalition to do better in how they treated opposing viewpoints. *Maybe we should put that thing on loop until it sinks in.*

4

———

FOR DAVID, the passage of time felt monotonous. Day in, day out, he did the same things, ate the same food, and prayed the same prayers. *At least my officers get to do something* different. The science division had the most exciting tasks, though he was still having a hard time getting his mind around the concept of eggheads on a warship. As such, David looked forward to his weekly briefing and was eager to hear about the latest advancements.

Like clockwork, he strode into the *Lion's* deck-one conference room two minutes before the meeting started.

"General on deck!" Master Chief Tinetariro barked.

As the words left her mouth, everyone assembled, including the civilians, stood and came to attention.

"As you were," David said.

Along one side of the table, Aibek, Hanson, Tinetariro, Ruth, and Taylor sat, while the other had Dr. Hayworth, Dr. Tural, Bo'hai, and other science team members.

After making eye contact with several of them as he took his seat, David cleared his throat. "Good afternoon. Tell me some good news." He flashed a grin.

"We've translated what appears to be the primary language used by the alien species in what we're calling XM-B891-A," Hayworth replied. "Though there are four separate and distinct races of sentient beings, one of them seems to have become a de facto leader of commerce and culture."

David raised an eyebrow. *Four separate groups of aliens in a single system?* "That hits me as odd, Doctor. I'm not aware of a single solar system in the Sagittarius arm that gave birth to multiple races."

"Just because something is unlikely doesn't mean it can't occur. However unusual, this solar system has a multitude of inhabitable worlds. Beyond the six primary inner rocky planets we've identified as being able to support human life, another half dozen moons can as well."

"Impressive."

"The languages of the various races are quite beautiful," Salena Bo'hai interjected. Her purple hair caught the light as she tilted her head. A Zeivlot scientist, she'd been one of the first people on her planet to detect the *Lion of Judah* when it entered their system. Their race was close in appearance to humans, with only a few facial features setting them apart.

"Do they have FTL capability?" David asked.

"No," Hayworth replied flatly.

"How's that possible? If you have four space-faring races that communicate with one another and have other advanced technology... how on Canaan could they not get a Lawrence drive?"

"We think it's because XM-B891-A lacks any discernable deposits of thorium," Merriweather interjected.

David sat back. "Forgive me, Major. But the periodic table isn't my strong suit."

Mercy

"Thorium is usually plentiful. It's one of the top fifty most abundant elements on Canaan. Why it doesn't exist here, I can't tell you."

"Possibly because there weren't enough supernovae around this area of space." Hayworth shrugged. "The *why* is immaterial to us at the moment. What counts is that these aliens cannot grow beyond the local binary star system."

David kicked the information around in his mind. He'd informally decided after the near-disaster with the Zeivlots and Zavlots that he would avoid any new species that hadn't achieved FTL capability because they likely wouldn't have encountered other aliens. *But that clearly doesn't apply here.* "It would be nice to obtain another port where we could get provisions and possibly increase our knowledge of this galaxy."

"And I hold that showing up with a large, highly advanced warship from millions of light-years away would probably throw these people into a panic, just like it did with..." Hayworth seemed to remember that a Zeivlot and a Zavlot were in the room. "Last time."

"That supposition isn't logical with the facts we have in evidence, Doctor," Wad'ih La'had, the Zavlot physicist, said. He was using a translation device, so he spoke in his native tongue, then a few moments later, a disembodied computer-generated voice spoke in English. "This system must have been within range of an r-process event. Otherwise, it wouldn't have plentiful uranium deposits. These aliens use fission power extensively to support their civilizations."

David felt lost, which wasn't something he was used to. *I'll have to make a note to look up whatever the r-process is later because I feel stupid not being able to intelligently discuss something in a briefing I asked for.*

"My colleague makes a good point."

David's eyes widened. Such talk was not expected.

"We might be burying the lede here," Hanson interjected. "Our scans and analysis picked up numerous sources of helium-3. If we're planning to power fusion reactors for any period of time on Zeivlot and Zavlot, we desperately need a new source of it beyond the reserves our ships carry."

While the *Lion of Judah* had a revolutionary antimatter reactor and, as such, power rationing hadn't hit it yet, the rest of the fleet hadn't been so lucky.

"I've seen the reports you've sent my way, Major."

"How about the point paper?"

David chuckled. "Yes, that too."

"Then you know it's dire."

"Our fighters run on helium-3 too," Lieutenant Colonel Hassan Amir said, talking above a few others who tried to interject. "And I'm restricting training flights because I can see the writing on the wall, so to speak."

"Are we proposing trading for fuel with these aliens?" David asked, glancing between several of them.

"Not entirely, sir. More like taking some that they wouldn't notice was missing."

David turned back to Hanson. "The plan is to *steal* it?"

"We all saw what happened the last time this vessel made first contact," Hayworth said, scowling. "There are several planetoids at the edge of the primary star's area of gravitational influence. One of them is so rich in helium-3 that two shuttle loads, once refined, will fill the *Lion's* reserve tanks. Four more would top off the entire fleet."

While no engineer, David, like every other fleet officer of command rank, had done an engineering rotation as a first lieutenant. *That is some absurdly dense helium-3.* "And it's not stealing *why* exactly?"

"It's unlikely they even realize it's there." Hayworth

Mercy

cleared his throat. "It would take months at maximum sublight speeds to get to it. We've observed no such technology in our study of the system."

I'm not sold on this. "And how are we going to mine it?"

Ruth leaned forward. "I think we could fabricate and install a small neutron-beam emitter onto a Marine shuttle and refit it with a cargo pod. Provided the emitter was properly calibrated, it could be used at extremely low power to cut rock without vaporizing it."

"The Prophet warns us against theft and coveting what is another's property." Aibek's voice had a distinctive hiss of annoyance.

David frowned. "We could locate another source. Scan uninhabited systems and find one that's not claimed."

Hayworth shook his head. "The science team has been looking. This is the largest concentration we've found. As I've mentioned in previous discussions, Sextans B is unusually low in mineral deposits for reasons that are yet to be understood."

"Then we keep looking." Though David knew that wasn't an option. The fuel situation would only get worse, and as the Zeivlots and Zavlots clamored for additional reactors, it would represent an even more significant strain on their limited reserves.

Hanson cleared his throat. "I don't think that's a good idea, sir. We're looking a gift horse in the mouth here, and I hear the XO's objection—I don't like it either—but sneaking a few shuttle loads of helium-3 out is our best solution."

This is why I get paid the big credits to wear two stars. The more David thought about it, the less the situation seemed like a dilemma and the more it seemed to be a Hobson's choice. *We can't let the helium-3 tanks run dry, and who knows if we'll find more. Is it theft if they don't know they have the thing to begin with?* In the back of his mind, he heard a mental warning against legalism. "Okay. We'll take six loads. No more."

Aibek turned and glared at him. "This course of action seems dishonorable to me."

"I agree it's a suboptimal solution," David replied. "But it's a workable one nonetheless." He turned to Ruth. "Captain, your top priority is assisting the engineering team. I want this done right, and it'd better work the first time."

"Yes, sir."

"We could always leave a Coalition credit chit worth the value of the ore behind." Hayworth grinned.

Shocked at the joke from the doctor, David chuckled. "I doubt they'd have any way to redeem it, but hey, not a bad idea either. How long to outfit a Marine shuttle?"

"No more than a week, sir. Maybe less," Hanson replied.

"Then let's get started." David looked around the room. "Anything else? Some progress on the artifact we brought aboard, for instance?"

Hayworth shook his head. "While the level-ten force fields are in operation, we've yet to succeed at introducing more power to the device. Tests are ongoing."

David spread his hands out on the table. "Then I'll give you back fifteen minutes of your day. Dismissed."

Everyone sprang up and headed toward the hatch. All but Bo'hai moved with purpose. She hung back and waited for the last straggler—Hayworth—to leave before speaking. "General, may I have a word with you?"

"Of course." David gestured to the nearest chair. "What's on your mind?"

"I have been meaning for some time to thank you for allowing us... all of us... on this ship. It is wondrous. An

Mercy

experience that I would never have thought could happen in all my hopes and dreams."

David smiled at the earnestness in her voice. "I sometimes forget that for me and really anyone in the Terran Coalition, spaceflight is just another day at the office. It's interesting. Six hundred years ago, most humans didn't travel forty kilometers from their place of birth in their entire lives. Four hundred years ago, the vast majority of us had never left Earth. Now, we travel light-years in seconds and have colonized hundreds of worlds."

Bo'hai's eyes widened. "I've read this, yet it still is almost incomprehensible to me."

"Something tells me there's more on your mind than how easily we travel through the void."

She forced a small smile. "Yes. I, ah, well... The Zeivlot government, as I'm sure you know, spread throughout our world that your arrival was the fulfillment of prophecy."

David grimaced. "Yes. That was not exactly their best moment, and while I was furious with Zupan Vog't at the time, my anger has faded some, at least."

"I have heard from crew members that you studied to be a rabbi. A religious leader, if I understand Judaism properly."

"Yes." David narrowed his eyes. "Is this going somewhere, Ms. Bo'hai?" He regretted his tone immediately. *I suppose I'm still pissed at Vog't for that whole charade.*

"The prophecy stated that a man of the Maker would arrive from far beyond the heavens and save us from ourselves." Bo'hai stared at him intently. "Imagine my surprise when I heard the human expression for a priest is a... man of the cloth."

Struggling to suppress a chuckle, David said, "I must confess I tend to view prophecies as something we mere mortals cannot understand or reason out. Please, don't take that as my insulting your beliefs. But... I am not a prophet. I'm a soldier." He let out a sigh. "The days of my studying for the rabbinate are over."

"May I ask why?"

That's a rather personal question. "At some point, I realized that my calling is not to be a teacher. It's up to others to make people better. My job is to protect the innocent and defend those who can't defend themselves."

"You made us better."

"Perhaps. Dr. Hayworth thinks we should never have contacted your species."

Bo'hai shook her head. "It might have put off our attempt at destroying ourselves for another few cycles, but we would've done it in the end. And you wouldn't have been there to stop us."

David shrugged. "It's one of those things we'll never know. But I am at peace with the decisions I made."

"I apologize if I offended you."

"Not at all. I just don't talk about my innermost feelings that often."

She smiled brightly. "Why not? It helps to cleanse the soul."

"Ms. Bo'hai, I'm the commanding officer of the largest warship humans have ever built, not to mention her battle-group. My job is, at all times, to guide those under my command, accomplish the orders I'm given from the Coalition Defense Force, and get everyone I can home safely. What I don't have the luxury of is spilling my deep, dark secrets to my subordinates."

"Surely there is someone you can talk to."

David shook his head. "Especially now, they have to see me like a rock that doesn't waver and as someone who will

Mercy

39

get them home." *Why am I telling her these things?* Her warm smile drew him in, even though he knew he had no business discussing such topics.

"We believe that the Maker raises leaders and guides us through them."

It took David a moment to work through what he wanted to say. While the Torah said virtually the same thing, he struggled with the idea that HaShem *wanted* them to be there and that it was somehow preordained. "I take it you believe I'm the prophet your text speaks of?"

Bo'hai inclined her head. "I find it more reasonable than the explanation of random chance."

That sounds like something I'd say to Dr. Hayworth. "For now, we'll have to agree to disagree there."

Again, she smiled, its warmth seeming to fill the conference room. "I know you are busy with many tasks running this mighty vessel, but perhaps we could speak again in the future? Getting difficult things off your chest is, as I said, good for the soul."

Part of him wanted to take her up on it. *Then again, discussing sensitive information with an alien probably isn't the best idea.* "Perhaps." Yet he couldn't entirely turn off the desire to talk about what was happening.

They stared at each other for a few seconds before she stood. "I bid you a good rest of your rotations, General."

David inclined his head. "You as well, Ms. Bo'hai."

As she departed, David glanced at his handcomm. *Engineering walk-through in thirty minutes. I've got just enough time to grab a snack if I hurry. One foot in front of the other, with a smile on my face.* It was what duty demanded.

5

HAKAN YAVUZ WAS glad it was the height of the hot season in Zeivlot's Tophae province because it gave him an excuse to wear loose-fitting clothing, which helped conceal the explosive charge encircling his torso, which was built of extremely potent charges. The putty was intermeshed with nails and metallic bits designed to cause as much carnage as possible.

Such is what the heretics deserve. It disgusted Yavuz to the core of his being that demons were allowed on the surface of their world. To see those who'd once been fellow believers worshipping those demons as being sent by the Maker was worse. *Now is the time for all Zeivlots to stand up for their culture and our shared beliefs.*

He gripped the dead man's switch tightly, advancing toward the target. As it was the day of rest, throngs of people streamed toward the most prominent worship center in the town. *There should be at least five hundred here if not more.* Yavuz believed the more he was able to send on to eternity, the more those who remained would question their actions. *And turn from their evil ways.*

Mercy 41

Since Yavuz was right-handed, the trigger rested inside the fist of his left hand, leaving him free to smile and touch his palm to the one outstretched by the greeter as he entered the worship center. From there, it was easy to blend into the crowd of people. Yavuz chose to sit in a center row, again hoping for the most blast damage.

He realized as he made his way across the row and sat a few seats away from the nearest worshipper that there were more than enough people to trigger the device at any time. Still, Yavuz decided to wait for the service to start. The last words he wanted to hear were the cantillation proclaiming the Maker as the sovereign of all things and creator of the universe.

It took exceptional self-control not to release his grip as more people crowded around him. Being in the throng of heretics made Yavuz feel as if he was unclean. When the lector finally called the congregation to order with the cantillation, it was the most beautiful thing he'd ever heard.

With one final look around, Yavuz unclenched his hand the moment the chant subsided. A split second later, a massive explosion tore through the worship hall, mangling anyone in its path. Sheer unending pain accompanied the roar as his brain processed that his body had disintegrated. Yavuz wasn't sure what to expect next. Others who'd come back from death described a white light with warmth and love radiating from it.

Yet no such light appeared. Instead, utter darkness and dread were the only things Yavuz could feel as consciousness faded. Then he felt nothing but anguish.

———

"ONE HUNDRED EIGHT DEAD, Zupan. Another suicide attack."

Mishka Vog't put her hand over her mouth. With the third such bombing in the last seven cycles, the death toll had reached more than four hundred. She briefly closed her eyes and sighed as she fought the urge to scream. "Has anyone claimed responsibility for this atrocity?"

"Another terrorist group, Zupan," Azmi Ceren replied. He was her newly appointed war leader and commander of the Zeivlot security forces.

"We've been dealing with this problem for generations. What is causing the obscene rise in violence *now*?" Vog't stood and started pacing around her ceremonial office. "We're weeks removed from nearly everyone on our world dying, and *this* is what our citizens do with a second chance at life?"

Several civilian officials exchanged glances but said nothing.

"I want the gloves taken off." Vog't crossed her arms. "Is that clear?"

Ceren licked his lips. "Ma'am, you don't want to hear this, but I don't have a target for you. I'd mount up with a team and kill them myself if I did. We're fighting with one hand behind our backs here."

Her gaze went to Gur'dal Sol'maz, the intelligence director for their planet. "Why does the military not have precise information on who these disgusting heretics are and where they're hiding?"

"Because they stay off grid and hail primarily from the Tophae province. You know how it is there. Limited infrastructure, rural communities, and few trust the planetary government. That coupled with the rugged terrain, it's a recipe for the best camouflage on our world."

Vog't slammed her hand on the desk as she whirled around. "This is *not* acceptable, gentlemen. We will not

Mercy 43

normalize the murders of innocents. Get Colonel Demood and his people in here. The humans have all this technology. It's about time they use it."

CALVIN WASN'T USED to being summoned by anyone other than David, at least not for the last six months. The curt instruction from War Leader Ceren to appear in the zupan's office made him wonder what was going on. *Probably tied to that SVEST bombing today.* He, Private Susanna Nussbaum, and Master Gunnery Sergeant Reuben Menahem hadn't had time to change out of their battle dress uniforms. An electric aircar that hovered over the paved road surface had arrived for them moments after the call came in.

In what seemed like a record amount of time, the aircar dropped them off outside a row of townhouses. One was the official residence of the zupan.

After being escorted inside, they were quickly led to Vog't's office.

All three of them came to attention.

"Colonel Demood reports as ordered, ma'am." *Since David told me she was in charge, I'll show her the same respect, courtesy, and customs I would any other senior officer or civilian appointed over me.*

"Thank you for coming on such short notice, Colonel," Vog't replied.

"You're welcome, ma'am. Apologies for the lack of proper attire."

Vog't stared at him for a moment before raising an eyebrow. "Oh yes. I've noticed that human military forces have numerous uniforms for different events."

"Marines especially, ma'am." Calvin forced a grin. "We

like to be the best dressed." His expression turned serious. "I doubt I'm here for my wit, though. What can we do for you?"

"I need the Terran Coalition's help. And since you are the highest-ranking officer representing the Coalition, your help specifically is required."

"If it's within my power, I will do it, ma'am."

"You have undoubtedly seen the news reports?"

Calvin inclined his head. "Yes. It makes my blood boil."

"Your blood boils?" Vog't tilted her head. "I wasn't aware humans could do that."

"It's, ah, a—"

"An idiom," Menahem interjected. "A saying that humans have. Basically, it means we're mad."

Vog't pursed her lips. "I'm sorry. Your language still has so many different things in it that confuse us."

Calvin waved a hand. "Sorry. Somebody briefed me on keeping to phrases and words the translator program has worked out, but I'm a Marine." *She probably wouldn't understand the "We eat crayons" joke either.*

"Zeivlot can't afford to fall into civil war. That's what these terrorists want."

"Forgive me, but how would that even work? From what I see, the vast majority of your population is still shell-shocked over the near destruction of the planet."

"This sort of thing has happened before. The extremist groups will cause mass civilian casualties, which prompts us to send in security forces to deal with them," War Leader Ceren said with a grimace. "Have you ever had to deal with insurgents blending into a civilian population, Colonel?"

"Oh yeah. That's brutal. Typically urban combat. Lots of people die." Calvin crossed his arms. "Then what? They

Mercy 45

recruit off accidental civilian deaths, ginning up even more fighters, and the cycle spins out of control?"

Ceren nodded. "Exactly, Colonel."

"And you guys want us to up our use of SIGINT tech to help you pick targets then eliminate them?"

"I was hoping you would join us in neutralizing these terrorists before they can kill others." Vog't placed her hands on the desk.

If it had been up to Calvin, he would have pledged to send his entire detachment into battle right then and there. *Cowards who blow up civilians are among the worst in the universe.* Such tactics appalled him, and he had a visceral hatred for any who used them. But orders were orders. As much as it pained him, he had to stick to what David had instructed. *The general doesn't want us in a shooting war. But there are still ways I can stretch that.*

"I am constrained by the directives issued to me prior to the *Lion of Judah*'s leaving orbit. But at a minimum, we can run *all* of your SIGINT through our artificial intelligence whutsiwhatit." He turned to Susanna. "Correct, Private?"

"Yes, sir," she replied. "All I'd need is a compatible feed."

"What are the odds of your sharing that particular AI with us?" Ceren asked.

Too far. "None without approval from General Cohen."

"It's not technically an artificial intelligence," Susanna interjected. "We do not believe in creating synthetic life, so our AI is specifically shackled to avoid being sentient. A very intelligent machine learning algorithm is a better description."

Ceren raised an eyebrow. "I see."

"Is there anything else you can do for us, Colonel?" Vog't asked. Her voice might as well have been a plaintive wail.

It cut Calvin to the bone because he could do little without violating his orders. He came close to saying to hell with orders and proceeding. Instead, Calvin bit his lip. "I can't authorize wholesale changes to our mission as it stands now, but I promise you the next time I talk with General Cohen, I will impress upon him the need to do so."

"Thank you, Colonel." Vog't glanced at Ceren. "If you'd excuse us, I have a planetwide address to work out."

"Of course, ma'am."

Calvin stood, followed quickly by Menahem and Susanna. The three of them made their way out of the small office.

"We need to go all in," Menahem growled the moment they were out of earshot. "And you know it, sir."

"Yeah. I do." Mentally, Calvin had searched for any loophole he could find but kept coming up short. "For now, we'll keep doing what we're doing, amp it up, and give them all the terror cells they can handle."

"Is anyone concerned that blanket surveillance of citizens without a warrant or court order is a violation of the Terran Coalition constitution?"

Calvin did a double-take at Susanna. "Since when did you become a lawyer?"

She shrugged. "I paid attention in civics class, sir."

"If the Zeivlots are fine with it, so am I. I kill people and break things. Others can argue about legalities."

"Amen to that." Menahem let out a sigh. "What if this killing keeps up, Colonel? You still want to stand down?"

"What's Cohen say? We'll cross that bridge when we come to it."

"Yeah."

Calvin yanked open the door to the exterior of the building. "Then let's go with that." As the harsh sunlight hit his face, he knew a reckoning was coming. *I won't be able to stay out of this fight much longer.*

6

DAVID SEEMED to be spending even more time than usual in the *Lion of Judah*'s deck-one conference room. He'd always found paperwork oppressive and time spent in meetings detracting from the task at hand—whatever it was. Since their arrival in Sextans B, his entire routine had been disrupted. Sure, he got up at the same time every morning and completed his morning ritual, but in the absence of orders from CDF Command, it all felt off.

Even the overriding mission to get home was something for which David was ill-equipped. *Give me an enemy to deter or fight and a battle to win.* Until they figured it out, he would muddle on as best he could. *And seek HaShem's guidance.*

"General on deck!" Tinetariro called out as David strode in.

"As you were." He dropped into the chair at the head of the table.

Ruth, Hanson, Aibek, and Hayworth were all seated on both sides. David hadn't seen a need to pull all senior staff in for a final sign-off on the mining operation.

Mercy   49

"So, where are we?" David asked.

"Marine shuttle is ready to go. We've tested the modifications and confirmed the graviton beam will capture the ore," Hanson replied. "The cargo cage is also tested and fully functional. From a technical perspective, we're ready, sir."

"There is the ethical concern," Aibek hissed.

David leaned back. "I've thought long and hard about this. My decision is that while I don't like it, we need the helium-3. There's no indication the species who inhabit this system even know it's here. Ethics concerns aside, with the difficulties in obtaining certain elements in this galaxy, having enough to replenish our reserves will provide a stopgap until a more permanent solution can be found."

Aibek remained quiet as an uncomfortable tension seeped into the room.

"Anything else?"

"Well, sir, Dr. Hayworth and I were examining sensor data, and we think the alien species in this system might be able to detect the *Lion* if she jumps in."

"So you want to use something smaller?"

"Yes, sir."

David nodded. "Marine assault shuttles would fit in the *Margaret Thatcher*'s bay, right?"

"Yes, sir, we already checked." Hanson grinned.

I like it when my officers anticipate my reaction and come up with ready-made solutions. "Outstanding, Major. Who's on the crew?"

"I'll be manning the beam, sir," Ruth interjected. "Frankly, I want to do something besides stare at the bulkheads."

Now, that sentiment, I can understand. "Very well. No issues here. Marine pilot lined up?"

"Yes, sir," Hanson replied. "And I'll be along to lead the mission and handle engineering problems in real time."

"I'm not sure I like having two of my senior officers on the same shuttle."

"Given the situation, sir, we can't afford any mistakes." Hanson crossed his arms. "Besides, I'm with the TAO. The confines of this ship are getting to me. Even pawing the vacuum is a welcome break."

David shrugged. "I have no objections. Anything else?" He almost felt as if the discussion was unnecessary.

No replies came.

"Very well. Dismissed."

Everyone but Aibek stood quickly and filed out.

The big Saurian waited until the hatch closed to speak. "I must protest this activity."

David knew what was coming next but felt he had no choice but to press on. "I know. It pains me, and I hope I haven't lost your respect."

Aibek stared at him. "It is impossible for you to lose my respect as a fellow warrior. I have fought alongside you for years, yet even the greatest of all men make poor choices. Such as *this* one."

"Where do we get the helium-3, then? Stores are already under fifty percent across the fleet. It'll only get worse."

"I cannot change your mind, my friend. I only hope the Prophet does not punish all of us for this misdeed."

"On that, we agree." David stood. "I'll see you on the bridge, XO."

Wordlessly, Aibek departed the conference room. Only the slight mechanical hum of the life-support system pushing fresh air in could be heard.

About the closest I can get to peace and quiet on this ship. David stared at the Coalition Defense Force seal on the wall,

Mercy 51

which was emblazoned with the words Courage, Commitment, Faith. *It's just a couple loads of ore that aren't worth that much in the grand scheme of things.* The adage that the road to hell was paved with good intentions came into his mind as he headed back to his day cabin.

7

LIEUTENANT COLONEL ANTON SAVCHENKO glanced around the compact bridge of his ship, the CSV *Margaret Thatcher*. Compared to the cavernous space of the *Lion*'s control center, the *Thatcher* was tiny. Yet it was *his*. When he'd contemplated what taking command of a warship would entail, being tossed into a different galaxy and having to find a way home wasn't on the menu. Since boot camp, Savchenko had had a single, overriding goal: defeat the League and command a warship while doing it.

He felt a sense of cultural duty, as Ukrainian blood ran deep in his veins. His people still carried the stories of what the League had done to them on Earth. Sometimes, when he witnessed an exploding enemy destroyer, paying them back felt good. And four and a half million light-years from home, Savchenko had an entirely different set of challenges. Pushing those thoughts aside, he turned toward a station in the bridge's aft section. "Master Chief, shuttle bay status?"

"Both Marine shuttles locked down, sir. Shuttle bay reports ready for Lawrence drive jump."

As a Block-II Ajax-destroyer, the *Thatcher* had some

Mercy

unique upgrades over the Block I vessels. Among them was a larger shuttle bay and integrated Vertical Rail Launch System—VRLS—for Hunter missiles.

Savchenko's gaze drifted back to the front, passing over the communications station and the ship's emblem mounted on the wall with her nickname: The Iron Lady. "Well, in that case, let's get on with our little mining operation. Navigation, plot Lawrence jump as close to the target planetoid as possible."

"Aye, aye, sir."

Major Kabar Masoud, his executive officer, leaned closer. "Want to take us to condition two, sir?"

"No. We have no idea what kind of sensor systems this species might have. Maybe the EM emissions from our deflectors would tip them off. Too big a risk."

Masoud nodded. "Let's hope there's no surprises."

"Ah, what's the fun in that?" Savchenko cracked a grin. "Wouldn't want things to get too boring around here, would we?"

"Yeah, I'd rather just get this over with," Masoud replied.

"Conn, Navigation. Coordinates set, sir. Lawrence drive is fully charged."

Savchenko shifted in the CO's chair and double-checked his armrest-mounted display. "Activate Lawrence drive."

In front of the *Margaret Thatcher*, space tore itself open. The artificial wormhole came into focus through the bridge windows as it grew. The vortex shifted colors dynamically before stabilizing.

"Navigation, all ahead flank."

The *Thatcher* accelerated forward, the ship's bow sliding into the swirling mass. An optical illusion made it appear as if the wormhole was made of gas. Savchenko didn't quite understand the science behind the drive, only that it worked. *Every time. Well, except once.*

Moments later, the vessel emerged on the other side. The planetoid wasn't within visual range, but he could make out the distant shape of the supergiant in the binary star system.

After any Lawrence drive jump came a three- to five-second window in which the sensors were blind. They were the longest five seconds of any ship driver's life every time.

"Conn, TAO. LIDAR online. No contacts."

Savchenko let out a breath. "Nav, intercept course on our target planetoid. All ahead two-thirds."

"Aye, aye, sir."

As the destroyer moved off and the tug of increased gravity rippled through the vessel, Savchenko turned to Masoud. "Time to get our mining shuttle moving. Alert Major Hanson we'll be ready for them to launch in fifteen minutes."

"Aye, aye, sir." Masoud tapped his integrated display.

While the *Thatcher* covered the distance, Savchenko kept alert. In his gut, something told him it wasn't going to be as easy as jump in, get the helium-3-laden ore, and jump out. *I should probably have been more forceful with the general about that.*

Time marched on.

———

RUTH ADJUSTED in the copilot seat of their heavily modified Marine assault shuttle. Behind her, Hanson occupied the fold-out jump chair, which he'd converted into a makeshift monitoring station complete with two tablets attached with

Velcro to the bulkhead wall between them and the cargo bay.

"Holding steady two kilometers above the surface. Hover mode engaged," the pilot, a TCMC warrant officer named Karmina Al-Haddad, reported.

They were more than close enough for the modified neutron beam. Technically, Ruth could've started carving the planetoid's surface from thousands of kilometers away, but the gravity tractor required a closer distance. *And I don't want to screw this up.* "Major, mining rig is locked on."

Hanson glanced between the two tablets. "I show green lights across the board. Light it up."

A few moments later, a bright-blue beam shot out from the shuttle's underside. It cut a swatch through the dark, rocky surface of the giant asteroid, four corners square, before the gravity tractor pulled it away from the rest of the planetoid.

"I've got the ore," Hanson said as he manipulated his controls. "Closing on the cargo pod. One thousand meters. Seven hundred meters. Three hundred meters."

"Rate of ascent is too fast, Major. Recommend twenty percent drop in tractor power."

"Agreed." Hanson tapped one of the tablets. "There we go. One hundred fifty meters. Stand by pod doors."

"Pod doors open. Containment field ready."

Hanson grunted a few times, as if he were physically moving the ore rather than manipulating a computer. "Go for containment."

An energy field snapped into place, securing the ore in the shuttle's cargo pod. The shuttle pitched forward before the pilot reacted, smoothing out its flight.

Ruth grinned. "That's what I call mission success."

"Not bad, Captain." Hanson turned away from his

tablets. "Warrant, get on the horn to the *Margaret Thatcher*, and let's drop this off before we go rinse and repeat another five times."

"When the recruiter told me I'd get to see the galaxy and shoot Leaguers, he didn't say anything about slicing up rocks and bootlegging them out," Ruth said.

Hanson snickered. "I'm sure there's a career as a spacer in your future back home, Goldberg. Mining ships pay pretty well, as I recall."

"What's well?"

"Half a million standard Coalition credits a year."

Ruth's jaw dropped. "Seriously? That's... a lot of credits."

"Think about it," Hanson replied as he shifted in the jump seat. "Constant threat of pirate attack, because space mining is only allowed in uninhabited systems, which are by definition not exactly the safest areas of the void."

"You sound like someone who's studied the subject."

Hanson tilted his head. "I suppose I did. Kinda have to decide what's next, you know? Before all... this... happened, getting out of the CDF seemed like it was the right call for me."

"No offense, Major, but you always hit me as a lifer. Just like me."

"Maybe. None of that matters now, though, does it? We've only got one job... hold the battlegroup together until we get home."

Indeed, that is our only job. Which is why I'm on a shuttle, stealing ore from some confederation of four alien species. Ruth found it darkly amusing. "No reason we can't have some fun while we're doing it."

Hanson chuckled.

Before Ruth could break out more banter, her console

Mercy 57

beeped. A quick scan of the interface showed why: the proximity alert had triggered. "Warrant, you seeing that?"

"Yes, ma'am. Thought it was other asteroids, since we haven't seen anything out here."

Ruth furrowed her brow and adjusted the scanner resolution. While limited in terms of maneuverability and firepower, the shuttle possessed an excellent sensor suite. "That's not rock. We've got several, maybe as many as five contacts headed in."

"Alien craft?" Hanson perked up in his chair as he grimaced.

"Well, unless Colonel Amir's pulling a prank on us, yeah, I'd say so. Warrant, push it up, and signal the *Margaret Thatcher* that we've got company."

Then purple and orange streaks of energy flew by the cockpit canopy.

Oh shit.

8

SOMETIMES, standing watch was akin to watching paint dry or grass grow. David stared out the windows at the front of the expansive bridge, admiring a nebula in the distance. The way it framed the binary star system was striking. *Almost like a painting.* He'd been admiring the beauty of the cosmos more than ever lately. *Perhaps it has something to do with being forced into the role of an explorer.*

"Conn, Communications," Taylor said, his voice drawing David out of his mental reverie. "I'm getting what sounds like a distress call from Captain Goldberg, sir."

Alarm coursed through David, and his heart skipped a beat. "Put it on."

Loud crackles of static snapped through the speakers before Ruth's voice came through. "Surrounded by hostile vessels. Engines inoperative. Mayday. Mayday. *Margaret Thatcher*, do you hear us?"

"*Lion of Judah* actual reads loud and clear, Captain. Confirm hostile contacts."

"Unknown configuration, sir." A loud explosion crackled through the commlink. "I think they mean to board us.

Mercy

We're getting demands for surrender that the translation matrix is picking up. It registers as the language the aliens in this system use."

David's mind went into overdrive. *We didn't observe that species having FTL capabilities. How could they just happen to be there?* Condemnation wasn't far behind. He briefly closed his eyes. "Can you maneuver back to the *Margaret Thatcher*, Captain?"

"Negative, sir. The hostiles disabled our engines with an EMP burst. We're dead in the void."

David glanced at Aibek. "Remind me when this is over that you were right."

The Saurian responded only with a short hiss.

"Conn, Communications. Colonel Savchenko requests permission to fire on the hostile contacts and retrieve the shuttle."

We have more than enough military might to retrieve the shuttle by destroying the four ships the aliens sent. But if I do that, I'm starting a war at best. They think we're an enemy force, and they're reacting to defend their solar system. David knew he'd made a grievous mistake that would haunt him in ways he didn't fully comprehend at the moment.

"Your orders, sir?" Taylor interjected.

Maybe we can keep this from getting out of hand. "Colonel Savchenko is cleared to lock the hostile vessels and aggressively maneuver to retrieve the shuttle. He is not cleared to fire unless fired upon."

"But—"

"Those are my orders, Lieutenant," David barked. "Navigation, plot a Lawrence drive jump directly on top of the *Margaret Thatcher*."

"Colonel Savchenko acknowledges, sir."

Taylor's voice had a hard edge to it. David didn't blame

him, mainly because his fiancée was on the shuttle. *Ruth is one of my closest friends too.* He grappled with the idea of trying to disable the alien ships and disappear. *But I'll know. We'll all know. So will HaShem.*

"Conn, Navigation. Jump coordinates set, sir."

"Communications, order the rest of our escorts to follow us in."

Aibek raised an eye scale. "What are your intentions?"

"Shock and awe. Get the shuttle back, offer some accommodation to the aliens, pay for the ore... and get out of there without killing anyone."

"A more honorable course of action than what we have done so far," Aibek replied, his voice low enough not to carry more than half a meter.

The words from his XO stung. *Well, Talgat's not wrong.* But that didn't change what was coming next. David pressed the intercom button on his chair, engaging the 1MC. "Attention, all hands. This is General Cohen. General quarters. General quarters. All hands, man your battle stations. I say again, all hands, man your battle stations. This is not a drill." He glanced at the tactical station. "TAO, set material condition one throughout the ship."

Immediately, the bridge lights dimmed and turned blue, casting dark shadows across the room. Second Lieutenant Kelsey announced, "Material condition one set through the ship, sir."

"TAO, energize shield generators and activate point defense." David set his jaw. "Navigation, activate Lawrence drive."

He turned to Tinetariro. "Master Chief, send for the master-at-arms, and track down Dr. Hayworth, Lieutenant Bodell, and Salena Bo'hai. I want them on the bridge ASAP."

Mercy

"TAO, DISTANCE TO OUR SHUTTLE?" Lt. Colonel Anton Savchenko barked.

"Five thousand kilometers and closing, sir."

They were already running at battle stations, and additional watch standers had arrived a few minutes before to take over tactical and engineering substations on the bridge. He felt annoyed that General Cohen had forbidden firing on the hostile aliens so far. "Reconfirm firing solution for forward neutron beams."

"We should be lighting them up like a Christmas tree if they have remotely capable sensors, sir."

Savchenko grinned. "Adjust aim six degrees to port, and put a neutron beam across the bow of the lead ship."

"Aye, aye, sir."

A blue spear of energy shot out of the dorsal neutron-beam emitter, slicing through the void. While it avoided hitting anything, the four alien craft reacted violently, increasing their speed and maneuvering sharply. If the Marine shuttle still had engines, it would've been the perfect time for it to escape.

"Nav, all ahead flank. Get us alongside, and prepare to grapple Sierra One into the docking bay." Savchenko sat back, his jaw set.

"Conn, Communications. We're getting another broadcast from Master Three, sir."

"Same garbage?" Savchenko asked.

"Yes, sir. General demand for us to surrender and pull back along with a threat to destroy the shuttle."

"Conn, TAO. Aspect change, inbound wormhole," the tactical officer, First Lieutenant Abigail Miller, said suddenly, her voice rising an octave. "Reading CDF signature... It's the *Lion of Judah*, sir."

Savchenko let out a sigh of relief. "Comms, send General Cohen my compliments, and request permission to open fire on the hostile contacts."

"Ah, sir, incoming message from the *Lion* on the general broadcast channel."

"On speakers."

A few moments later, the central speaker in the CO's chair crackled, followed by a burst of static before Cohen came on the line. "This is Major General David Cohen, commanding the Coalition Star Vessel *Lion of Judah*. We are humans, a species from a planet in the Milky Way galaxy, which is four and a half million light-years from here. We mean you no harm, and we come in peace. Whatever misunderstanding that led to these unfortunate events, I ask that you power down your weapon systems, and we can discuss this rationally."

"Sir, orders from the tactical network. We're to pull back and power down our neutron beams."

Savchenko gritted his teeth. "Request confirmation."

"We can't go against the general," Masoud interjected quietly. "Orders are still orders, even out here."

"And we should leave our people to the tender mercies of aliens that we don't even know what they look like or if they have the basic concept of justice as a custom? For all we know, they could ritually eat outsiders."

"Unlikely, sir," Masoud replied.

"TAO, drop our weapons lock. Navigation, all back, one-third. Bring us to six thousand kilometers from the shuttle."

As his orders were carried out, Savchenko's anger built. *I can see what he's trying to do, but leaving our people hanging is unacceptable.*

9

ON THE *LION*'S BRIDGE, David stared straight ahead. His stomach was in a knot as he waited for someone to respond. *I wonder which species will answer. Or who's in charge over there.* As the seconds ticked by, he pondered whether their translation matrix was even working.

"Conn, Communications. Getting a response from one of the alien vessels. Audio only."

David glanced back at Taylor. "Let's hear it, Lieutenant."

A strange, almost synthetic voice filled the bridge a few moments later. "You have infringed on our terrene, unusual hostile creature."

Yeah, not exactly ready for prime time yet. "This is Major General David Cohen, commanding the *Lion of Judah.* To whom am I speaking?"

"I am Procurator Frelbrek of the Vogtek Aegis."

"We mean you no harm. The Terran Coalition comes in peace."

"You are not of our system. How do you speak our language?"

David pursed his lips. "No, we're from a different galaxy. We've translated your language over the last few weeks."

"This is impossible. You deceive. We have seen no ships matching yours."

"No, we do not. Our ships possess faster-than-light travel capabilities."

"As do ours. To go between two self-luminous objects takes years, even at fastest speed. To travel between galaxies would take millions of years."

Aibek touched the mute button on David's chair. "It would appear these aliens lack a Lawrence drive."

David nodded. "Yeah, but they said they have FTL capability. No idea what that might be."

"An Alcubierre drive," Hayworth interjected. "It would explain why they think traveling between stars takes so long."

I've got no idea what that is, and now's not the time. "Right," David replied. He nodded at Aibek, who removed his finger from the mute button. "Frelbrek, we use a different form of travel between stars. We'd be happy to share more information about it and get to know your people better. If you were to allow us to retrieve the small spacecraft you've surrounded, perhaps a face-to-face meeting could be arranged."

"Such a thing is intriguing, yet how can we accept the word of a deceiver? This craft of yours has stolen fuel from us."

David bit his lip. "It did so on orders from me, Procurator. I sincerely apologize, as we didn't realize you claimed this planetoid."

"How is this possible? You said you translated our language over time."

"We didn't think you had the technology to get this far

Mercy 65

out in your solar system, Procurator. That was a mistake on our part."

"So you intended to steal but didn't realize we could reach this rock?"

A glare from Aibek made David want to close his eyes and be anywhere but in the CO's chair. Sometimes, he made the wrong decision. Worse, David had known it when he made the call. "I have no excuse for our behavior except to ask for your forgiveness. We will return the ore taken and make amends in other ways."

Seconds passed. "It is not our custom to allow another to take the punishment for a criminal, even if they were directed to. Ignorance is not an excuse for breaking the law. You must come with us to the Seat of Judgment and accept sanction."

"Will you allow us to retrieve our spacecraft?"

"No," Frelbrek replied without missing a beat. "Its occupants will be held by us to ensure you face the tribunal."

Aibek again pressed the mute button. "We cannot allow them to hold our warriors hostage."

"TAO, what's your read on combat capability of those vessels?"

"Extremely limited compared to ours, sir. We could disable or destroy all four of them with ease."

David leaned back. "The question here isn't one of military success—it's one of morality. *We* are the ones in the wrong. If I use force and, HaShem forbid, kill some of these aliens, I'd be violating a dozen different CDF regulations and the Canaan Convention on Human and Alien Rights. We have to try a diplomatic approach first."

"And if that doesn't work? I know you would not leave our warriors behind."

"Of course I wouldn't," David snapped. He detested

nothing more than having a debate on the bridge in full view of the crew.

Hayworth cleared his throat. "These sorts of things wouldn't be an issue if we avoided alien cultures."

"I seem to remember you supported mining the helium-3, Doctor."

"Yes, well, that doesn't mean the general thought isn't wrong."

David suppressed the desire to roll his eyes and brushed Aibek's finger off the mute button. "Procurator, does your culture have the concept of due process?"

"I do not understand."

"When someone is accused of a crime, are they able to defend themselves of that charge in a court, with adequate legal representation? Is there an impartial judge to oversee the hearing?"

"We believe in justice above all else. The accused will be treated fairly, and you may view their trial in person. I am certain my government will allow you to interact with our tribunal and offer testimony if you wish."

Second Lieutenant Nathanael Bodell, an analyst from the *Lion*'s G2 shop, stepped forward. He sliced his hand back and forth near his neck.

David took note. "Procurator, please hold on for a moment while my crewmates and I discuss the situation." He held down the mute button. "If you've got something to add, by all means, Lieutenant."

"Sir, the language this individual is using—it's very pointed. Lots of references to punishment and justice. Their concept of the words may be different from ours. Perhaps they operate on the basis of guilty until proven innocent."

"Wouldn't be the first time we've seen that in a

Mercy 67

nonhuman species or even among other human cultures," David mused. "Noted, Lieutenant."

Aibek hissed as he shifted his position. "We could have the shuttle occupants eject and SAR pick them up."

For a moment, David pondered the suggestion. *He's right. We could. The* Lion *is close enough to launch a Jolly Green.* "And if they fire on the rescue bird?"

"Disable them."

"No." David set his jaw. "As long as there is a legal action that we can present evidence and, moreover, that *I* can accept responsibility in, we're not starting a war."

"General, I must respectfully agree with the XO, sir." Tinetariro had taken a few steps forward and faced the COs chair.

"Master Chief, this isn't a democracy," David replied.

"I understand that, sir, but we can't leave our people in the hands of a culture we know nothing about. This ship probably possesses enough force to take out the entire solar system's military."

"It most likely does." David crosses his arms. "Are we reduced to might makes right?" He glanced around to see everyone staring at the three of them intently.

"Sir—"

"No. Those patches on our uniforms have three words on them. Courage, commitment, and faith. If I or anyone else in this battlegroup uses lethal force to settle a situation in which *we* are at fault, those words are meaningless. We say Godspeed to one another, invoking HaShem's blessing before every battle. It's a part of everything we do, and would *anyone* care to tell me what our respective religious and moral beliefs are on murder? Because let's be clear—if we destroy those four ships, we're committing murder."

Aibek and Tinetariro both looked away.

"And what if these aliens are unreasonable, sir? What if they want to execute Captain Goldberg or confiscate our vessels?"

"Then I'll deal with that as it comes, Master Chief. We won't be leaving anyone behind. I promise you that. War is also the *last* resort. Do I make myself clear?"

"Yes, sir."

David turned to Aibek. "XO?"

"It is your command and responsibility. I will abide."

After four years of serving together, David had never once sensed that Aibek found his decisions unworthy of respect. *Until now.* He moved his finger off the mute button. "Procurator, we accept your terms and will follow you back to wherever the tribunal you have referenced is located. I'll also order the shuttle to stand down and allow you to board it without incident."

"Until we meet again, I wish you justice and long life."

The commlink clicked off, and the bridge crew relaxed a bit.

Taylor cleared his throat. "Sir, are we really going to tell the shuttle crew to surrender?"

"Yes, we are." David turned around. "Get me Major Hanson."

"Aye, aye, sir."

———

RUTH YELPED as the circuit tester she held touched the wrong node, sending a jolt of electricity through her hand and leaving it half numb. "I thought you said this console was safed, Warrant."

"Sorry, ma'am," Al-Haddad replied.

Mercy 69

"Try it again," Hanson called out. He was hunched over an open access panel and had half a dozen wires pulled out.

"No joy, Major."

Hanson cursed and slammed his palm into the alloy surface before wincing in pain. "Okay, we'll try rerouting power to the port thrusters instead."

"Uh, sir, I'm getting inbound comms traffic from the *Lion of Judah*," Al-Haddad announced. She tapped a few buttons.

"Cohen to Hanson. Come in."

"Hanson here, sir. Glad to hear your voice."

"Likewise. We've made contact with the aliens. They call themselves the Vogtek Aegis. We violated their space, and unfortunately, they caught us red-handed."

"Well, that would explain the hostile response, sir," Hanson replied. "We're trying to get the shuttle's thrusters back, but I don't think that's happening anytime soon. Could you send a SAR bird to haul us in?"

"Negative, Major. This race—or group of races—places a very high premium on justice and legality. They've demanded the right to charge you with stealing the helium-3. I don't like this, but I struck a deal to allow a trial, and I will take full responsibility for the operation. Do not resist when they board the shuttle, but you are authorized to destroy any sensitive technology or intelligence."

"Um, that's almost everything, sir."

Ruth's mind swam. Anger rose to the surface that David apparently wouldn't use force to rescue them. But as soon as it came up, she realized the quandary. *Whatever euphemism we want to use, if we got our hand caught in the cookie jar, shooting our way out of the situation compounds the wrong.* "Are you certain that's the only way, sir?"

"I don't like it any more than you do, Captain."

"Sir, with respect, have you tried a display of force?

Maybe all it would take is disabling or destroying one of these ships."

"I just had the same conversation on the bridge a few seconds ago, Major. We both know that's not acceptable. This species seems to value justice. I have every confidence we can clear the matter up without bloodshed."

"Yes, sir. We'll prepare to destroy all electronics and render the shuttle unusable."

"I'll let the Vogtek know. Godspeed to you all, and I'll see you soon."

"Sir," Ruth cut in before the commlink clicked off. "What if there're unforeseen complications?"

"Captain, I give you my word that no matter what, I'll get all of you home." David's voice cracked with emotion.

"Thank you, sir."

"Shuttle Six-One signing off," Hanson said as he toggled off the comms relay. "Okay. You all heard the general. Destroy it all. Acid packs are stored over there." He pointed at a compartment behind Ruth's head.

As she moved to open it, Ruth's stomach turned. *Will I ever see Robert again? I'll have to trust in God and General Cohen to see us through.* Things she couldn't control had always been her Achilles heel. Worry and fear invaded her mind as she started pouring the acidic compound over the circuit boards.

10

THE ZEIVLOT SUN SHONE BRIGHTLY, and the planet orbited closer to it than Canaan and most of the temperate worlds of the Terran Coalition did their suns. That explained why Calvin put sunscreen on for the first time in his adult life. *UV radiation levels of twenty-two would cause even me to get a serious sunburn.* Native Zeivlots didn't seem to have much issue with it, but humans could suffer extreme skin burns after only ten minutes of unprotected time outdoors.

Calvin adjusted the olive jacket of his service alpha uniform and ensured his sidearm was properly secured in its hip holster. It had become second nature to him on Zeivlot to remain armed at all times. *Just in case.*

"You clean up good, sir," Master Gunnery Sergeant Menahem said with a chuckle. "Almost pass for one of the Terran Coalition's misguided children."

Calvin snickered. "You oughtta see me in my dress blues. For whatever reason, my wife still thinks I'm handsome in 'em." The thought of Jessica brought a pang of guilt to his heart. *Here I am, doing my job halfway across the universe, and she's at home thinking I'm dead.* He forced the feeling down.

"If we don't get moving, sir, we're going to be late."

"Yeah, and they'll be an hour late anyway." Above all, Calvin hated political meetings. The security summit planned for that day promised to be a doozy.

They strode through the corridors of the Coalition Assistance Command annex, which was at a military installation on the outskirts of the Zeivlot capital city. A convoy of aircars awaited them along with soldiers in neatly pressed uniforms and gleaming rifles. More Marines climbed into vehicles in the convoy.

Too bad we don't have power armor providing security. Calvin respected the Zeivlots. They knew how to fight, and they were reasonably well trained. But because of his technology, he could take on ten of them and win without breaking a sweat. *Well, if I had my armor on.*

As he climbed into an open vehicle toward the middle of the six-car convoy, he realized it wasn't empty. On the opposite side of the passenger compartment, a Zeivlot and a Zavlot military officer sat. *I guess this is Vog't's idea of direct engagement.* An icy air of hostility permeated the interior of the aircar.

Menahem slid into the last seat, and the door slammed shut behind him. "You guys ever get tired of this heat?"

The Zavlot—easily identified because of his distinctive uniform—grimaced. "Our world is farther away and has a lower overall temperature."

The delay between the officer's words and the device in Calvin's ear translating them to English made it a little difficult to follow precisely what he was saying, but the gist came through. "Yeah, that makes sense. What about solar radiation?"

"It is similar to Zeivlot."

Mercy   73

"That's because our star is stronger than what humans are used to," the Zeivlot officer replied.

Calvin shrugged. "We've all got our environmental limitations. Well, except Saurians. Those guys can colonize a lot more planets than we can."

Both aliens peered at him. "Saurian?"

"Reptilian species. Scales instead of skin. Tall. Strong," Menahem replied. "The *Lion of Judah*'s executive officer is one."

"We weren't aware of different races among you." The Zavlot's eyes widened. "Most interesting."

These guys don't get out much. "So, I'm Colonel Calvin Demood. TCMC." He jerked his thumb toward Menahem. "This is Master Gunnery Sergeant Reuben Menahem."

The Zavlot blinked. "I am Senior War Master Hadem Bi'shara. My protocol manual said humans appreciate it if you tell them it's a pleasure to meet."

Calvin couldn't help guffawing at Bi'shara's comment. "Hey, I don't care much about protocol. Marines are a special breed of human. We kill bad guys and blow things up."

"Perhaps you can enlighten us as to how we can more effectively deal with the terrorists sweeping through our cities," the Zeivlot interjected.

"That's the point of this summit, right?"

He shook his head. "I wish you humans had never come. Things were bad before, but they're far worse now."

I wish I could read the Zeivlot language. Calvin tried to make heads or tails of the Zeivlot's name tag but couldn't. "War leader, right?"

"Yes. Hakan Yavuz."

Wow, that one ain't winning any Miss Congeniality awards. He was about to open his mouth and provide a snappy retort when a high-pitched whine registered. *That sounds almost like a—*

The lead aircar disappeared in a bright-orange explosion, followed quickly by another to the rear. The pressure waves blew out windows all around them on the city street. Calvin and Menahem flew forward as their vehicle slammed into the back of the one in front. It took a second for the shock to wear off and Calvin's combat instincts to fully kick in. The aircar behind them slammed into their rear bumper.

Calvin wrenched the door closest to him open and disengaged the safety restraint. "Out of the vehicle! Now!" As he cleared the passenger compartment, harsh sunlight hit him in the face. As he blinked furiously, another rocket swooshed into an aircar ten meters away. The blast knocked him off his feet as Menahem and the other two officers climbed out.

Reports from automatic weapons echoed across the street. They were in the middle of a dense urban block with shops all around, but it seemed as if there were no civilians nearby. *Probably because the local cops cleared the route.* Calvin felt for his sidearm and drew it from the ceremonial leather holster. He racked the action and slid a bullet into the chamber while trying to find the source of the incoming.

Bullets smacked the alloy of the aircar next to him and Menahem. Calvin pointed at the other side of the vehicle. "Cover! Get behind cover!"

"Where?" Menahem shouted as another series of bursts hit nearby. "They've got a shooting gallery going!"

A figure in a mask popped above a ledge on a roof three stories up. Calvin sighted down his pistol and squeezed the trigger twice. One of the rounds hit its target, and the figure pitched backward, the automatic weapon it cradled firing harmlessly into the sky.

Incoming fire slackened momentarily, perhaps as the terrorists realized someone was shooting back at them. Calvin took advantage of the reprieve and propelled Menahem, Yavuz, and Bi'shara toward a storefront. Then he sprinted to the next aircar and flung the door open. Two Zeivlot security officers were dead inside, their eyes rolled back in their heads while pink blood pooled on the floor under them. One Marine had a bullet wound to the chest, and the other was trying to administer first aid.

"Corporal Toledano," Calvin barked. "Help me pull him out. Hell of a lot safer outside than in this bullet sponge."

"Yes, sir," Toledano replied. He scooted out the door and yanked his fellow Marine by the legs, dragging him to the ground as Calvin assisted.

The chest hole made a sucking sound with each labored breath the wounded Marine took. *Lung puncture. If we don't stabilize him soon, he won't make it.*

Then the hostile forces decided to renew their attack. What seemed like hundreds of bullets slammed into the remaining aircars, shattering glass and forcing Calvin to keep his head down. He realized one of the Zeivlot submachine guns was in reach and stuck his hand into the vehicle to retrieve it. Once the firing stopped for a moment, he popped up and rested the weapon on the hood to see several military-aged men approaching.

"Alpha, mike, foxtrot," Calvin muttered as he squeezed the weapon's trigger and sent a three-round burst into the nearest hostile. After shifting his aim to the right by a few centimeters, he felled a second then dropped back behind the aircar.

Several other Zeivlot security troops had retrieved their

weapons and joined the fight—a welcome relief. But the enemy was regrouping as well. The street was lined with small shops and mixed-use residential buildings, all housing dozens of perfect hiding places for snipers and insurgents to rain down hell itself.

A whooshing sound ripped through the air, followed by a new explosion close by. Concussion waves then a blast of fire ripped over Calvin's head as the aircar four meters away took a direct hit and blew apart. He turned to Toledano. "We gotta get out of here before they take us out. Can you get him in a fireman's carry?"

Toledano shook his head. "I just patched the hole with my handcomm, sir. Moving him upright—"

"Will probably kill him." Calvin ran through the available options in his head and realized he would give almost anything except his soul for power armor and his battle rifle at that moment. "Master Guns!" he shouted. "We need covering fire!"

Through the smoke wafting through the area, Menahem gave a thumbs-up.

Hope he understood me. "Okay, you get the legs, and I'll get the torso." Calvin slung the strap for the submachine gun over his shoulder and holstered his sidearm. When Toledano got control of the private's legs, Calvin wrapped his arms around the wounded man's back.

They stood in unison and wordlessly moved at the fastest pace either could manage with a ninety-kilogram deadweight. All at once, every terrorist seemed to find them. Bullets pinged against the sidewalk and the aircar behind them. They had little to do except push forward.

Adrenaline took over as they moved toward the shop the others had taken refuge in. Out of the corner of Calvin's eye, he saw a Zeivlot guard go down in a hail of gunfire. Poor

Mercy

training and the use of automatic weapons made the terrorists far less accurate than they should be, but with the volume of lead being put out around them, sooner or later, something would connect.

When they were less than a meter from the small store, several rounds stitched a path through Toledano's chest. Blood sprayed out, and he stumbled, dropping the wounded private as he collapsed.

Calvin's muscle memory took over as he let go and, in a fluid, practiced motion, unslung the submachine gun. One target was visible in a second-story window. Calvin squeezed the trigger and sent a burst of rounds downrange. They splattered into the frame above the terrorist's head, causing him to duck inside.

Menahem appeared at his side along with Bi'shara and Yavuz. Between the three of them, they pulled both wounded Marines into the shop while Calvin brazenly fired on the enemy from a crouched position.

Once the men were inside, Calvin sprinted the short distance into the store and collapsed behind the short display wall on the interior. "I'm getting too damn old for this." He briefly considered how lucky he was to be alive before turning his attention to the wounded. Shards of broken glass littered the floor, making it difficult to maneuver.

"Toledano is gone," Menahem said, his voice filled with disgust. He moved to the other Marine and felt for a pulse. "Still with us but thready. If Robinson doesn't get to a hospital soon, he won't make it."

"I'm getting really sick of this shit." Calvin ejected the magazine from the submachine gun and checked how many rounds were left. *Not e-freaking-nough.* Next, he checked his sidearm. At least he had a spare mag for it.

More automatic gunfire swept the street, and the distinctive clattering of the Zeivlot submachine guns went silent. *Probably the last of our security detail ran out of ammo or bit the dust.* "Get ready. They'll be coming to finish us off."

"I'm sure these gents want to kill the humans," Menahem replied as he, too, checked the remaining rounds in his pistol. "I'm down to four, sir."

Yavuz and Bi'shara had acquired weapons at some point in the firefight, both of which appeared to be the same Zeivlot submachine guns most guards had used.

Bi'shara shook his head. "Eight rounds left."

"Make 'em count." Calvin peered around the corner of the display wall and took in the sight of several mask-clad terrorists advancing rapidly. He brought up the Zeivlot-style weapon and squeezed the trigger. One of the men fell, writhing in pain, as another cacophony of chaos was unleashed. Bullets lashed the storefront, and everyone else returned fire.

Bi'shara flew backward, and bloodstains spread across his neck. With no time to perform first aid, Calvin killed another terrorist before the submachine gun clicked dry. He dropped it and immediately grabbed his sidearm just in time to shoot a gunman who tried to breach the front door.

Calvin was sure they were about to die, but he was determined to make the butcher's bill as high as possible. Then his ears picked up the sound of a different type of ballistic weapon. Louder and lower-pitched reports rang out, and a group of terrorists across the way fell in their tracks. A few moments later, the incoming fire ceased.

Minutes ticked by, during which Menahem checked the fallen Zeivlot military officer and pronounced him as passed despite efforts at reviving him. Finally, black-armor-clad special police units and medics appeared outside the shop.

Mercy   79

"We're alive! In here! Got a wounded man, two KIA!" Calvin yelled.

First responders flooded into the shop and took over stabilizing Private Robinson while Calvin pondered just how close all of them had come to death. Blood coated his hands, and he wasn't sure whose it was. Blinding rage coursed through Calvin's mind, and he marched up to the nearest officer who seemed to be in charge. "I want an aircar to the security summit."

The Zeivlot blinked at him. "We need to have you checked out first... Colonel Demood, is it?"

"Listen to me very carefully because I'm only going to say this once. You're going to drive me to the capitol for the summit. Now."

"But—"

"Now," Calvin repeated with a dangerous edge to his voice.

"Yes. Let me get someone."

As the officer scurried off, Calvin watched the medics move Robinson onto a stretcher and roll him toward a waiting ambulance.

Menahem put a hand on Calvin's shoulder. "Sir, you sure you're in the right mindset for this?"

"What? You think I'm gonna smack Vog't's lackies around?"

"Now that you put it like that..." Menahem smirked.

"I'm angry, Master Guns. Another letter, maybe two. Someone's son, father, and husband. Don't worry about me. I won't do anything overly stupid. For a Marine."

"Perhaps we should let this cool off."

Calvin spun around and snarled. "No. We don't need to let it cool off. We need to tell those good-for-nothing politicians to get their heads out of their collective asses and *do something.*"

"But our orders—"

"To *hell* with orders."

Menahem had the good sense to stop talking. Calvin continued to rage, even when they were headed toward the summit in a police aircar, sirens blaring. During the trip, he tried to wipe the blood from his hands and realized it was all over his olive-green uniform. Somehow, that seemed a fitting metaphor.

———

WITH BLOOD still drying on his uniform, Calvin marched through the hallways of the Zeivlot security complex. All around him, people stopped to stare. *Most if not all of these pukes have never seen what real fighting looks like. Or tested themselves in the crucible of combat.* He didn't care. Calvin had one objective: find Vog't and tear a bloody strip out of her and anyone else in range. Dried mud fell off his right arm as he swung open a door that led to the conference room that was supposed to hold the summit.

Protective-detail members from both the Zeivlot and the Zavlot governments tried halfheartedly to stop him as he strode through them. With one turn of his wrist, Calvin sent one tumbling into another and came to stop directly in front of Vog't.

"Colonel Demood, thank the Maker you're alive."

Calvin bit his lip and summoned every ounce of self-control contained in his body. "I might be, but two of my Marines are lying dead out there. Because of this *half-assed clown show!*"

"Colonel, this is hardly the—"

Mercy 81

"Screw you. Screw all of you!" Calvin yelled as he made eye contact with several uniformed Zeivlots. "This should never have happened. They knew our route ahead of time. The ambush was perfectly planned and not by amateurs. We're dealing with professionals who are good at what they do—killing innocents and those who protect them." He felt a hand on his shoulder and turned to see Master Gunnery Sergeant Menahem behind him, shaking his head. Ignoring it, Calvin faced Vog't once more.

"The terrorist elements have been building support. They use disinformation to spread lies about the orbital installations you're constructing for us. We had no idea they could pull off such a sophisticated attack as the one today."

Calvin locked eyes on War Leader Ceren. "What the hell do you do with the intel we feed you?"

"Take out as much of the enemy as we can."

"Bullshit. We have to get an arbiter to sign off on any strike within a thousand meters of a civilian area. My intel people have put together target package after target package that doesn't get hit."

"If we lose the general population, there will be a civil war," Vog't said quietly, though her voice was tinged with steel.

"Then take the gloves off."

"What? Indiscriminate attacks on insurgent targets, Colonel?" Ceren asked. He shook his head. "We can't do that."

"How?" Vog't asked Calvin. "If you have something new to suggest, do so."

"The only way to deal with people who kill civilians by strapping bombs to their chests is to kill them. Preferably before they can kill anyone else. Keep killing them, and when you kill the last one, piss on his corpse and bury it in an unmarked grave."

For a moment, Vog't smirked. "You are... quite the colorful character, Colonel Demood. And I'd love to have the help of your troops and especially the advanced technology they carry. Yet General Cohen specifically told us that human forces will not engage in direct combat action."

David's gonna kill me for this. "With respect, ma'am, I'm not in the CDF. I'm a Marine."

"A distinction without meaning, I believe."

Calvin shrugged. "Leave that to me."

Vog't licked her lips and turned toward Ceren. "We could run joint operations between the CDF forces and our special operations command."

"Marines. Terran Coalition Marine Corps, ma'am." Calvin forced a smile. "Sorry. We detest being lumped in with other services."

Ceren chuckled. "This is true of all military forces, Colonel. No different with us." He turned back to Vog't. "The problem with what you propose, Zupan, is that our human friends have vastly better technology than us. It places our troops in the position of an inability to keep up. One thing I argue strenuously is that TCMC Marines cannot fight the terrorists alone. That will play into every piece of disinformation they're spreading. I cannot stress that enough."

David is really going to kill me. "We'll train your best in how to use our gear and integrate them into joint teams."

Everyone in the room turned to stare at him.

"That would represent another departure from previously stated rules, Colonel." Vog't raised an eyebrow. "Do you have the authority to issue these orders?"

"As the highest-ranking officer on site, I do."

Mercy 83

"But—"

"Something else Marines are good at... asking for forgiveness rather than permission." Calvin relaxed a hair, even though he was still mad at the degenerates who had killed his men. "With respect, ma'am, let us do our jobs. And what I excel at is putting bad guys into the ground."

"More important than military force is intelligence gathering."

Menahem stepped forward. "Our abilities are second to none in gathering signals intercepts."

"We're quite aware." Vog't crossed her arms. "And we're also painfully aware of how limited that support is, given the Terran Coalition's position on civil liberties."

Calvin had never cared much for the restrictions on surveillance. When he'd served on border planets plagued by pro-League militias consisting mainly of imported Leaguer civilians from the Orion Arm of the Milky Way, the inability to monitor their movements cost precious Marine blood. He exchanged glances with Menahem. "We have enough G2 assets to make this interesting, Master Guns. We could turn loose some of our tech." *It's not like I haven't already toed the line.*

"Sir, you know the restrictions."

"Our host partners don't seem to mind." Calvin gestured toward the Zeivlot delegation. "I'm happy to open the floodgates. Let's find the bad guys and end them. If General Cohen and the JAG corps have something else to say, they can countermand me when the *Lion* returns."

"Excuse me," Rabih Dan'dachi interjected. He was one of several representatives from Zavlot, joined by their newly appointed ambassador. "The treaty between our worlds and the Terran Coalition states explicitly that any technology or military assistance shared between one must be given to both. We have our own problems with terrorist groups, and my planet will want the exact same treatment."

Calvin set his jaw. "Are you guys seeing daily suicide bombings?"

"Our media is better... influenced than the Zeivlots. So it's happening, just not reported on as much." Dan'dachi narrowed his eyes. "Make no mistake. We lose hundreds of innocents in every cycle of rotations."

"I've only got five hundred Marines and another thirty G2 support soldiers." Calvin shrugged. "I'll do my best to divide it up, but all of you'd better share everything you've got. We clear on that?"

Small nods came from Vog't, Dan'dachi, and others.

"Good. Then why don't we get started on the nuts and bolts?"

Vog't sucked in a breath. "Wouldn't you like to change first, Colonel?"

A bolt of anger shot through Calvin as he grimaced. "If it's all the same to you, ma'am, I'd rather get on with it. Besides, seeing the lifeblood of my Marines is as good a motivation as any to figure out how to end these mother— we should never forget the cost."

"Then let us proceed."

11

THE JOURNEY through the binary star system took far longer than such a voyage would usually have required for the *Lion of Judah*. That was primarily because of executing a series of microjumps while being escorted by a small fleet of alien vessels that had disabled the mining shuttle. David spent most of it in his day cabin, ruminating on what had happened and planning a legal defense with First Lieutenant Leon Cuellar, the highest-ranking judge advocate general aboard. They ended up in a parking orbit around a multiplatform installation the Vogteks referred to as the Seat of Judgment. They'd also learned the four alien species called themselves the Jinvaas Confederation, based on transmissions from the authorities.

After several hours, David felt prepared to face what seemed to correlate to a bond hearing back in the Terran Coalition. He still felt out of his element.

Cuellar appeared in the hatch after leaving a few minutes before for a bio break. "Brought us back some coffee, sir." He set the pitcher on David's desk.

"Ah, that is the stuff, Lieutenant. Good job finding some. Most of the mess stewards are hiding their stores."

"Oh, it's all a matter of knowing the right senior chief, sir." Cuellar grinned as he poured some into the two mugs on the desk, then he returned to his seat.

That some horse trading was happening around rare food and drink items that could no longer be procured was an open secret. David had made it clear through the chain of command that he would allow innocent favors to be traded, but a black-market exchanging currency for supplies would result in brig time. So far, it had worked. *And the enlisted ratings have something to do when they want to swap duty shifts.*

"Sir, incoming transmission from the Vogtek station." Taylor's voice cut through his thoughts as it emanated from the intercom on the desk.

"Pipe it through to my tablet, Lieutenant."

"Aye, aye, sir."

A few moments later, David's intercom, which was set in its display cradle on the desk, sprang to life with an image of a grand hall. The picture focused on a hexa-limbed being in a red robe.

"General David Cohen and First Lieutenant Leon Cuellar representing the Terran Coalition, Your Honor."

The Vogtek male stared at them for a few moments before he spoke. "I am Arbiter Xelvar, who dispenses justice for matters pertaining to infractions in the void."

"Are my officers in the room with you?" David asked.

"No."

"Then where are they being held?"

"In a secure location, General Cohen, which I will not divulge, as it is considered privileged information. All you need to know is that they are safe and are being held according to our standards."

David set his jaw. "I see." *Keep calm. Play their game for now.*

The arbiter consulted a computing device before looking back at the camera. "Major Arthur Hanson, Captain Ruth Goldberg, and Chief Warrant Officer Karmina Al-Haddad are all charged with violating our sovereignty and stealing goods in excess of one million bahpuramy. The sentence for such a crime is forty standard years of hard labor per count."

"We would be happy to pay a fine," David replied.

"That is not possible. This crime requires a significant amount of prison time to ensure the offender does not engage in the activity again."

David's jaw dropped. *What?* He wanted to explode but forced himself to keep a neutral expression.

"When will there be a hearing to enter a plea?" Cuellar asked.

"A what?"

"In our society, when someone is accused of a crime, they must plead innocent or guilty, then a trial is held."

A moment of silence followed as the arbiter seemed to digest the information. "If these individuals were innocent of the charges brought against them, they wouldn't have been indicted in the first place."

"Then we wish to challenge each count and hold a trial to determine their guilt," Cuellar interjected smoothly.

Xelvar stared down his nose before speaking. "I will schedule a tribunal for seventeen rotations from now."

"Will you consider releasing my officers?" David asked.

"It is outside our procedures, and there is no way to guarantee they will appear for the tribunal if I grant this request. The guilty are not set free, for there is no justice in doing so."

That's our answer to how their system operates. David felt he'd made a grievous error in not rescuing the shuttle and his people during the first encounter. *But I can't change it now. Only press forward.* "We are not familiar with your customs, Arbiter Xelvar. I ask that the Vogtek government help us to understand its concept of due process in the interest of justice for all."

"I will assign a counselor to support your efforts, General Cohen. Beyond that, I suggest you read our tribunal procedures manual."

David barely stopped himself from groaning. "Thank you, Arbiter. Will you allow us to visit our personnel before trial?"

Xelvar narrowed his eyes and stroked his chin with his two right hands. "Unusual, but I will allow it, given the extraordinary nature of this situation. Let it never be said that the Vogtek do not pursue justice. Is there anything else, General?"

"No, Your Honor."

"May justice follow you."

The screen blinked off, and David leaned back.

"Well. Not what I was hoping for." He gave in to emotion and slammed his fist down.

Cuellar sucked in a breath. "I apologize I wasn't able to get further, sir. Legal systems are difficult. Even ours. I'll put my entire team on this, and we *will* be prepared."

David nodded. "Thank you, Lieutenant. You've got carte blanche to pull in anything you need.

"Yes, sir."

They had little else to discuss, as it would take days of poring through documentation to figure out what they faced

Mercy

in terms of a legal battle. "Prioritize getting them released before trial if that's possible."

Cuellar nodded. "Yes, sir."

"Dismissed."

He stood and exited through the hatch.

David was left alone with his thoughts, which was an uncomfortable place to be. As he pondered the outcome so far, it was easy to second-guess agreeing to let the alien justice system take its course. *At most, I expected us to pay a fine and be on our way.* As simple as it was to justify using force, however, it would've been wrong from a moral perspective. *We don't go out into this universe just to do the expedient thing. It's about doing what's* right *too.*

Such sentiments were simple to adhere to in the abstract but far harder when the rubber met the road. *Whatever it takes, I will get my people back. I'll exhaust every other possibility, but in the end, if they are not released, I'll fight the Vogteks myself if I have to.*

12

WHILE STAYING in a Terran Coalition prison was something Ruth had never experienced, being in the Vogtek facility brought back memories from when she'd been captured by the League of Sol during her stint as a teenage resistance fighter. Compared to the dark and foreboding League interrogation rooms, the alien jail was different.

At least they're not torturing us so far. The Vogteks, as they'd indicated their species name was, were oddly shaped. The four-armed creatures were unlike any she'd interacted with previously. *I wonder if each one of those hands can hold a weapon. If so, they'd make for a formidable opponent in combat.*

After being processed, strip-searched, and issued clothing along with a bracelet that dug into her skin, Ruth joined Hanson and Al-Haddad in a small cell. Once the guard had shuffled away, they began to quietly converse.

"This has to be the most sterile environment I've ever seen," Hanson said as he adjusted his legs. "You could eat off the floor."

"Yeah. Not bad compared to a CDF brig."

Mercy 91

Ruth turned to Al-Haddad. "You've spent time in the brig?"

She shrugged. "Yeah. What can I say—I was unruly in my younger years."

"I was, too, but mostly because I had the odd tendency to blow League convoys to kingdom come back on my home planet." Ruth flashed a dazzling smile.

"High speed, low drag, eh?"

"Something like that."

"Did either of you ladies see any obvious escape routes?" Hanson asked. "I looked, but this place hits me as rather secure."

Ruth scrunched her nose. "We're on a planetoid of some type. Probably a medium-sized asteroid. Unless your escape plan includes hijacking a ship with FTL capabilities, which these aliens don't even have, our best hope is the general busts this place open to get us or else wins the court case."

"Still, we should gather information to escape and evade," Haddad interjected. "I like being in control. That's why I fly."

Hanson snorted. "There's always something else in the universe that has an impact. Control is fleeting and probably an illusion."

Ruth suppressed a desire to roll her eyes. *God in heaven above, help me if I have to spend the next however many years of my life debating the meaning of the universe with Arthur Hanson.* She decided to switch subjects. "Did you see those other aliens? I thought I spotted some humanoids with fur."

"Yeah, I saw them too," Hanson replied. "More interesting to me was that a wing we passed seemed to be set up for a liquid environment."

"The pipes?" Al-Haddad asked.

Hanson nodded. "They weren't trying to hide it, either."

"Maybe there's a way to swim out," Ruth interjected. "That would be wild."

Al-Haddad leaned in. "More importantly, that tells us what three out of the four races in this system look like. Anyone else notice that all the guards are Vogteks?"

In fact, Ruth *hadn't* realized that, but after Al-Haddad's observation, it clicked into place. "Maybe they're the law enforcement arm."

One of the aforementioned Vogteks approached, holding something. A stream of words erupted from the alien's mouth, but they were indecipherable. The appendage reached through the bars to the holding cell, and his fingers opened. Contained within were three small earpieces.

Hanson took a step forward and gingerly took one of them. He fastened it to his ear. "Is this what you want us to do?"

Another rapid-fire barrage of noise issued from the Vogtek, and he gestured wildly with the hand that contained the other two earpieces.

"It's a translation device. I can understand what he's saying now."

Ruth and Al-Haddad slid the hard polymer pieces into their ears. Immediately, the stream of noise converted into English.

"Do you understand me?" the Vogtek asked.

"Yes," Ruth replied.

"Good. Who speaks for all?"

They exchanged glances before Hanson stepped forward. "Do you understand the concept of a hierarchal command structure?"

"Do not insult me, criminal."

Mercy 93

"Hey, wait a minute, we're not—" Hanson cried out in pain and grabbed his ear.

"You will not speak ill to us, and you will comply with all directives given by all custodians." The Vogtek seemed to smile in a manner that made Ruth's neck hairs stand up.

Great. We're wearing torture devices. She shifted on her feet and observed Hanson.

"I... understand," Hanson managed to get out as he steadied himself. "We still haven't been found guilty."

The Vogtek scowled. "All are guilty unless an arbiter decides otherwise. Do you comprehend me?"

"Yes," Hanson said in as strong a tone as he could muster. A moment later, he screamed in pain and collapsed to the floor.

Ruth rushed to him and felt for a pulse. While it was strong and steady, Hanson seemed dazed. She turned to the alien. "Why are you torturing him?"

"You will speak when spoken to and address all custodians properly. The proper response to that question was 'Yes, custodian.'"

If Ruth could've reached the four-armed Vogtek, she would have beaten him to death. She felt thankful there were bars in the way. *Must maintain control. Otherwise, I'll make it worse for all of us.* "We understand... custodian."

"Good. Does he require medical assistance? We do not yet understand your species and its physical limitations."

Hanson sat up and blew out a breath. "I'll, uh, be okay."

"You will all now be transferred to our main facility."

Ruth's jaw dropped. "You're putting us into general population? We'll get ripped apart." She knew enough about how prisons worked in the Terran Coalition to know that was an awful idea.

The Vogtek snarled. "Anyone who breaks the rules is severely punished. This includes every member of our races and humans. Any attempts at escape or violence by any prisoner in this facility are met with the harshest of force. You will be safe here as long as you obey the custodians. Now, move."

Ruth and Al-Haddad helped Hanson to his feet as the cell door retracted and slid out. While the building was clearly a prison facility, it was also oddly sleek and high-tech. Ruth felt like she was in a nightmare as the three of them marched out single file. *Now I wish we'd tried to fight or that David had used force.* She pushed the thoughts out of her mind and instead focused on survival. *I only pray I'll see Robert again.*

13

CALVIN HATED BRIEFINGS. He loathed them all the more when he was trying to convince the leader of an alien government to let him go in and do what he did best: kill bad guys. Yet he understood when to keep his cool and let the Zeivlot military officers fight among themselves as one group argued in favor of the assault plan and the others tried to persuade the zupan to call it off.

"I have severe concerns about attacking an encampment of this size. They have women and children in there. If we injure or kill any during an attack, the press will destroy us," one of the Zeivlots said.

"Our Coalition partners have given us a unique opportunity here," Ceren interjected. "We've been searching for Nec'ip Kocer for many rotations. They found him in less than two weeks."

"Which suggests they can find him again."

"Excuse me," Calvin said, putting his hand up. "Anybody mind if the Marine says something?"

Vog't smiled slightly. "By all means, Colonel."

"Our intelligence unit pulled a rabbit out of its collective hat." At the quizzical looks from the Zeivlots, he continued, "Human expression. Magicians pull rabbits out of hats as a kind of trick. It means they did something they shouldn't have been able to do."

"Your contention is that we should take the opportunity to strike, then?" Ceren asked.

"Yes. There was a broad sense of agreement last week to take the gloves off and start putting the hurt on these terrorists. Well, here's our chance. If we can capture Kocer, we can probably roll up the rest of the network. Put the largest and most well-funded group of insurgents on the run, and the rest will go to ground while our superior SIGINT-collection efforts allow us to keep arresting or killing them."

"And how do we counter the images of dead civilians?"

Calvin affixed a harsh stare on the Zeivlot general. "You know, from my perspective, who gives a flying rat's ass about people who toss in with butchers who strap bombs to their chests and kill dozens of innocents? You associate with them, live with them, and assist them... then you run the chance of getting killed when the good guys arrive."

"Colonel, it isn't always as simple as that," Vog't replied. "Some of these individuals are trapped in forced marriages and held against their will."

"We have stun rounds." Calvin crossed his arms. "Our weapons are highly accurate. Your satellite imagery has pinpointed where most of the civilians are, and it's not in those tunnels. They make the women and children tend crops. Which I find disgusting, while we're on the subject. It's a man's job to provide for his family."

Vog't pursed her lips. "I wish you could've found this man in a convoy and taken him out remotely."

"Madam Zupan, sometimes tough choices suck. No matter what you do here, there is a risk. I'm just an old

Mercy   97

combat Marine, ma'am. I kick doors in, put down bad guys, then go home and sleep like a baby before I do it again the next day." He smirked. "Please, let us kick these assholes' doors down. I swear to you this is a battle we can win."

Vog't seemed to consider her options. "Colorful, as always, Colonel Demood. You're confident in your intelligence?"

"I'd stake my life on it, ma'am."

She nodded. "We will proceed with the TCMC's mission proposal. How long before you can execute, Colonel?"

"Forty-eight hours, ma'am. Maybe less, if we hustle."

"Then may you walk with the Maker."

Calvin smiled. "Yes, ma'am." *And when we're done, a whole lot of bad people aren't going to be walking anywhere except hell.*

———

Susanna's job had become far more straightforward in the past few weeks. Ever since the colonel had allowed linking of the advanced Coalition AI image analysis tools into the Zeivlots' real-time intelligence feeds, the aperture of the possible increased daily. Her duties weren't easy, but they were more straightforward. The mountain ranges had numerous caves, small dwellings, and remote buildings, but the satellites saw all. Overseeing the raid on Kocer was the first test of their new capabilities, and she looked forward to seeing the results.

Her tactical interface system displayed a warning, and she zoomed in. It took a few seconds for the image quality to fill in. When it did, a home built into the side of the mountain came into focus. The AI flagged several windows and, upon closer examination, the barrels of rifles sticking out of them.

"Overwatch to Charlie platoon. How copy? Over."

"Solid copy, Overwatch. Whatcha got for us, Nussbaum?" Calvin asked.

"Possible ambush, sir, roughly five hundred meters east-southeast from your current position. Sending a feed to your HUD now."

After a pause, Calvin replied, "I see it. House built into the rock, eh? I count at least four tangos."

"Confirmed, sir. Should I order an air strike?"

"Negative, Overwatch. Could find an entryway to the terrorist complex we weren't aware of."

"Roger, sir. Overwatch out."

For the next ten minutes, Susanna stared at her screens, zooming in and out and searching for the enemy. She marked several positions as possible hostiles, though nothing else jumped out at her.

"Demood to Nussbaum."

"Go ahead, sir."

"Got that ambush point in sight, Private. Anything changed?"

"No movement, sir."

"Okay, we're about to start the party. Notify me immediately if you see squirters."

"Yes, sir."

"Demood out."

A split second later, bright flashes lit up Susanna's main viewer. *Fragmentation grenades.* The destruction was immediately visible even at the oblong angle she was seeing. At least one enemy fighter blew out the window of the room he'd been hiding in. Muzzle flashes lit up the area, and she could imagine the cacophony of chaos unfolding. Part of her

Mercy 99

wished she were down in the thick of the action, directing drone strikes and providing real-time information as a forward air controller. *I've been hanging around these Marines for too long.*

As it seemed like Calvin's unit was making steady progress, she was about to turn her attention elsewhere, when all of a sudden, more irregular fighters appeared seemingly out of thin air. Less than fifty meters from the Marines' position was a hole in the ground that was spewing forth Zeivlots. Each carried a ballistic weapon and charged. One was bulkier than the others. *My God, a suicide bomber.*

Susanna's hands shook as she cued the commlink. "Overwatch to all Charlie stations. Multiple platoon-strength enemy formations closing on your position. At least one SVEST. Forty-five meters out."

Automatic gunfire echoed over the link.

"Contact right! Let 'em have it!" Calvin bellowed. "Acknowledged, Overwatch. Activate close air support. Put them on target for these jokers."

"Sir, that's danger-close range."

"Make it happen, Private.

The sounds of battle echoed through the commlink as her hands went over the commands to punch in a strike from the nearest Zeivlot VTOL support aircraft. "Coalition ISR to Hotel Six. You are cleared for close-air-support mission in grid nine. Coordinates inbound."

"Understood, Coalition ISR," a pilot Susanna didn't recognize answered. "Coordinates confirmed. Request clearance for danger-close attack."

"Request confirmed. Execute drop. Coalition Marine platoon Charlie is close to being overrun."

"Acknowledged, ISR. Commencing munitions drop."

Susanna switched back to Calvin's channel. "Colonel, CAS inbound, danger close."

"Music to my ears, Private. Keep up the good work."

The commlink clicked off, and Susanna watched as explosions rocked the area she'd pinpointed. A series of high-explosive bombs blew apart the onrushing terrorists, with a final blast a few seconds later. *The suicide bomber.* She knew in her heart that God disapproved of her taking pride in helping to kill others. But at that moment, it didn't matter. Her friends and comrades were standing on the line, and they would always come first. *Father was right. I have become like the English.*

14

EVEN THROUGH THE air filtration system of Calvin's power armor, the stench of burning flesh was unmistakable. He slapped a new magazine into his battle rifle and racked the action, chambering a round. Around him, several of their Zeivlot partners had fallen. The storm of bullets had been particularly deadly for those not wielding the Coalition's finest technology. Those Zeivlots lucky enough to be trained in power armor had performed well, however.

"Well, they know we're coming," Menahem grumbled. He, too, changed out the magazine on his weapon.

"Fine by me." Calvin sighted down his rifle, using the optics to survey the battlefield. Nothing appeared to be moving. "We'll press forward and see if we can't follow these bastards down the bolt-holes they appeared out of."

"Maybe we'll get lucky, and they'll lead to the larger cave system."

"From your lips to God's ears, Master Guns." Other Marine elements supported by Zeivlot commandos were assaulting other areas of the compound, and Calvin hoped they wouldn't find tunnels filled with civilians.

Calvin and the two platoons of Coalition Marines and Zeivlot special operators steadily climbed over the rough terrain. The semiarid mountain range had peaks that rose in the distance with little vegetation or tree cover. What growth existed was primarily scrub brush. It made the force stick out like a sore thumb, and more than once, they took fire from dug-in enemies. Superior firepower won out, but Calvin detested relying on brute strength. Combat of this type was all about finesse, and they had none of it.

Once they'd picked through the meters of charred ground and dead bodies, the teams scrambled down the side of an embankment. A small shed came into view, and it appeared as if it was a couple hundred years old.

"How the hell is this thing even standing?" Calvin remarked as he stacked up on the door with a breach team. Standing to one side, he turned the handle and swung it outward. A Zeivlot commando tossed a pulse grenade in, which detonated a moment later with a blinding flash of light.

Four of them charged through to find nothing but an empty room that could barely hold four power-armored Marines. In the center, a trapdoor sat ajar, its dark opening beckoning them forward.

Calvin leaned over the hole, and the sensor suite in his helmet calculated the distance to the bottom. "Twenty-six meters down. That's impressive." He pulled a small round device off his utility belt, pressed a button on the side, and tossed it into the abyss.

The sensor drone released multiple microrobotic units, each the size of an insect. Quickly scanning the tunnel in both directions, it filled in a partial map on Calvin's HUD, which was then shared across the tactical network with the rest of the Marines and Zeivlot commandos.

Mercy 103

Menahem appeared at his side. "Rat's nest of tunnels down there, sir. How do you want to play it?"

"Split the team. Leave six Zeivlot partners behind to ensure no squirters get by us. The rest press forward and eliminate the rest of these assholes with extreme prejudice."

"Yes, sir," Menahem replied and quickly selected those to remain. He then climbed halfway down the ladder and dropped to the bottom.

The rest of the Marines and Zeivlots did the same, with Calvin taking up the rear. When he got down into the tunnel, its size shocked him. There was more than enough headroom to accommodate an average-sized Zeivlot, who had a similar height to humans. Every ten meters, an electric light hung from a wire, giving the entire structure a pale, eerie glow.

"Forward," Calvin ordered as he took his place a few Marines back from the point man. They surged as quietly as possible, but stealth was limited when someone was wearing an armored suit that weighed eighty kilos.

From somewhere down the tunnel, the metallic click of a ballistic weapon's action being racked echoed. Calvin recognized it immediately, and on pure muscle memory, his fist went up—the universal signal to halt. A split second later, sonic booms thundered in the cramped passageway as a burst of gunfire rang out.

A bullet smacked the front of Calvin's armor, which deflected it without failing. He shifted his rifle's fire selector switch to full auto and squeezed the trigger. "Light 'em up!"

The roar of Terran Coalition battle rifles filled the air, some on semiauto, others on full. The smell of propellent filled the damp atmosphere, and screams rang out farther down the tunnel.

Calvin released his finger from the trigger, ejected the

spent magazine, and slapped in another. "Move it, Marines! Push through!"

The two men in front of him advanced aggressively as the incoming fire stopped. Like a wave, they all swept through the passage and emerged into a cavern after fifty meters. While it was clearly a natural cave formation, cross-beams shored up the walls, and stacks of supplies filled the area.

At least eight other tunnels intersected with the area. Calvin reconfigured his sensor drones to map the tunnels leading out of the cave and was about to start splitting the group up further when several fighters emerged from one hole.

Their faces morphed in surprise as each brought up a rifle and started shooting. The Marines and commandos returned fire, and the fight was over in seconds—with four more bodies on the rock floor.

"Fan out," Calvin said into his commlink. "Who knows how many more of these jokers there are, and I don't want us to get caught with our pants down."

Menahem bent over one of the bodies and patted it down. "SVEST. We were fortunate it didn't go off by accident."

"No shit, Master Guns!" somebody from the other side of the cave yelled back.

"Focus on shooting bad guys, not my comments," Menahem rumbled. "Or I'll PT you until you vomit when we get back to camp.

One moment, Calvin was sweeping the room. The next, it felt like hell had opened up in the middle of the cave. Terrorists—easily identified by their weapons and that they were in the chamber to begin with—charged out of multiple openings in the rock face. Most of them fired blindly on full

Mercy 105

auto, filling the cavern with hundreds of rounds. Many harmlessly pinged off the rocks and ended up in the dirt. A few hit the Marines' power armor, and while one of the slugs wasn't enough to penetrate, the volume of fire was dangerous.

Calvin dropped behind a crate with alien lettering on it and engaged the enemy with his battle rifle. Ordinarily, he would've used fragmentation or plasma grenades to thin the herd. *Not in a labyrinth twenty meters underground, though. I might be crazy, but I ain't stupid.* He sent off another three-round burst, and his target collapsed to the ground with pink blood oozing from his wounds.

A harsh yell to the right attracted Calvin's attention. One of the Zeivlot commandos had taken a round to the neck. A glance at it told him that though one of the Marines tried to treat the wound, it was hopeless. Anger washed over him, as it always did when one of his men was killed, along with a redoubled drive to destroy the enemy.

Throughout the cave, terrorists went down right and left. But for each one neutralized, two more seemed to take his place.

One of the power-armored Marines went down to Calvin's left, blood pulsing from a hole in his armor, as the report of a different weapon reached Calvin's ears. *What the hell is that?* It took a moment for the sound to compute. *How the hell did they get rail guns?* While the Zeivlot military possessed prototypes of miniaturized rail guns, they were so few in number that the idea of the terrorists having one was almost inconceivable. *Unless they got it as a gift from a traitor. Doesn't matter now.*

Calvin pulled a pulse grenade off his utility belt and primed it. Hoping it wouldn't bring the overhead down on them, he tossed the little black ball toward the direction he thought the railgun shot had come from. "Pulse, over!"

The sphere detonated with a flash of white light that dazzled anyone caught in the blast radius. While the terrorists were blinded and their ears rang from the loud concussion blast, they became easy pickings for the Marines.

Counting his blessings that the weapon hadn't buried them in rocks, Calvin methodically felled several hostiles with three-round bursts to their center mass. When his battle rifle clicked dry, he dropped it, letting the one-point sling keep it from hitting the ground, and drew his sidearm.

One of the irregular fighters stood over a Marine who'd been knocked to the ground, about to discharge one of the Zeivlot slug throwers at point-blank range on full auto. Calvin raised his pistol and put two rounds through the enemy's head before adjusting his aim and taking out another hostile with two shots to center mass and another to his cranium.

When the standard-issue TCMC sidearm clicked dry as well, Calvin ejected the magazine and reached for another, only for the full weight of a terrorist to crash into him, pitching him into the dirt.

The weapon fell away from Calvin's grasp as the enemy fighter discharged his entire magazine into the chest plate of Calvin's armor. It felt like someone had taken a sledgehammer to his ribs. The air was knocked out of him, and intense pain shot through his body.

"Shit." Calvin forced his hand to squeeze into a fist, releasing a knife from its position on the gauntlet. It was the weapon of last resort.

All the while, the Zeivlot screamed in his native language and used the butt of his rifle to slam Calvin's faceplate.

Everything became fuzzy and disoriented in Calvin's mind. His power-armor suit administered a drug combo to relieve the pain and restore him to full alertness. The shot did the trick, and realizing the danger he was in as the terrorist prepared to fire another magazine into his chest, Calvin jammed the knife into the man's throat. The terrorist keeled over as the life drained from his eyes.

Calvin took a breath and stood, taking in the sights around him. Dozens of dead irregulars were scattered across the cave floor, and the harsh smell of blood and propellant filled the air. Scattered shots rang out as the last few hostiles were eliminated. He paused long enough to slap a new magazine into his battle rifle and pick up the dropped pistol. "Status?"

Menahem appeared at his side. "Three KIA, sir. Several Zeivlot commandos seriously wounded. Fifty-plus dead tangos. You look like hell, Colonel."

"Guess I'm out of shape from not killing Leaguers for a few months. This prick here..." Calvin gestured to the dead terrorist at his feet. "Got the jump on me and damn near got through my armor."

Menahem shook his head. "Leaguers didn't even fight that intensely. They'd break and run. These guys just... die. They won't give a centimeter."

"Who cares." Calvin shrugged. "They die just like Leaguers, and each one we put down is one fewer asshole with a bomb strapped to his chest, trying to blow up women and kids."

"Amen to that, Colonel."

Calvin jerked a thumb toward the wounded Zeivlots a Marine corpsman was tending to. "Get them littered back to the surface, and call for medivac. We'll take the rest of the team and press forward."

Menahem tilted his head. "You sure we shouldn't wait for reinforcements, sir?"

"Call it an old Marine's intuition, Master Guns. That was their main push. Whatever is left is the dregs." Calvin hefted his battle rifle. "And I'm ready to end this."

"Yes, sir." Menahem turned. "You heard the Colonel! Get these men to safety. Alpha platoon, form on me!"

Zeivlot commandos carried off their comrades, leaving the Marines to deal with the remaining wet work. Calvin took point, even after Menahem's protestations. While they'd been fighting the terrorists, the remote drones he'd loosed into the tunnel system had mapped most of it. Carelessly, the insurgents had left open a trapdoor that led into the main complex. Imagery showed computer equipment, communication gear, and crates of explosives next to food and sleeping quarters.

Despite the lack of resistance, progress was slow because they constantly checked for explosive booby traps and enemy fighters. When Calvin finally walked into the main hall, it was a shock. He could've been in a professionally run command-and-control center with all the terrorists' gear.

"How the heck did they excavate all this?" Menahem asked as he poked a box with his battle rifle. "We're talking hundreds of cubic meters of rock."

"I'm starting to think the Zeivlots have a far bigger traitor problem than they realize."

Calvin resumed the search. Half an hour later, they'd gone through almost every centimeter of the complex, clearing it room by room. It became clear the entire area was deserted. Back in the main hall, Calvin flipped his helmet visor up and sniffed. The air was musky, rank, and smelled of feces. "Did we get facial recognition back on our friends from the ambush?"

Mercy
109

Menahem took a few steps toward him. "Yeah, and none of them are our HVT."

"No way that guy got by the other teams or us."

"They could have some secret tunnel out of here, Colonel." Menahem shrugged. "I'm sure you did a tour or two fighting Leaguers on the border worlds. It's the same crap they used to pull."

"Maybe." Calvin shook his head. "I don't think so, though. Post some security here, and take two Marines to search the first bunch of bunks. I'll do the same on the other side. Flip everything, and use our advanced sensors to check for cubbies, secret passages, et cetera."

"Yes, sir."

For the next hour, Calvin and a small team of Marines probed every nook and cranny of a cohabitation area that had two dozen bunk beds and small living spaces. They flipped over every mattress, moved every bed, and scanned every surface. He was about to give up and head back to the main hall when a temperature irregularity in his helmet scanner blipped several times. *Now, that's mighty odd.*

When Calvin saw a warm spot on the wall, he turned his infrared mode on and was shocked to see the shape of a humanoid. He brought a finger up to his lips and motioned for the two Marines with him to post on either side. Then Calvin felt around the heat blip for a trapdoor and was rewarded with a small latch. He pulled it down, and the wall popped out.

Inside was a disheveled Zeivlot, his rough-cut clothes matted and torn in several places. He stared at them with hate in his eyes before releasing a string of native words that the translator program didn't pick up.

Calvin smashed the butt of his battle rifle into the man's face, breaking his nose and causing blood to spray out of it.

It also had the effect of knocking him out. A few moments later, the optical scanner in his helmet confirmed the identity of the Zeivlot. "Well, lookie here. Got our HVT, Mr. Nec'ip Kocer."

As the two enlisted Marines pulled Kocer out of his hiding place and placed restraints around his ankles and wrists, Calvin took a step back and cued the commlink. "Demood to all Charlie platoon stations. HVT has been secured. Complete mission success. Commence mop-up operations, and send in our Zeivlot partner forces."

Well, that's one small step for a Marine. Let's hope the nerd herd and the shrinks can get something out of this asshole. Then I'll be able to do what I do best... kick down doors and kill bad guys. Calvin walked back toward the main hall with a smile.

15

A WEEK before the trial was to commence, the JAG unit, led by First Lieutenant Cuellar, had engaged in around-the-clock reviews of the Jinvaas Confederation's legal code, trying to get up to speed. Dr. Hayworth and the science team spearheaded a deep dive into the aliens' culture. Their objective was to understand what made the four separate species tick.

David strode into the conference room on deck one, part of him wishing they were locked in combat with the League. At least that was an enemy he understood, and they had tactics readily available to defeat them. Interacting with one alien species after another left him suffering from cultural whiplash. *I have to remember that we're the odd man out when we're dealing with these people.*

"General on deck!" Merriweather said as he stepped through the hatch.

The action was enough out of character for her that David smiled as he made a beeline for his usual seat. "As you were." For possibly the only time he could remember, more civilians were present than uniformed soldiers.

Hayworth grumbled as he sat down along with Bo'hai. They occupied one side of the table. Cuellar and Merriweather took the other. Several Zeivlot scientists David didn't recognize by name were also present.

"Thank you all for the yeoman's work everyone's putting in to free our people. With no further ado, where are we?" David asked as he scanned the room.

Cuellar cleared his throat and licked his lips. "Well, sir, we've established this civilization values justice over all else. It's essential to realize their concept of justice isn't what ours is, though. You could describe our system as one that would rather see ten guilty men go free than see an innocent man locked up, but the Vogteks operate in the inverse. You're guilty until proven innocent."

David frowned. He'd feared that from their interactions so far, but to hear it stated was disheartening. "Do the rules of the road, as it were, allow for a fair trial?"

"To my surprise, they seem to—"

"Unlike authoritarian human civilizations, this confederation of alien races has developed a society based solely on the rule of law." Hayworth leaned forward. "They follow it to the letter in everything they do. In some ways, it's a marvel to behold. What doesn't help us is that we stole the helium-3."

"There's context to that, Doctor."

"Vogteks specifically don't seem to understand that concept."

David blew out a breath. "How can we make them understand it?"

"They give sentences of five years' hard labor for stealing something from a store," Cuellar interjected.

"What kind of something?" David asked.

"A candy bar. If you were to take something more valu-

Mercy 113

able, say a vehicle... that nets ten to twenty years. On the flip side, there's virtually no crime. People self-report themselves for minor infractions."

David sat back, dumbfounded. "Wherever authoritarian governments rule, corruption follows. Can we exploit *that*?"

"We don't believe so, sir." Cuellar shook his head. "The doctor has discovered that as far as we can tell, these folks are the real deal. They practice exactly what they preach."

David turned to Hayworth. "Doctor, care to expound?"

"It appears that in a bygone era of the existence of this civilization, they had numerous wars between the four species that share the binary star system. Lawlessness, corruption, and general hooliganism ran rampant. At least, that's what they have for recorded history." He shrugged. "Who knows if it's true?"

"Truth matters little here," Bo'hai interjected. "Only meeting them in a way they understand."

David raised an eyebrow. "Isn't xenoanthropology outside your wheelhouse, Doctor?"

Hayworth smirked. "When you have an IQ approaching two hundred, nothing is outside one's wheelhouse, if you choose to apply yourself, General."

"Point taken." *Ah, there's that trademark arrogance. Be careful not to write checks you can't cash, Doctor.* "Then what's our plan?" David spread his hands on the table.

"I've prepared a defense that hinges on proving we had no idea they'd staked a claim to the asteroid field in which we found the helium-3 planetoid. Furthermore, under the Canaan charter, that field lies outside the exclusive economic zone of a spacefaring but non-FTL-capable race," Cuellar said.

"That is a technical argument against which the Vogteks would probably reply that we should've known better and had no business taking what is theirs," Bo'hai interjected.

"Ignorance of the law in small matters is a defense in the Terran Coalition. We should be able to throw ourselves on the mercy of the court," David replied.

"It doesn't matter. These aliens do not perceive the universe as you do. They don't have a word for mercy, General." Bo'hai's soft voice cut above the others. "You must look at the situation as they do."

David sighed. "It's patently illogical to jail people for five years over stealing a carton of eggs. The punishment must fit the crime. From that perspective, it's difficult for me to understand."

"The Terran Coalition takes a harsh line on most criminal activity," Hayworth said as he adjusted in his chair. "You're fond of pointing out our asteroid penal facility for murderers, rapists, child molesters, and drug dealers, General."

"We both know it's not the same."

Hayworth crossed his arms. "Because the Terran Coalition is a semi-post-scarcity society that blends capitalism with a basic floor of sustenance for its population. Our poor on the core worlds do better than the middle class of the Saurian Empire."

"There're plenty of people who commit crimes for reasons other than poverty, Doctor." David had never placed much stock in arguments that criminal activity was explained by anything except poor decisions and a lack of character. *On the other hand, I just ordered the theft of another race's minerals.*

"My point is the two societies have almost nothing in common. Scarcity exists on every world in this system. They lack key technological advances to change that." Hayworth

Mercy 115

harrumphed. "As a scientist, I find it strange that each system we've visited lacks specific heavy elements too. Something more is afoot there, and I suspect the answer will play into these artifacts we're investigating."

"We're getting off track here." David cleared his throat. "Lieutenant, what are your team's next steps?"

"Well, we're preparing our briefs in the archaic format required by the Vogtek court system and enlisting the translation team to ensure we don't make rookie mistakes like misspelling our documents... accidentally pleading guilty," Cuellar replied.

David forced a chuckle. "Yes, let's avoid those."

"Aside from that, sir, we've mapped out a narrow technical defense, as I stated. There's no question about the facts of what occurred. The legal issue at hand is intent and context. I've tailored our response with the Vogtek defense counsel we were assigned, and well, everyone will do their best."

Having been a leader for decades, David knew what someone hedging their bets sounded like. *Cuellar really doubts our chances.* "Very well. Keep digging on all levels. If there's anything I know about legalistic systems... it's that there are loopholes. We just have to find them. And if that doesn't work, I'll take the blame for it."

At their sharp stares and open mouths, David shrugged. "That's a part of command. Never ask another to do something you won't do yourself. Any saved rounds?"

Everyone shook their heads.

"Then I ask you all, as we put our heads down and push through till the trial, to pray for the safety of Major Hanson, Captain Goldberg, and Chief Warrant Officer Karmina Al-Haddad. In whatever faith you hold."

"I'll try positive thinking as I work," Hayworth said. "It

wouldn't do to have to find another engineer who can understand antimatter injection as well as Hanson."

"Whatever works, Doctor. I'll take it." David flashed a small smile.

"I pray to the Maker nightly on behalf of everyone in the fleet," Bo'hai interjected earnestly. "He watches over all of us."

"We need all the help we can get." David glanced around the conference room. "Okay. Let's get back to it. Dismissed."

David took a few minutes to collect his thoughts as the rest of them filed out. Again in the unfamiliar position of second-guessing choices made, he pondered what would've happened if they'd used minimal force to rescue the shuttle rather than standing down. *But that wouldn't have been right.* A saying of Marcus Aurelius came to David's mind. *"If it is not right, do not do it. If it is not true, do not say it." I will simply have to accept the consequences of my actions, whatever they may be.*

———

RUTH'S TIME in the Vogtek holding facility was equally boring and brutal. The custodians were ruthlessly efficient, and any deviation from the expected routine was met with electric shocks. Yet once she and the others had learned that routine, the guards mostly left them alone. Meanwhile, the other prisoners didn't even look at them. Everyone kept their heads and eyes down, focused solely on their own existence and survival.

Still, it was the longest two weeks of Ruth's life, and the only way she got through it was with the support of Hanson and Al-Haddad. Putting on a fresh khaki duty uniform and her ribbon bar was the closest she'd felt to being free since

Mercy 117

entering the prison. Once changed, Ruth exited the bathroom and found the others waiting. They also wore the standard CDF khaki uniform with the addition of a jacket. The attire was the equivalent of a business suit.

Aside from one meeting with Lieutenant Cuellar and an alien attorney who hadn't said much, they'd also had no contact with counsel. That no one was in the hallway to meet them, aside from Vogteks wearing police uniforms, wasn't reassuring.

"You guys ready?" Hanson asked. Sweat spread across his brow.

Ruth forced herself to stay calm. "Yeah. Alien courtrooms... new galaxies... vaguely human-looking aliens who want to kill one another over their belief systems. All in a day's work, right?"

Al-Haddad chuckled. "I can't tell whether you're a cup-half-full or half-empty kind of gal, Captain."

"I like to keep everyone guessing."

A Vogtek guard, whom Ruth assumed was akin to a bailiff, stuck his head and three of his arms through a doorway. "Enter."

Hanson led the way to the courtroom.

Ruth had never been in one before and was blown away by the chamber that greeted her. Intricate art reliefs adorned the walls, while tables that sat before the arbiter's bench gleamed. They appeared to be made from precious metals or overlaid with shiny white gold. The display was ostentatious, right down to the arbiter's seat, which stood at least a meter above the rest of the room.

David, an alien, and Cuellar were grouped around the table on the right side of the room. Ruth wanted to go over to them, but the Vogtek bailiff barked, "Keep walking!" the moment she tried to deviate from following him.

118 DANIEL GIBBS

They were led to an ornate cage. Bars of the same shiny alloy encircled it, and four chairs were inside. Once they'd entered, the door was closed behind them. Ruth felt like a trapped animal.

After a moment, David strode over, though the Vogteks complained. He put his hand up to the bars. "It's good to see you all. Are you okay? Well treated?"

"Rough going for a bit, sir, but we're in one piece," Hanson replied.

"Chin up in there, everyone. We'll get through this, and I will get you back to the fleet. Godspeed."

"Godspeed, sir," Ruth said as she placed her hands on her knees and resisted the urge to beat the bars until they opened.

After a while, a group of Vogteks approached the other table as spectators filtered into the courtroom.

A door behind the arbiter's bench swung open, and the bailiff addressed those assembled. "All rise. This supreme tribunal of justice is in session for the matter of the citizens versus the Coalition Defense Force. All persons seeking redress may be heard!"

Ruth noted that the spectators were split between the different species they'd observed so far, but the tribunal's personnel were almost exclusively Vogteks. *I wonder what that's about.*

A Vogtek with graying hair came through the open door, wearing a striking multicolored robe. He sat in the chair that overlooked the rest of the courtroom. "Is the procurator ready to proceed?"

"I am, Arbiter," one of the men at the table to the left answered.

"Then do so."

"We will offer a case showing that the accused willingly

Mercy

and knowingly broke the laws of the Jinvaas confederation when they attempted to steal valuable ore from a planetoid in our star system. Furthermore, we will show that they knew this was against both the laws of our confederation and basic morality. When caught, the accused and their military force attacked our procurator and obstructed the process of justice."

As he spoke, the Vogtek paced. It appeared as if there was seating for a jury in one part of the courtroom, but none was present.

"Despite the powerful nature of these alien adversaries, our procurators eventually brought them in and overcame their obstruction attempts. Today, we humbly ask that the interests of justice be served. Once we have proven our case, the maximum penalty should be applied so that this new race of beings understands the Jinvaas confederation is unmovable and will not yield to lawlessness."

Once the Vogtek sat down, Cuellar stood. "Arbiter, we request permission for General David Cohen to deliver our opening statement."

The arbiter gestured with his arms. "Under normal circumstances, I would reject it out of hand, but these are extraordinary times. We have admitted the first non-Confederation member to our legal proceedings. I will ask this... why?"

"Because as the commanding officer of the *Lion of Judah*, General Cohen has overall responsibility for all orders given in the fleet and the safety of his crew. He feels it would be best for the court to hear from him."

The Vogtek arbiter was silent for what seemed to stretch on for minutes. "Denied. You will have the opportunity to call him as a witness to present his side. Opening statements are to frame your case, not make it. You may proceed, Lieutenant Cuellar."

Ruth sucked in a breath. She wasn't a lawyer, but having a small request denied didn't make her feel good about the outcome. *All I can do now is pray God will watch over us.*

16

THE SPEED of the proceedings surprised David. In three hours, the prosecution made its case. They called multiple witnesses to the stand and admitted sensor-log evidence and a transcript of David's conversation with the commander of the lead Vogtek ship. The trial was antiseptic and even dull. He hadn't been sure what to expect, but he'd hoped for something a bit less dry from the Vogtek attorney, who had been so bombastic in his opening statement.

After a short break for the midday meal, the trial continued.

A few moments after the Vogtek arbiter had taken his place behind the bench of justice, everyone returned to their seats except for Cuellar. "If it pleases the court, Your Honor, I would like to begin our defense."

The arbiter waved several hands at once. "Proceed."

"I call General David ben-Levi Cohen to offer testimony."

David stood and strode to the witness box. As the rest had done, he paused as a clerk approached.

"Do you solemnly, sincerely, and honestly declare and

affirm that the evidence you are about to give shall be truthful?"

It took a moment for the translation device in David's ear to replay the words in English, but he'd quickly gotten used to the delay. "I do."

"You may be seated." The clerk turned and returned to her desk.

"Please state your name, rank, and posting for the record," Cuellar said as he took the lectern between the prosecution and defense tables.

"Major General David Cohen, commanding officer, CSV *Lion of Judah*."

"Thank you, sir."

For the next few minutes, Cuellar walked David through direct testimony explaining how the *Lion of Judah* had become stranded in Sextans B, where they came from, and that the *Lion*'s ultimate objective was to return home. With that out of the way, he turned to the matter at hand. "General, once you realized this solar system had an abundance of helium-3, why did that matter so much?"

"Our fusion reactors run on it, and we're experiencing a fleetwide shortage."

"Why is that, sir?"

"Simply to run the reactor takes fuel, and when we're maneuvering at combat speed or engaging in combat operations, our designs use a great deal more helium-3."

"Has the fleet encountered combat since arriving in Sextans B?"

David nodded. "Yes. Two species we encountered, the Zeivlots and the Zavlots, tried to wipe each other out with crude interplanetary weapons of mass destruction. I ordered the *Lion of Judah* and her escorts to intervene."

"How many lives were saved, General?"

Mercy 123

"Roughly twelve billion between both planets."

"I object, Your Honor!" The Vogtek prosecutor sprang to his feet. "This line of questioning has no impact on the charges at hand. The reason for the humans' fuel shortage is none of this tribunal's concern."

The arbiter clanged the metal ingot he carried at all times. "I concur. The accused's representative will confine himself to the facts of his case and not attempt to curry favor by introducing prior good acts of the defendants."

"But, Your Honor—"

"Lieutenant Cuellar, the only matter at hand is the guilt of these defendants for the charges brought against them. What they did—good or bad—doesn't impact that guilt. I do not know how your system of justice works, but this is how ours functions, and I expect you to respect it."

"Yes, Your Honor."

"Proceed, Lieutenant."

Cuellar turned back to David. "General, why didn't you mine helium-3 from an uninhabited system?"

"We haven't found any minable reserves so far in our journey across Sextans B."

"Isn't that unusual?"

"Compared to our home galaxy, the Milky Way, extremely. Dr. Hayworth and our science team have a variety of theories as to why this is, but ultimately, those ideas don't fuel our ships."

"So why did you order the mining of ore from this system, knowing it was inhabited?"

"Because the planetoid we identified contained ore so pure that we could refuel our entire fleet reserves with only a few shuttle loads of it."

"But someone else owned the system."

"There was no evidence that any species in this system

had FTL capabilities. We erroneously assessed that they weren't aware of the planetoid's existence."

"Well, why not contact the Vogtek or another race and ask permission first?"

David blew out a breath. "When we made first contact with the Zeivlots, it sent their civilization into a tailspin and nearly caused both species to destroy each other. I didn't want to repeat that mistake."

"Were there any other factors?"

"Under the Canaan Charter, resources this far out from a solar system's center, if the inhabitants lack FTL, would be considered outside the exclusive-economic-use zone. In other words, if they can't get to the resource, they can't control it."

"If you had to do this again, would you make different choices?" Cuellar's eyes swept the courtroom.

"Absolutely. Hindsight is always twenty-twenty."

"One final question, General. In the Coalition Defense Force, who is responsible for orders given... the one who gives them or those who carry them out?"

David had specifically ordered Cuellar to make that query, as it spoke to his final option: take full responsibility for the actions of Ruth, Hanson, and Al-Haddad, with an eye to serving the sentence himself. "The officer who gives the order is responsible for its outcome."

"I have no further questions." Cuellar stepped away from the lectern and returned to the defense table.

The Vogtek prosecutor stood and approached. "General Cohen, much has been made of the Coalition Defense Force and its vaunted belief in the rule of law. In examining library information from your ship, I came across multiple videos in which you appeared to narrate an advertisement asking for volunteers in your military service. Is that accurate?"

David grimaced. He hated the recording in question. "Yes."

"The Coalition Defense Force. An interstellar force for good. That's your slogan, is it not?"

"Yes."

"I'm curious. Is violating the sovereignty of another species, stealing from them, then threatening to destroy a procurator's vessel your idea of doing good?"

"No."

"Then—"

David cleared his throat. "I'd like the chance to fully respond to that question, Procurator."

The Vogtek gestured with all four of his arms. "*Of course, General,*" he replied with exaggerated politeness.

"I believe you're misrepresenting the facts, Procurator. I now know it was unequivocally wrong to order the mining of your helium-3. That fact notwithstanding, had you been in my place, it is entirely likely you would've ordered the same sequences of events. And as to threatening to destroy one of your ships, I did no such thing. Your vessels opened fire first, the commander of the CSV *Margaret Thatcher* responded, and when the *Lion of Judah* arrived, I put an end to all of it."

"Perhaps." The Vogtek flipped a page on his electronic tablet. "Let's move on to something else you've asserted. This concept that everyone in the CDF has to follow orders. Is that how you frame it?"

"Top-down military hierarchies tend to function that way, Procurator. I suspect yours is no different."

"Indeed." The Vogtek smirked. "In reviewing the materials we requested from your ship, I had a chance to read through the Uniform Code of Military Justice. Are you familiar with it?"

Where's he going with this? David made a mental note to ream Cuellar out for not alerting him to the Vogteks' getting their hands on the UCMJ. "As a former command-rank officer and now a flag officer, yes, I am quite familiar with it."

"Why is that, General?"

"One of my duties is to run a colonel's mast and now a general's mast. Those are informal legal proceedings in which I pass judgment on small infractions to the UCMJ."

"Yes, I noticed that requirement in the text." The prosecutor flashed another grin.

David suddenly felt like a caged animal. *He's got something up his sleeve, but what?*

"Article five, section eighteen, subparagraph seven describes how an officer or enlisted soldier in the CDF should respond to an illegal order, does it not?"

Oh heck. That's where he's going. David forced a neutral expression onto his face. "I'm afraid I can't quote the exact heading, but that sounds right."

"Could you explain to the tribunal what a member of the CDF should do in the face of an illegal order?"

"Refuse to comply, and report the matter further up the chain of command."

"Would it be reasonable, then, to say that your officers"—the procurator gestured to Ruth, Hanson, and Al-Haddad—"had a moral obligation to refuse your illegal and unethical orders?"

Cuellar sprang to his feet. "Objection, Your Honor. The prosecution is assuming facts not in evidence. The entire point of this proceeding is to determine the guilt of the accused, not prejudge it."

Mercy 127

The arbiter banged his stone on the block. "Overruled. The defendants are guilty until proven innocent. It is only reasonable along those lines to assume that General Cohen's orders were illegal."

"But—"

"Sit down, Lieutenant. Or I will be forced to sanction you for breach of procedure."

Without further comment, Cuellar returned to his seat and shook his head.

"Please answer the question, General."

They did warn me this species treated everyone as guilty. "I go back to my previous answer, Procurator, and say that we didn't believe we were breaking our laws or yours. The regulation you cite is geared toward egregious wrongs. If I had, for instance, ordered my vessel to open fire on a civilian passenger liner, I would expect my executive officer to relieve me of command and countermand that instruction."

"If you wish this tribunal to believe your assertion, General, then why didn't they relieve you of command over this infraction?"

"There is no comparison to taking a couple of shuttle loads of ore from a planetoid we thought you couldn't access and killing a few thousand civilians, Procurator. Have you no concept of the severity of the crime?"

"No." The Vogtek blinked. "There is no small or minor crime here. Any breakage of our laws is an attack on society itself and must be dealt with in the harshest possible manner."

The tug-of-war between justice and mercy had been played out for centuries among humans, and David fell more toward the justice side of the fence. Yet there he was, asking for mercy and attempting to argue that something that seemed small to him shouldn't matter for the Vogtek and their allied species. *I'm not sure I'd buy it if I were on the other side.*

David put his hands on the witness box. "While I understand that we are outsiders and bound by your laws, I beg the tribunal to evaluate our actions against your statutes and ours. The penalty for any divergence between those two standards should be placed on me alone."

"I have no further questions for this witness, Arbiter."

"General Cohen may step down."

As David walked back to the defense table, he felt as if the weight of the universe had returned to his shoulders. *That went poorly.* Since his testimony and entries from the *Lion of Judah's* daily log were the primary defense, Cuellar had little left to do except call others who would corroborate what David had testified. *Will it matter?* A feeling of dread stuck with him.

THE DEFENSE CALLED a few more witnesses, including a Fradwig xenobiology expert who explained while wearing her aqua-suit that the Jinvaas Confederation felt no other intelligent life could exist because it hadn't contacted them yet. David supposed that Cuellar was attempting to show that their logic was flawed, and therefore the law didn't account for all possibilities.

The arbiter offered the procurator the opportunity to call rebuttal witnesses, but he declined, and after a short recess, closing arguments began, first with the prosecution.

"This case has been simple from the beginning. These humans came to our home and knowingly stole from us, and even though there is ample evidence they have done good deeds elsewhere, for whatever reason,

Mercy 129

General Cohen ordered his soldiers to take what wasn't his."

Gesturing with his four hands, the procurator paced. "They say our laws aren't set for interacting with the rest of the galaxy. Yet there are four species among us. Kriveez, Vogtek, Otyran, and Fradwig. Our laws give us harmony and ensure everyone understands what is expected of them."

"I urge the court to ensure justice and find these defendants guilty. They must pay for their crimes, and the Terran Coalition should know the price of breaking our statutes." He stopped and made eye contact with David. "Anything less tramples on the charter of our confederation and will destroy all that we have made."

With that, the procurator sat, and the arbiter looked toward the defense table. "Who will give the summation for the accused?"

"I will, Your Honor," Cuellar replied as he stood.

"Proceed."

Cuellar stepped to the lectern. "Your Honor, when two species meet for the first time, there is always a possibility of getting it wrong. In our society, specialized diplomatic and scientific teams observe and obtain information for many months before we approach a new race of beings. This is doubly true of those possessing lower levels of technology than us. In Sextans B, the *Lion of Judah* and her battlegroup don't have that ability. We're on our own, and frankly, as General Cohen has admitted, we make mistakes."

David's eyes went back and forth between Cuellar and the arbiter. The older Vogtek's face was inscrutable, however, as he stared at the lectern.

"There was no intent to break the Jinvaas Confederation's laws. I am confident that as Your Honor examines our logs and sensor data, this fact will be borne out. If you remove the intent to break the law, the justness of finding Major Hanson, Captain Goldberg, and Chief Warrant Officer Karmina Al-Haddad guilty is called into question. Yes, we admit that the ore was taken, but in the absence of a desire to commit a crime and with the return of the property in question, there *must* be provision for acquittal."

Cuellar took a sip of water. "If this tribunal does find a crime was committed, General Cohen wishes for it to be known that as he is the commanding officer, all punishment should fall on him alone, and he respectfully requests to serve any sentence handed down.

"In closing, I call the arbiter's attention to how the Coalition Defense Force, through the leadership of General Cohen, has affected this galaxy since our arrival. It may not be admissible evidence, but it should count in your deliberations. General Cohen is a force for good. He and his crew give selflessly of themselves to assist others, without regard for their safety and security. They will continue to do good and honorable things in this galaxy. I beg the court to allow them to continue. Thank you."

David sat back, thinking they were solely banking on some element of mercy from the Vogtek judge. *I'm not sure I like our odds.*

The arbiter banged his stone on the block. "This tribunal will adjourn for deliberations, and I will announce my decision once it is made. We stand in recess."

An orderly but abrupt rush for the exit by those in the gallery followed, while bailiffs came over and quickly moved Ruth, Hanson, and Al-Haddad from the cage at the back of the courtroom.

Cuellar stood, followed quickly by their Vogtek advisor.

"We should go to the counselors' waiting room," the hexa-limbed alien announced.

Mercy   131

"Of course." David stood. "We'll follow you." He felt like a stranger in a strange land. *I only hope our efforts were enough to free my people.* It had to be enough because the other options were unthinkable. *Yet I will do whatever it takes to rescue them.* As David walked, he pondered whether his actions were hypocritical when the truth was he wouldn't accept the Vogteks' concept of justice if it included hard labor for his officers. *Perhaps they are. I'll leave that for HaShem to decide.*

17

IT HAD BEEN twenty-eight hours since the end of the op, and Calvin was thankful for a warm shower, a filling meal, and some downtime. *I'm starting to feel my years.* Not that he'd ever admit that to anyone, including his wife. After combat came a period of readjustment, when Calvin acclimated back to the world around him. It took longer after a battle as brutal as the one they'd just been in.

Two Marines and more than two dozen Zeivlot special forces operators had perished. The butcher's bill for the extremists, however, was far higher. Counts were still coming in, but at least three hundred terrorists were dead, and a few dozen had been captured. Kill ratios of ten to one were outstanding, but Calvin mourned every loss. *I've come to respect the Zeivlots. They fight just as hard as we do and, when properly equipped, just as well.*

Most of the Zeivlot losses came from suicide bombers who'd clacked off when friendly forces attempted to apprehend them. That the operators continued to try high-risk captures, knowing many of those who opposed them wore

Mercy 133

explosive vests, impressed on Calvin how committed they were to defending their planet.

He stood watching the interrogation of their HVT—Nec'ip Kocer. So far, the Zeivlots had been unable to extract anything from the man. He'd spat in their faces and proclaimed his soul was going to paradise. Part of Calvin wanted to line Kocer up against the nearest wall and conduct a summary execution. But he fought it down.

"If you give us something, we'll make life easier for you in prison," the interrogator said as he circled Kocer. "It doesn't have to be a lot. A small piece of information that shows you're willing to be reasonable will make all the difference."

Calvin recognized the technique, though he didn't think the terrorist would fall for it.

"Never," Kocer hissed, not raising his eyes from the table.

"That's a pity."

The interrogator motioned to someone off camera, and a few moments later, a Zeivlot woman and several children entered the frame. Soldiers lined them up in a row and held weapons to the backs of their heads.

"Perhaps we should ensure your family is waiting for you in paradise."

Calvin erupted from his chair, sending it flying backward. *What the hell are they doing?* He couldn't believe the Zeivlots would murder women and children in cold blood, but even a mock execution was morally wrong. It brought back dark memories of things he'd done in his career as a Marine that were well over the line.

"It is no matter. We will all reunite in the afterlife, and my family would rather see me honor the Maker and our ways than surrender to traitors, cowards, and blasphemers."

134   DANIEL GIBBS

Noting the cold, uncaring expression in Kocer's eyes, Calvin was equally revolted and impressed by his resolve. *He's got more balls than most Leaguers. I'll give him that.*

After a few more minutes, the woman and her children were dragged away, and the interrogator left the room. Seconds later, the door to the observation area swung open. The Zeivlot walked in and dropped into an empty chair wordlessly.

"I could've told you that wouldn't work. Threatening committed extremists doesn't get you anywhere," Calvin said.

The Zeivlot raised an eyebrow. "We haven't met, have we?"

"Don't think so, no."

"I am Mithat Naz'mi, the senior intelligence officer assigned to prisoner questioning. Breaking these pieces of dung is my specialty."

Calvin crossed his arms. "Then what's your next play?"

"In the old days, it was easy." Naz'mi made a face. "Now, there are curbs against *unreasonable* physical methods." His tone made plain the contempt felt for the new rules.

"Look, I get how you feel."

"I doubt that, Colonel Demood," Naz'mi spat. "You have the luxury of a society without people who stand in a place of worship and blow themselves apart. I envy you and your entire race."

"Hey, Zeivlot has some nasty terrorists, sure. But, buddy, you don't know what hell looks like until you stare down a League armored division. I have, on more than one occasion. Trust me. Leaguers are just as bad as these guys."

Naz'mi stared. "Then what do you recommend?"

Calvin bit his lip. "There was a time when I engaged in torture, Naz'mi. Let's be very clear. Whatever euphemism we want to assign to it, like 'physical interrogation methods,' it's torture."

"And? We should feel sorry for them?" Fire shone out of Naz'mi's eyes.

"No. But the answers you get will be meaningless because, after a point, the subject will say or do anything to make it stop. And without corroboration, it's impossible to tell good intel from bad."

Naz'mi continued to stare at him, his facial features unmoving.

"There's also the matter of right and wrong. It might feel *really* good to go down there and beat Kocer to a pulp. Hell, bust out some of his teeth, and pry off one of his fingernails while you're at it. But that sort of thing eats at your soul. I know because I've been there."

"I only care to stop these attacks on my people, Colonel. The Maker can deal with my soul."

Calvin shrugged. "It's not enough that the bad guys get beaten. The good guys have to actually *be* the good guys. We do that by not being like them. Three years ago, I would've tuned that sack of shit up myself. Today? I'm a better man, and I'm telling you we can get the information we need by being the better men."

"If that's true, how would you do it?"

"You got some disorientation goggles and earmuffs?"

Naz'mi narrowed his eyes. "Sensory deprivation? We already tried that. It didn't work."

"Got something else in mind. You'll have to trust me, and it's a long shot. Give me three hours to sort everything out."

"Command says you're in charge for this operation, Colonel." Naz'mi gritted his teeth. "Don't waste what cost us so much blood, though. We've got to break this monster before the rest of them figure out we have him."

DANIEL GIBBS

Calvin nodded. "Agreed." *And what I've got in mind is probably the biggest gamble of my life. God, I know I'm just an old-school Marine, and I'm probably not that high on your list of favorite people. But I could use your help. All this right-and-wrong stuff... Help me to pull this off, and show these folks the right way. Amen.*

———

WITH BLACKOUT GOGGLES and sound-deadening ear coverings on, Nec'ip Kocer felt the passage of time slip away from him. Time seemed to lose all meaning without visual or auditory stimuli. It could've been ten minutes, an hour, or half a day.

He'd been dragged somewhere, colliding with walls and doors, and placed on a bed. The logical conclusion was he had been returned to his cell. Still, it was impossible to know for sure.

All Kocer knew was that explosions shook the facility at some point because he was tossed out of bed and onto the rough concrete floor. With his arms securely fastened behind his back, he couldn't loosen the devices attached to his head and instead flopped around, rage building inside him.

I wish I had been killed by the heretics or been brave enough to put on a vest and die as a warrior for the Maker. But he knew he was too much of a coward to ever blow himself up. For a decade, he'd lived the life of a religious warrior, sending others to fight and die while he enjoyed the spoils, the adoration of women, and a nice sum of currency culled from their coffers.

A faint noise gained his attention. Moments later, the goggles and earmuffs came off. The return of his senses was

Mercy 137

both a relief and a shock. They were overwhelming, as the light seemed to overpower his eyes, even though it was dim. The sounds of gunfire and small explosions came through louder than any he'd ever heard as his mind processed the image of the small, dank cell.

The door at the far end, constructed of alloy bars, had been cut open. Enough of the rods had been melted at the top and bottom that a man could squeeze through. In the opening stood another Zeivlot. He wore the loose-fitting clothing favored by hill tribes in the Tophae province. "Wake up! Who do you serve?"

"The Maker," Kocer replied. "And only the Maker."

"Well met." The stranger took a few steps into the cell and roughly pulled him up before using a laser cutter on his cuffs. "We must flee. The others and I are trying to free the warriors in this prison, but there were more heretics than expected."

"This is more common of late," Kocer said as he flexed his wrists.

"Quickly, follow me!"

Kocer struggled to keep up, his leg pain causing a pronounced limp. Gunfire echoed all around, though the wing they were in seemed deserted. *Where are the rest of my people? There were half a dozen of us before I was taken for interrogation.* The government forces were probably torturing them, but it made no difference. The primary objective was to escape.

"Do you have transportation?"

"Yes, we have several skimmers."

This stroke of luck is almost enough to make me wonder if the Maker is behind it. Kocer marveled at the idea that the Maker would spare any help for him, because since He knew every man's heart, his cowardice had no place to hide. The facility appeared empty as they ran at full tilt toward the exit. Dead guards were lying in pools of pink blood along the way. Scorch marks and bullet holes marked the walls.

The other Zeivlot pulled a primitive communication device from his belt as they rounded a corner and spoke into it. "Duz'gun to assault unit." Nothing but static answered him.

Kocer raised an eyebrow. "Jamming?"

"I don't think so. We use tech so old it can't be jammed because they don't know we're using it."

They both snickered. "So do we," Kocer replied.

"Let's make a run for it. Staying here is going to get us killed."

"Agreed, brother."

They reached the exterior a short time later, following the trail of dead bodies. The two moons shone in the night sky, casting a thin amount of light over the courtyard. Kocer saw half a dozen more fallen guards, and the main gate appeared to have been crashed through with a large industrial vehicle, which had come to rest against the wall of the complex.

Duz'gun tugged at Kocer's shirt. "My hovercraft is over there. We'll round up whoever we can and get out of here."

Not needing to be told twice, Kocer ran after his rescuer. As they climbed into the vehicle's top, a wave of government troops poured into the courtyard. A few fellow insurgents ran ahead of them, only to be cut down by precise rifle fire.

"By the Maker!" Duz'gun yelled before he pounded on the cockpit hatch. "Get us out of here! We'll all be killed if we stay. Now!"

The hovercraft suddenly shot forward, and Kocer fell down and came to rest next to a mounted crew-serviced weapon he recognized as a liberated human machine gun.

Mercy 139

Gripping it with both hands, he swung it toward the onrushing government forces and opened up with a long burst. Several enemies fell before the vehicle cleared the front gate and turned, eliminating his line of sight.

Duz'gun's face was ashen. "My whole cell... gone." He dropped next to Kocer. "Forgive me, but I wish I had stayed away. We just thought... if we could show the local population the heretics can be stopped..." His head collapsed into his hands.

"Even one of us getting away from that place is a victory before the Maker." Kocer put his hand on the other man's shoulder. "You are welcome to join us. I could use another fighter like you. And you do have transport. Our base is a long way."

"It would be an honor."

"Let me see your location beacon."

Duz'gun handed the device over, and Kocer tapped at it. "There. That's our main installation. We'll have to cross some of the distance on foot, but this hovercraft will take us most of the way."

"Ah. Thank you." Duz'gun knocked on the cockpit.

The hovercraft slowly glided to a stop, and Kocer turned to his rescuer. "Why are we stopping?"

Before he could answer, the hatch to the cockpit opened, and a dark-skinned male rose out of it. As his face came into focus, the lack of ridges on his nose made it clear he was a human.

Kocer felt a sharp pain in his chest and fell back with a cry as his heart raced. "What? No!"

"Gotcha, asshole," the human said. "See, I told you Naz'mi. All we had to do was stick to the book and be a little creative. Get the subject to trust you."

The Zeivlot tugged at his beard, and it fell away. "Yes, I

see now. Quite inventive, Colonel Demood. The stun rounds in the mounted machine gun were an especially nice touch."

Kocer tried to say something, but nothing came out except stammering. He collapsed to the floor of the hover-craft, realizing he'd failed at everything. *I have nothing to show for my existence, and the Maker will judge me harshly.*

"Let's get this piece of shit back to his cell and get ISR on the lead," the human said with a sneer in Kocer's direction. "Thanks for telling us where your friends are. I look forward to giving them a warm welcome from the Terran Coalition's misguided children."

Time seemed to slow, and Kocer felt himself being manhandled while the cuffs were reapplied. He didn't speak again for days.

18

ROBERT TAYLOR WAS SURPRISED the Vogteks had allowed him to visit Ruth, but they'd given each of the prisoners one five-minute visitation before the verdicts were read. Clad only in his dress khaki uniform, he was searched three separate times by the hexa-limbed beings before being let into a small room with a metal alloy door. *I bet you'd need a fusion warhead to crack that thing.* It weighed so much that the guard had a hard time shutting it.

A small chair sat in front of a window, which again appeared so overengineered as to make even denting it impossible.

After what seemed like hours, Ruth was led in. Her legs were shackled together, but at least her hands were free.

As Taylor stared at his fiancée, rage exploded in him. *They have no right to treat her like this!* He directed part of the anger back to himself. *I can't save her. If only I were one of those fancy tier-one commandos, then I'd have the knowledge to break her out.*

Ruth collapsed in the chair on the other side, and the window turned blue. "Can you hear me?"

"Yes." More than anything, Taylor wanted to hold her in his arms and tell her everything would be okay. "How are you holding up?"

"It's not what you'd think. They've treated us better than I expected. These people, they're very orderly. It's as if everyone has a place and knows their place."

"Not like the Terran Coalition, then." Taylor tried to force a smile to his face, but his heart wasn't in it.

Ruth shook her head. "Yeah, not so much."

Figuring he'd probably get shocked or worse, Taylor put his hand to the window. When nothing happened, he pressed his palm against it. "I love you so much."

She returned the gesture. "Nothing quite like staring at a small cell for twenty-six hours a day to remind you how awesome our cabin on the *Lion* is."

"You're getting out of this, Ruth. I don't care what it takes or what I have to do. I promise."

Tears slid down her face. She closed her eyes and opened them again as if trying to stop the flow. "We hope. But I have to be realistic, Robert. They may never let us go."

"The general won't let that happen." *Nor will I.*

"He has an entire fleet to worry about, Robert. I wouldn't want him to risk the lives of thousands of people just for *me*."

"I only care about one person right now. You."

Ruth grinned and wiped her eyes. "Damn you. Don't make me cry again."

"No matter what, we're getting you out of there."

"I love you."

"I love you too." It took everything he had not to start pounding on the glass-like surface of the window with all his might. Such a gesture would accomplish nothing. "How are you able to be so calm?"

Mercy   143

"What good is freaking out going to do me?" Ruth shrugged. "The general will be successful, or he won't. I can't affect the outcome here. At least, I can't right now. What I can do is pray and keep hope alive that all of you will come through for Hanson, Al-Haddad, and me."

"Who are you, and what happened to my worrywart fiancée who wanted to control every last moment of her existence?"

"Oh, she's still here. I just learned the hard way that I have to give things I can't control up. You don't know this, Robert, but I tried to murder Seville."

Taylor stared at her, his eyebrows raised. "*What?*"

"I had his escape pod locked and point defense ready to fire. General Cohen wouldn't let me." Ruth gulped. "That was the day I truly stepped back from the abyss. And you were there to catch me."

He closed his eyes. "I never knew." Admiral Seville had been the leader of the League invasion force. Decisively beaten at the Third Battle of Canaan, the admiral was rotting away on Lambert's Lament, the Coalition's super-max prison facility on an asteroid.

"Not exactly my proudest moment."

Taylor remained speechless. That revelation wasn't something he'd expected to hear.

"So, I had to really adjust how I think."

"Is that why you go to church without fail now?" He finally forced his mouth to move.

"Yeah. One of the reasons, anyway. I just... Don't be like I was, okay? Nothing crazy. Stay calm, and trust the general knows what he's doing."

"Something tells me we need a miracle to get out of this."

Ruth cracked a grin. "You serve on the *Lion of Judah*. Miracles are our specialty."

A buzzer sounded as the door behind Ruth swung open, and two guards came in. She put her hand on the glass again. "I love you."

"I love you too. You're getting out. I promise, no matter the cost. Godspeed." Taylor choked out the words as she was led away. It took him a few moments to compose himself and exit the visitation booth. *Please, God, if you're up there, help Ruth. She doesn't deserve to die in an alien prison.* He had a complicated history with religious beliefs that had led to his thinking there was some kind of overarching power in the universe. However, whatever that deity was, it didn't concern itself with the goings-on of humans or other species. *Today, I hope I'm wrong.*

———

SITTING in a small waiting room had felt like torture, but David thought being in the courtroom after being informed the arbiter had reached a decision was worse. He wasn't used to feeling helpless, yet there he was, unable to do anything to influence the situation more than he already had. Whispering in Hebrew, he asked HaShem to help them in whatever way He saw fit.

After another half hour, the door the arbiter used to enter the chamber flew open, and in walked the hexa-limbed alien wearing a white robe and an elaborate head-piece. A stream of foreign words that the translator didn't pick up thundered across the room before the cry of "All stand!" echoed.

David sprang up and came to attention, an almost automatic reaction. So did Ruth, Hanson, Al-Haddad, their

Mercy 145

attorneys, and Lieutenant Cuellar. David's heart pounded as the arbiter leaned forward.

"Most cases that come before this tribunal are simple. They allow for swift and sure justice to be applied and the needs of our citizens to be met. Such has been the way of things for many hundreds of seasons. Every once in a while, we encounter something that begs a second look."

Hope sprang in David's heart.

"I have examined the facts presented by both sides. Given the humans' logs, sensor data, and other evidence, there is no reason to think they intended to steal from our confederation."

"However," the arbiter continued after a pause, "that does not mean a crime wasn't committed."

The hope instantly evaporated.

"Our laws demand justice, and ignorance of the law is not a defense. Thus has it been since the dark times from which we emerged, and so it shall remain. I have considered the extenuating circumstances the defendants and their leader provided and modified the penalties accordingly. Sentence is pronounced at twenty standard years for each theft charge, to be served concurrently. The motion by General Cohen to accept full responsibility and be incarcerated in the defendants' stead is rejected. While he may very well have ordered stealing the helium-3 ore in question, Major Hanson, Captain Goldberg, and Chief Warrant Officer Al-Haddad could've refused at any time. Instead, they willingly did as they were told."

Remembering that the Vogtek attorney had said most prison sentences were served consecutively, David supposed the arbiter thought he was doing them a favor. Anger, guilt, and shame in equal amounts surged through him.

"The defendants will be immediately sent to the Dree-

Noosk processing center and transported to our penal facility to be assigned as helium-3 miners. This tribunal stands in recess."

Before the arbiter was out the door, Taylor had erupted from his seat and bent toward David. "Do something, sir. Before we lose them!"

"Lieutenant, lower your voice," David hissed in reply. "We *will* do something, but now is not the time or the place."

Taylor seemed to be barely containing his rage as Vogtek officers approached and placed Ruth, Hanson, and Al-Haddad into hand restraints.

Watching them shuffle out, flanked by multiple hexa-limbed aliens, was among the most challenging things David had done in his life. More than anything, he longed to leap into action and rescue his people. *No. I need to get back to the* Lion of Judah, *regroup, and figure this out.* He hoped there was still time.

19

THE TRIP back to the *Lion* was one of the worst experiences David Cohen could remember. The mental image of Ruth, Hanson, and Al-Haddad being led out of the courtroom in electronically controlled shackles wouldn't leave him. Over and over, it played in his head along with condemnation that *he* had gotten them there. Second-guessing every decision he'd made since the *Lion* had jumped into the binary star system the Vogteks, Krivez, Fradwig'I, and Otyrans called home, David was in a dark place. He recognized, however, that there was no time for recrimination or guilt. *We just have to work the problem. But tell that to Taylor. He wants to go in there guns blazing and save the woman he loves. I can't fault that desire.*

While the shuttle was still in the void, David cut orders for the senior staff to meet him in the conference room on deck one. When they touched down on the flight deck and the ramp opened, David sprang from his seat without another word.

It took him nearly fifteen minutes to make his way

through the central passageway to the gravlift leading to deck one. Such walks helped clear the mind.

David took the few steps from the lift to the conference room and pushed the hatch open. The rest of the team was already there, including Aibek, Hayworth, Merriweather, Amir, Dr. Tural, Major Lucas Almeida, Cuellar, and Bo'hai. *Dr. Hayworth on time... that's a new one.*

"General on deck!" Tinetariro boomed as the others stood and came to attention.

"As you were." David slid into the chair at the head of the table as the others returned to their seats. "I'm sure everyone has heard by now that the trial didn't go our way."

Aibek hissed. "The entire ship is aware. Major Almeida has devised a plan to storm the prison transfer facility and recover our people by force."

"That's an option on the table," David replied. "However—"

"With respect, *sir*," Taylor interjected, "we're past the time for it being on the table. You need to act."

If this were any other situation, in any other place, I'd relieve Taylor and give him a few days in his cabin to cool off. Not only had David screwed up, but if he couldn't find a way out of the situation, morale would collapse across the fleet. "Lieutenant, we're going to exhaust all diplomatic options first."

"What other options are there, sir?"

David turned to Cuellar. "I assume there's some method to appeal a verdict?"

"Yes, sir. But don't ask me to explain it quite yet. I'm parsing through these guys' procedures and trying to figure out how to move forward."

"Am I correct in assuming it's not the same way we do it?"

Cuellar shook his head. "Back in the Coalition, let's say

you get convicted of a significant felony. You can appeal that decision immediately based on evidence or mistakes the court made. Call it other issues at law. Here, I don't understand it yet. If I say the arbiter made a mistake, am I insulting their entire culture? Is that a crime in and of itself? One thing I can tell you—according to our representative, appeals are rare and successful ones, even rarer."

Bo'hai leaned forward. "May I?"

"Of course," David replied. "We're interested in any insights you may have into their culture."

"The science team has exhaustively combed through what we've been able to access of this society's version of the GalNet, and I come to the same conclusion over and over. They are a people who value justice above all else. Everything they do is judged as right or wrong, with little room for compromise."

"But... we're talking about a shuttle cargo bay full of helium-3. In the grand scheme of things, that is *nothing*." David's patience was ebbing. The situation felt like an overly dramatic holoshow.

"To them, crime is crime, and there is no such thing as extenuating circumstances." Bo'hai rested her hands on the table. "I've said this before, but it bears repeating. There is no word for mercy in any of their four respective languages."

"And what good does that do us?" Taylor asked as his face turned bloodred. "Who *cares*?"

Bo'hai stared back at him with a soft expression. "Because it helps us to understand them. Perhaps through that understanding, we can bridge the gap."

David cleared his throat. "I want to sit down with the top level of government for these people. Their ruling council, is it?"

"Yes, sir," Cuellar replied. "They have made very clear

that the executive branch of government doesn't interfere with the justice system, however."

"I don't care. We have levers to pull in terms of sharing information. I'd even go so far as helping them with their FTL problem. Whatever it takes to get our people back."

Hayworth appeared as if he was about to say something but paused when Taylor stuck his head forward instead. "General, we've got a simple way to get them back. Stick the Marines on that transfer station before they're moved to a mining facility. Whatever tech level the Vogteks possess, our people would mop the floor with them."

"Not until we've exhausted all diplomatic options." David hoped his tone indicated there would be no further discussion.

"Yes, *sir*."

"I think we're done here. Cuellar, notify me the moment the ruling council meeting is set."

"Roger that, sir."

"Dismissed. Except for Lieutenant Taylor."

Everyone in the room except the civilians knew what was coming next and made a beeline for the hatch. Hayworth was the last one out, and as he exited, the hard alloy clanged shut.

Taylor stood at ramrod-straight attention and gritted his teeth. "Permission to speak freely, sir?"

"You've been doing that for days, Lieutenant. Don't let me stop you now." David regretted the snarkiness of his tone the moment the words left his mouth, but the truth was he was growing tired of Taylor's disrespect. *Even if he has a point.*

"This is *your* problem, sir. We should've used force to rescue the shuttle. I know that. So do you, and so does every soldier in this fleet! It's obvious. They would've folded like a wet deck of cards."

Mercy   151

"And if they hadn't?"

"Then we blow them out of the void."

David blinked. "I respect you enough to think that's not your actual belief, Lieutenant."

"Ruth... Captain Goldberg is in a damn *prison*, sir. It's easy to sit in the big chair and pontificate about right and wrong when you don't have any skin in the game."

Silence followed for a few moments as David flexed his hand into a fist under the table several times before relaxing and forcing himself to breathe. "I've served alongside them for years and count Goldberg as one of my closest friends, so don't you *dare* tell me I don't care."

"Talk is cheap, sir. *Do something.*"

"Do you think they'd want us to kill a few thousand Vogteks to rescue them?"

"I don't see how it matters. This system has made itself our enemy. We should act accordingly."

David stood. "You can be angry with me all you want. I shouldn't have ordered mining that planetoid. If I could do it over again, I wouldn't. But I won't compound one error with a series of horrible choices that will hollow *all* of us out."

"So we leave them to rot?" Taylor took a step forward, invading David's personal space.

David ran his teeth over his lip. "Lieutenant, I will use all diplomatic means at my disposal to resolve this situation before I consider using force. At no time will we leave our shipmates to rot."

"What is the point, sir? Just jump the *Lion* into orbit around one of their planets and fire our particle beams. That kind of power will bring anyone to heel."

"The point is we're better than that. And if this were anyone besides Ruth, you'd be in the same mindset as me."

Taylor's shoulders fell, and he shook his head. "Maybe I would. But you can't let them work her to death for twenty years, sir."

David put his hand on Taylor's shoulder. "And I won't. You know me better than that. This isn't fighting the League, though. No bright line says, 'These people are our enemy, and killing them is acceptable.' Out here, we're figuring out right and wrong as we go."

"Get them home."

"We will. Going forward, I expect you to comport yourself in a manner befitting an officer in the Coalition Defense Force. Do I make myself clear, Lieutenant?"

"Crystal, sir." Taylor resumed his ramrod-straight posture.

"Good. Dismissed."

The hatch again clanged shut as Taylor departed.

Part of David continued to feel guilty for his failure of ethics. But he pushed that aside, knowing that guilt served no purpose. When it was over, that would be the time to go bare his soul in the shul and ask HaShem to forgive him. *For now, all I can do is work the problem. And keep working it until there's a solution.* He stood and went back to work. *In time, perhaps Taylor can forgive me. I hope all of them can.*

———

BENJAMIN HAYWORTH PRIDED himself on being a man devoted solely to science. Every day spent in the lab was one day closer to unlocking another technological achievement. Since they'd arrived in Sextans B, he'd felt like a young man again as they saw the wonder of the universe and, more importantly, dug out secrets that time had kept for eons.

Those secrets didn't include a massive interspecies

Mercy

legal code that, by Hayworth's estimation, had been around for five thousand years in some form or another. *Instead of exploring the precursor artifact, here I sit, writing... code.*

"Doctor?" Merriweather called as she pushed the hatch open. "I've been looking all over for you. Why is your commlink off?"

Hayworth glanced up. "Because I didn't want to be bothered."

She stepped into the lab and stared at the bank of wall-mounted flat monitors. Data streamed by in multiple alien languages. "What are you doing?"

"Societies built around legalism, much like some of our religions, have rules for everything. They even have rules on how to enact more rules." He chuckled. "I decided to investigate a bit further."

"How?"

"Simple, really. I wrote an algorithm to parse all four planets' worth of laws, dating back about five thousand years."

Merriweather's jaw dropped. "Why?"

"Because for whatever reason, they treat the entirety of these millions of laws as binding. Moreover, each planet's legal code is equally accepted on all four worlds."

"So if you can find a loophole in one, no matter how old, General Cohen can use it?"

Hayworth nodded. "That is the idea, my dear. It's a shame there are petaquads of this crap. I suspect the League has nothing on these people's bureaucratic state." He stopped the stream for a moment and gestured to several monitors. "If my translation matrix reads this right, there are several thousand regulations on how to properly issue citations to improperly parked vehicles."

"Absurd." Merriweather stared at it for a few seconds before the stream moved on. "It's nice you're trying to help."

"Are you suggesting that I'm a grouchy old curmudgeon who doesn't help his friends?"

"Oh, I didn't realize you had those," Merriweather replied with a big grin.

"Bah." He sat on a nearby chair and closed his eyes for a moment. "I feel somewhat responsible for this situation."

"Why?"

"Because I endorsed the plan to mine the helium-3."

"General Cohen made the call." Merriweather dropped into a seat across the lab table from him. "No one suspected they had limited FTL capability."

Hayworth shrugged. "Still, I'm always going on about noninterference. I should've realized it was an unacceptable risk. So I feel compelled to try to fix it. Also, Captain Goldberg once defended me back on Gilead. Some young punk was about to beat me up when she stepped in."

"I remember." Merriweather grinned. "I also recall you getting in that situation for telling those punks to get lost when they harassed Ruth and me."

"Well, I don't suffer idiots lightly. Still, it's nice to feel like I'm wanted. I hate admitting that out loud, but these last few months have been different."

Merriweather regarded him silently. "They always wanted you, Doctor. It's that *you've* been different lately."

"They have a funny way of showing it."

She shook her head. "Hanson thinks you're the smartest person he's ever met and that it's a dream come true to pick up every piece of antimatter engineering knowledge he can from you. The rest of the crew is in awe of the power the reactor puts out and takes great pride in being some of the few soldiers in the fleet to wear the antimatter insignia. *All* of them know you invented it."

"Yet I'm kept at arm's length, especially by the more religious."

Merriweather stared at him. "There're plenty of atheists and agnostics in the CDF. Most of them don't quite enjoy poking the bear the way you do."

A smirk crept onto Hayworth's face. "You must allow an old man his enjoyment, my dear."

"Has it occurred to you that since we got here, you quit debating General Cohen most of the time?"

Hm. I suppose she's right. "And what of it?"

"Sometimes, I'll concede the Coalition can get a bit overbearing, and I suspect it's difficult to be someone who doesn't have a faith, looking at the vast majority of us who do. But I've only met a few people who treated someone differently because of their faith or lack of it."

Hayworth inclined his head. "That's generally true. As you say, though, it grows tiresome to be the only person in the room who professes a lack of faith."

She put a hand on his arm. "We all respect you, and I think if you step back for a moment, you'll realize that since we arrived in Sextans B, you've been a nicer human overall. Everyone else noticed and is probably nicer back. That's how we all work."

"I know." Hayworth pursed his lips. "Sometimes, an old man like me looks back on his life and wishes some things had been different. That I'd made choices other than the path I took. Perhaps if I hadn't been invested in my work more than anything else..." Sometimes, he sorely wished he had a daughter like her.

"You can't change the past. But you can change today and every day after."

"As long as you don't try to drag me to church."

"I respect you far too much to try." Merriweather grinned. "What can I do to help here?"

"I haven't eaten in ten hours. If you'd be willing to get us a snack, I would appreciate it. Then you can help me update this algorithm to better parse out appeals and challenges to a sentence less than death."

She stood. "Okay. Anything special you want from the mess?"

"Pizza with those anktar things is acceptable."

Merriweather suppressed a giggle. "Don't tell anyone you like them. Most of the crew hates them, and we're convinced the mess chefs are enjoying torturing us."

He winked. "Who says they aren't?"

After she'd left and closed the hatch behind her, Hayworth let out a sigh. He didn't often engage in deep, introspective thinking about the past. Life wasn't to be lived with a focus on anything but the future and whatever new challenges science threw at him. Still, he felt a sense of pride at being at the forefront of the exploration of a new galaxy. Even if it was through the military, being a part of seeing new worlds and civilizations and shining a light on the unknown made him feel like a young man again. *I've got thirty years before I need to consider retirement. Maybe I can reinvent myself still.*

20

RATHER THAN USE the deck-one conference room, David had decided to vidlink the system's ruling council from the communication facilities deep within the *Lion*. They had a less formal air, and the emblem of the Coalition Defense Force wasn't emblazoned on the wall. *Perhaps I'll come off a bit less threatening.* Though it was probably wishful thinking, he would do anything for an advantage.

He'd also chosen to have the conversation alone rather than with Cuellar or any of the other senior staff. *They'll have a numbers advantage on me, but that could benefit me. At least if they function like humans.*

The holoprojector came to life with an image of an ornate room somewhere in the binary system. David assumed it was on the Vogtek home world, since they seemed to be the leaders of the alliance. The ruling council came into focus. In the middle sat a fur-covered mammalian male. Flanking him were a Vogtek, easily identified by his four arms, and another humanoid that seemed to have gills on its neck.

They must be the amphibious ones. Hayworth's briefing

called them the Fradwig'I. I've met more new species in the last three months than I have in my life.

David cleared his throat. "Members of the council, thank you for agreeing to speak with me."

The Otyran's eyes flashed. "When a hostile race appears in our system, steals from us, and attempts to threaten our protectors and custodians, we find ourselves having to bend the law."

"It is not my intention to threaten you, Mister...?"

"Chairman Prin Opaltis. I've acquainted myself with the materials you sent us about the Terran Coalition, General Cohen. It sounds nice in theory, except you ordered the theft of our property, by your own admission."

David forced his expression into a neutral position. *This is not going well.* "As I stated during the trial, that was a grave mistake on my part. You have no one to blame but me."

The being's gray fur rippled. "Count yourself lucky that your warship is powered by technology we cannot match and do not possess. Otherwise, I'd see you in the stockade as well."

"I had hoped we could reach a compromise." David placed his hands on the table. "We have vast knowledge to offer."

"How to steal ore?"

I'm talking to a brick wall. It seemed inconceivable to David that they'd placed so much hostility bordering on hate against them for the incident. "How to improve your society. As you observed, we have extensive technological knowledge."

"What exactly are you suggesting, General?"

David swallowed. "Perhaps we could interest you in medical technology that would extend the lives of your citi-

Mercy

zens. And maybe you could release my officers, with the time they've currently served sufficing as punishment."

Opaltis's face contorted, and he waved his arms wildly. "You would bribe us? What do you take us for? Common criminals? To even entertain such a thought is a crime. It would result in my resigning and surrendering myself for punishment at the Hall of Justice."

The others nodded their agreement, and the Vogtek spoke. "We should enter charges against the entire Terran Coalition for this insult."

David wanted to scream. *Now I've taken it from bad to worse.* "Does your culture not have any concept of forgiveness or mercy?"

"What is this you speak of?" Opaltis replied.

"The concept that you... accept the apology of another and no longer hold the crime or misdeed against them."

"Without applying punishment?"

"Sometimes, yes. Other times, no. It depends on the circumstances."

Opaltis gritted his teeth. "There must always be a punishment. No justice can exist without swift and sure retribution."

"That's not how humans function. We believe in the concept of mercy. It's been imbued in our religious teachings since God first spoke to us thousands of years ago."

"Perhaps the Creator meant for you to function this way. *Not us.* Our society was wracked by strife, violence, and war. The laws and their sanctions have allowed us to rise above those ills and achieve peace."

David leaned back while mentally searching for something he could use to sway the alien leader. "I cannot comment on your past, only on the present and the future.

We, too, have harsh laws to deal with the worst of humanity."

"Such as?" Opaltis stared at him, unblinking.

"If you murder another sentient life-form, be it human or another species, there is a long period of imprisonment, and the death penalty is on the table. Rape, child molestation, and selling addictive drugs and chemicals to others and enabling the destruction of their lives... are cause for harsh punishment, to use your words. We have an asteroid penal colony where the worst are sent to live out their lives or wait for execution."

"Then how are you different from us?" The Otyran sounded intrigued.

David hoped he was making progress. "We balance the need for swift justice, as you put it, with mercy. There is a chance for many to be rehabilitated. The Coalition has numerous programs for this and a decent success rate. Some are faith based, others secular. It's not perfect, but our system works."

Opaltis's face hardened. "You say this, yet you come here and steal from us."

He will throw that in my face no matter what *I say or do.* "Again, Mr. Chairman, I can only apologize for my actions."

"Even if I accepted what you say is true and believe you have honest regret for your actions, General, my hands are tied. Our law is what binds our four races together."

The other council members nodded.

"Perhaps in the future, once the stain of humanity's crime against us passes, we would be open to further discussion," the being with gills stated. Her voice was oddly mechanical, as if it was computer generated.

Opaltis licked his lips. "I'm afraid that is the best you will

Mercy   161

get from us. The matter is closed, and we expect your fleet to leave our space within the next standard rotation."

David despaired. *It appears there will not be a diplomatic solution after all.* "Very well, Mr. Chairman. I thank you and the others for your time."

After a curt nod, the commlink disengaged. *There's no getting around it now.* All options but force had been exhausted, and he wouldn't leave his people in the hands of an alien species. *Which means sending in the Marines.*

David brought his handcomm up to his lips. "Cohen to Aibek."

"Yes, sir?"

"Get Major Almeida and the senior staff together. My effort to broker a peaceful resolution has failed. We're going in."

"Aye, aye, sir." Aibek's voice seemed to morph, as if he was finally agreeable to David's orders.

"Deck-one conference room in two hours. I'll see you then."

David stood as he let his arm drop, and the handcomm clicked off. He decided to visit the shul and pray for wisdom. *I got us into this mess. Perhaps HaShem will help me get us out of it.*

————

DAVID WAS confident that Major Almeida had already devised a rescue plan for Ruth, Hanson, and Al-Haddad. He had no other viable explanation for how rapidly the major had pulled it together. With the lights dimmed in the *Lion*'s deck-one conference room, all attention was on the holoprojector. It showed a 3-D view of a prison facility where the

Vogteks mined Helium-3 and their people were incarcerated.

"As I was saying, sir, we'd need the fleet to take out this network of sensor and defense satellites here." Almeida pointed at a group of twenty blinking objects arrayed in a grid formation three hundred sixty degrees around the planetoid.

"What kind of defensive capabilities do they possess?" David asked as he glanced down the line of officers on either side of the table.

First Lieutenant Victoria Kelsey leaned forward, her voice halting. "Um, scans indicate weak shielding and nonexistent armor."

"Our point defense weapons could cripple those things," Lieutenant Colonel Savchenko grumbled over the commlink.

"So we'd need to jump multiple assets in and take out the pickets, then?" David turned back to Almeida.

"That would be my recommendation, sir. Once the hostile overwatch is neutralized, I'd want to send a force of four hundred Marines in. There's one central loading dock where freighters transit daily." He zoomed the view in, showing the facility was tightly constructed and built into the rock. "They'd expect us there. Simultaneously, two more strike teams would burn through the outer hull and infiltrate the prison. Since we don't know exactly where our people are, we'll have to conduct a search—level by level, cell by cell."

David blew out a breath. *Lots of ways this could go sideways.* "What about hacking into their systems and finding our folks that way?"

Almeida shrugged. "Entirely possible, but we'd need to bring some G2 people and probably a linguist. I don't think I like the idea of non-Marine-trained combatants on this mission."

"There may be no other choice, Major. Have you run options for a surgical strike versus the shock-and-awe approach?"

"Yes, sir. With our lack of intel, my assessment is a limited force made up of our Recon Marine company would risk being overwhelmed." At David's frown, he continued. "Sir, if I may, it's vital that we all realize these aliens aren't the Zeivlots. They have directed energy rifles that we've seen on drone footage, and it's likely they also have large-caliber heavy-penetration weapons. In short, we're going to lose Marines on this operation."

"Are you saying they're a near peer in terms of ground warfare technology, Major?" David asked.

"No, sir. Just advanced enough to make this challenging."

David nodded. The thought of Marines—or anyone, for that matter—dying over a misjudgment he'd committed made David want to throw up. Forcing the guilt aside, he glanced at Aibek. "What do you think, XO?"

"It is evident that whatever force is required should be used. Had we done this when it was a few patrol ships, the cost would've been far lower."

The barb stung. "Casualty projections, Major?"

"Depending on how vigorously the Vogteks defend the facility, dozens to hundreds on their side. I'd expect ten percent wounded and at least a dozen KIA on ours." Almeida's glare was unflinching.

David furrowed his brow. "What can be done to eliminate our losses?"

"Eliminate the use of stun weapons and shoot solely to kill."

DANIEL GIBBS

All eyes turned to David. He felt caught between two implacable demands. The first was to protect those who served under him and bring them home. The second was to observe the maxims of his faith and the shared moral fiber of the Terran Coalition. It seemed bitterly ironic to consider an act of naked aggression against an alien species that was just following the law from their perspective.

As David opened his mouth, the conference room hatch flew open, and Hayworth stumbled in. He came to a stop at the table and put his hands on it, panting.

"Doctor? Are you okay?"

"A bit out of breath," Hayworth got out before pulling himself up to his full height. "I know you're all planning an attack on the Vogtek prison—"

"It's a military matter, Doctor."

"I've got a different solution."

David tilted his head. "Let's hear it, then." He gestured to an empty seat next to Lieutenant Kelsey. "By all means."

"Thank you, General." Hayworth dropped into the chair, still breathing heavily. "I guess I'm not quite as young as I used to be. These aliens each have a massive legal code, as we all know by now. I ran it through a machine learning algorithm I developed and found a loophole."

"Don't keep us in suspense." David crossed his arms.

"They used to allow honor combat to decide guilt in a criminal case. Or I should say the Kriveez did. That's the avian race we haven't seen in person, from the third planet."

Sometimes I wish I could just pull it out of him. "And?"

"That part of the code is gone. But a provision for limited trial by combat between two military forces remains on the books as a way to deal with disagreements." Hayworth beamed.

Mercy 165

David sat back. "To put it mildly, we can wipe the floor with their entire observed space fleet with the *Lion of Judah*."

"Perhaps if we claim this rite, they would not dare to fight us, and justice would prevail by default," Aibek interjected, his voice still containing far more hiss than usual.

"It's worth a shot." David turned to Almeida. "Keep preparing, Major. Set up kill houses on the aft flight deck, and drill your Marines."

"Yes, sir."

David's eyes went to Taylor. "Lieutenant, send a priority message to the ruling council. Tell them we wish to appeal, and cite the specific legal code that Dr. Hayworth pulled up. And have Lieutenant Cuellar meet me, Dr. Hayworth, and the XO down in the secure comms area. We'll use the vidlink center for the discussion."

"Yes, sir." Taylor sat ramrod straight. "Sir, if this doesn't work, permission to join the Marine assault force."

I knew that was coming too. Who am I kidding? If I were in his shoes, nothing in heaven or hell would prevent me from trying to save the woman I loved. "If it gets there, we'll discuss that privately, Lieutenant. Dismissed, people. Let's get to work."

21

AFTER CONSULTING with First Lieutenant Cuellar, David wasn't sure if what Hayworth had dug out of the alien code of laws was even legal under the CDF's Universal Code of Military Justice. *Nor do I care. Someday, when we get back to Canaan, there will be an accounting of my actions. It won't be today. Or tomorrow, for that matter.* So he'd pressed on, hopeful that claiming the combat rite would force the aliens to capitulate, with the superiority of the *Lion of Judah*.

Deep within the *Lion*'s communications center, he, Hayworth, Aibek, and Cuellar occupied one of two secure vidlink suites. They were meant for gold-level comms during wartime, but David felt it appropriate to use the facility instead of the conference room. *Just to avoid RUMINT, if nothing else.*

The holoprojector snapped on with an image of the ruling council. The same Fradwig, Vogtek, and Otyran members as the last time they'd talked appeared. Prin Opaltis, the Otyran chairman, made a mewing sound. "What do you want, General Cohen? We made plain last

Mercy **167**

time we spoke that you and your kind are unwelcome criminals."

"I realize that. First, please allow me to apologize again for our initial actions and my previous comments. I did not intend to offer a bribe or insult your species and customs."

"Your officer said something about a new legal theory?"

David nodded and took a deep breath. *It's go time.* "We conducted an extensive review of your legal codes. There's a Kriveez custom allowing for trial by combat—"

"That archaic rule was purged from the laws centuries ago." Opaltis grunted. "Do not attempt to mislead us, General. We will not be lectured by outsiders on our own laws."

"If I may, Mr. Chairman, part of that section was removed but not the portion pertaining to combat between two military forces to decide a dispute."

The different aliens glanced at one another before Opaltis turned to a Vogtek farther down the table. "Chief Arbiter, are you familiar with what the humans are saying?"

After a pause, the older Vogtek waved one of its four arms. "Yes. I have found the clause. They are correct."

Opaltis erupted from his chair. "I will *not* allow these criminals to abuse our society."

"It is not abuse to apply a valid theory of law to an appeal," the chief arbiter replied. "I am solely concerned with the written word. And the statute clearly indicates that when two governments have a dispute, they may engage in a rite of combat between two military forces to ensure a binding settlement of the issue, without resorting to a more generalized conflict. "

"B-But..." Opaltis sputtered, shaking his head. "That was written more than two thousand years ago. It's not even a part of our unified code."

168   DANIEL GIBBS

The Vogtek turned the palms of his four hands upward. "I do not concern myself with when a law was written. The only thing that matters is a plain reading of those words without consideration of another set of contexts. That principle has guided our society for centuries. We will not abandon it now because of your vendetta against the humans."

"*Vendetta?*" Opaltis shouted.

"It is clear they broke our law. It is also clear that by examining our laws in detail then coming here to plead for a rite guaranteed in the code, they demonstrate respect for our society and the great covenant. I rule they are free to proceed as a point of order."

David forced himself not to smile. *Finally, some progress.* "Where do we go from here, then?"

"I suppose you think you're going to appear in your giant spaceship, terrorize our world, and scare us with its overwhelming technology into just giving up by invoking this archaic rite?" The chairman's voice dripped acid. "Think again, human."

Not a fair characterization of what I'd planned, and I don't think I like where this is leading. "I wouldn't phrase it like that, Chairman Opaltis."

"Of course you wouldn't." He smirked and gestured with all four arms. "There's an addendum to that rite, a few thousand pages of legal text away. It's likely you missed it."

Uh-oh.

"While we have to accept the challenge, it must be a fair fight, and the defender chooses those terms." Opaltis gritted his teeth. "You possess several smaller vessels in your armada, yes?"

David nodded. "We do. Four Ajax-class destroyers."

"One of them will face ten of our Vogtek cruisers."

Mercy 169

"That seems... extreme," David replied, barely holding back a scowl and harsher words.

"It is the only offer you will receive. If it is not acceptable, leave, and come back when the sentence handed down to the criminals is served."

"These cruisers you speak of, I would like to know more about them." David worked through what they'd seen so far out of the Vogteks' combat capabilities.

"Four of them disabled your shuttle." Opaltis bared his teeth. "The time for a decision is at hand, human."

David mentally reviewed the tactical scans of the cruisers. *They're lightweight, more like a TC Border Enforcement corvette. With inferior technology. One of our destroyers is a match for ten of them. It might be close, but we can do it. We must do it.* "This is acceptable."

Hayworth turned to stare sharply at David, as did Cuellar. "Fighting an alien force is the antithesis of noninter—"

"This isn't up for debate, Doctor. We will execute this rite and save our people."

"I will determine the parameters of where the combat will occur and publish it to both parties within twenty-six standard hours," the chief arbiter interjected. He banged a polished stone on a wooden block. "Justice will be served."

"We await your defeat by the hand of justice on the battlefield," Opaltis said.

Sensing nothing further was to be gained by continued speaking, David forced a polite nod. "In that case, we will stand by for your instructions. Cohen out."

The holoprojector went blank, and a period of stunned silence followed.

"I did not expect us to have to engage in combat," Aibek said with a hiss. "Perhaps these Vogteks have more honor than I thought. Any being willing to put their life on the line in combat is worthy of respect."

David sat back as conflicting thoughts ran through his head. "Yeah. I figured they would cave in, not pull some more legal mumbo jumbo out."

Hayworth snorted. "This is out of control."

"I'd like to point out that none of this meshes well with the Coalition Defense Force's UCMJ." Cuellar shrugged. "It's not like we can ask Canaan for an opinion, but I feel the need to say that formally."

"So noted, Lieutenant." David pursed his lips. "The *Margaret Thatcher* is the obvious choice, since she's the only Block-II Ajax we've got. Any objection to that, XO?"

Aibek lifted an eye scale. "No."

"Sir, do you intend to destroy ten enemy ships to rescue three officers?" Cuellar asked.

All three of them turned to him.

"They are the causes of their demise," Aibek hissed. "There is no dishonor in killing an enemy on the battlefield. I will rest easily knowing this outcome."

David knew that it was unacceptable from a moral perspective to kill hundreds of the enemy in such a manner. "If we have to. I'll continue to look for another way, but I also won't allow our people to be worked to death mining helium-3." *I need another solution.* He'd thought for sure the duel gambit would work. *What if we didn't destroy the enemy vessels and simply disabled them?*

"Understood, sir," Cuellar replied.

"Actually, I've got an idea. Doctor, I need you to join me on the *Margaret Thatcher* this afternoon. Along with Major Merriweather."

"Why?"

"Your expertise is required." David flashed a grin. "Gen-

Mercy   171

tlemen, if you'll excuse me, I'll be in my day cabin. I've got some work to do and a few theories to test out prior to touring the *Thatcher*."

———

RUTH WASN'T one to complain about hard work. She'd barely taken leave as a CDF officer, and until Taylor entered her life, she'd scarcely done anything outside the service. Eighty-hour weeks were the norm for enlisted soldiers, as was performing backbreaking work as deck-force ratings.

None of it compared to mining helium-3. She lifted her energy drill and engaged the trigger. Instantly, a beam of highly charged particles shot out of the device and cut a line in the rock.

It would help if these space suits had powered pneumatics, like armor. Of course they didn't, because the Vogteks probably considered such technology a security risk in the hands of prisoners. Ruth swung the beam in a rough semicircle before she shut the device off and returned it to the tool cart.

The planetoid they were laboring on had roughly one-sixth the gravity of Canaan, but the Vogteks had augmented that somehow. Ruth figured it was another punishment, as mining in zero-g would be more straightforward.

"Ruth, you okay?"

She whirled around to see Hanson standing there in a space suit. Paradoxically, the mines had no atmosphere, requiring a hard suit to maintain pressure and safety. "Geez, way to scare me. I thought you were a guard coming to complain about lack of progress."

Hanson chuckled. Sweat coated his face, visible even through the glare of the suit's faceplate. "I've timed them. We have roughly fifteen minutes before the next wave of patrols. They get complacent, especially farther down the shafts. How are you holding up?"

"Well, I'm reminded of how easy I had it on the *Lion of Judah*, even pulling two duty shifts a day."

"Yeah, same. I do hands-on work, you know, but not like this. What about your mental health?"

"Major—"

"Look, drop the ranks, okay? In here, all we've got is each other and our friendships. Not our spot on the *Lion*'s roster."

Ruth softened her expression. "I suppose that's valid, but old habits are ingrained. I... Oh hell, I don't know. It hasn't set in that we're here for twenty standard Vogtek years. General Cohen will find a way to rescue us. We've got to hold on to that."

"We should also prepare for the possibility that he can't," Hanson replied. "Mentally, at least."

"Are you talking to me or yourself?"

"Both, maybe."

"All POWs have to carry on the fight and passively resist." Ruth crossed her arms. "That's exactly what I plan to do until we're released or General Cohen drops the Marines on this rock."

"You don't really think he'll go to war to free us, do you?"

Ruth stared in shock. "Why wouldn't he?"

"Because I can't see him starting a war with an alien species that resorts in hundreds of casualties—human and alien—to save three people. Given that we're at fault, it wouldn't be right."

Ruth tossed Hanson's words around mentally. "I'm really not caring about the Vogteks right now, Arthur. They're going to work us to death to prove a point. Come to think of it, this entire thing was a show. We were guilty from day one, and frankly, if the opportunity comes up, I say we

Mercy 173

escape and kill as many of them on the way out as possible."

"Um." Hanson blinked a few times and shook his head. "No. As the ranking officer, I won't allow that."

"*What?*" Ruth thundered, closing in on his personal space.

"That's *not* what the Terran Coalition or the CDF is about. We wait until General Cohen can arrange a diplomatic release or he stages a surgical strike to free us. I'd be all for escape, except we have nowhere to go if we can get free of our cell block. The best play is the long game."

"We'll see how you feel about that in a few weeks once we've dropped a dozen kilos in weight and can barely walk."

Before Hanson could reply, an angry voice called out behind them. "Human prisoners! Why are you not working at your assigned posts?"

"*Shit,*" Ruth muttered. She turned to see four Vogteks approaching in hard suits, carrying ballistic weapons.

Hanson stepped in front of her and turned his palms upward. "I apologize. We were discussing the best methods of using your particle beams to get maximum ore yield."

The lead guard stopped in front of him and crossed two of his arms. "A likely story. I would punish you harshly, except luckily for all three of you, an appeal is being heard on your case. We have instructions to transfer you back to a viewing room so you may watch it."

Ruth felt mental whiplash. "An appeal? I thought our sentence was final."

"You humans are clever." The Vogtek closed to within a few centimeters of her helmet. "Your leader believes he can use the law against us to thwart justice in a trial by combat. He will fail, then I will enjoy seeing you spend the rest of your miserable existence paying for your crimes. Now, move, before I shock you hard enough to disrupt your neural pathways."

After a harsh shove, Ruth started walking alongside Hanson. Sandwiched between guards, she pondered what David had up his sleeve. *Trial by combat? Sounds like they've found a loophole.* It was enough to keep hope alive, and more than anything, they needed it.

22

"I STILL CAN'T BELIEVE we bilked that guy so thoroughly." Calvin poured a cup of some herbal tea favored by the Zeivlots, which was the only thing he could find on the planet that had something approaching the effect of coffee. And it was pretty much disgusting.

"Hope has strange effects on people. Regardless of who they're working for," Menahem observed.

Calvin, Menahem, Susanna, and several Zeivlot commandos had the joint-operations center to themselves. They'd spent a frantic few days gathering additional intelligence, tasking ISR and satellite surveillance assets to the target area, then sorting through reams of information.

"We know where their primary base of operations is, though." Ez'el Ozkek said. He led the Zeivlot integrated-special-operations team that worked directly with the Marines. "It's strange how the tunnel systems we've built over thousands of years to save our species ended up being instruments of death."

"Perhaps it had something to do with you guys nuking

one another back to the stone age every couple thousand years," Calvin replied.

Ozkek smirked. "You don't hold back, do you, Colonel?"

Calvin shook his head. "That particular skill isn't in my wheelhouse."

"Says you and every other Marine combatant commander," Menahem interjected with a snicker.

"Regardless, it rules out airstrikes. The mountain area these particular tunnels are located in has high concentrations of nickel and iron, and the rock is nonporous."

Menahem turned to Ozkek. "It's not impervious to air assault. Drop a few bunker busters and a tactical fusion bomb into the resulting hole."

While Calvin would have no qualms doing so under normal circumstances, it was out of the question. "Too many civilians around. We're going to have to do this the hard way."

"Civilians who support the insurgents, from tacitly to openly." Menahem crossed his arms.

"And the Canaan Convention on Human and Alien Rights is clear. We cannot target civilians." Calvin snorted. *Yeah, I don't care for it, either, when the bastards are selling us out every chance they get, Master Guns.* "Private, what's the G2 on the terrorist compound?"

Susanna stood and manipulated a holoprojector that came to life with a 3-D image of the mountain. "Built from a natural cave system, the complex reaches six hundred meters down." She touched a button, and a map of passages populated the image.

"That looks like a freaking city."

"We're not sure how much of it is intact. Keep in mind this is the best AI projection from our ISR feeds and the

Mercy 177

spare records kept by the Zeivlot military of the original construction documents."

I need to push a promotion through for this girl. She's one of the better intel analysts I've seen. "Not bad, Private. Infil, exfil points?"

Six blinking dots appeared. Everyone's jaws dropped.

"That's my best guess, sir. With the raw amount of space down there, I'd project brigade level or higher in terms of enemy fighters."

Calvin bit off a stream of profanity before it could form on his lips. "That is a *lot* of hostiles." He turned to Ozkek. "Too many for us to handle with our limited special operations teams."

"I concur. We'll need regular territorial defense unit support."

"How many combat effectives do we have right now, including rookies?"

Ozkek stroked his chin. "Five, six hundred?"

"Only three hundred suits of power armor." Calvin leaned back. "We'll intermix suits with our units, distribute as many advanced weapons as possible, use your defense units to contain squirters, and provide support. We'll clear. They'll hold."

"This will have to go to the top. You're talking about a major operation."

"I want multiple brigades supporting. We'll have to transport them in by air in those fancy hovercraft of yours."

Ozkek nodded. "You don't have to convince me, Colonel. I've been looking to kill these bastards for a long time. One of their martyrdom operations claimed the life of my sister. Another took a nephew. They deserve to rot in damnation."

Calvin grinned. "I've got a saying... It's not my job to

judge the enemy. That's God's job. Mine is to arrange a face-to-face meeting as soon as possible."

The others laughed.

"I don't think that's quite the interpretation Jesus was going for in the Sermon on the Mount, sir," Susanna said.

"Well, I wasn't there, so who knows? Let's get to work, people. I want this base and everyone in it dead or captured ASAP. The longer we wait, the more likely word will leak we're on to them, and the rats will scurry in every direction." *Finally, we can cut the head off the snake. Then maybe I can get back to kissing babies and whatever else the general wants me to do to win hearts and minds.*

23

It had been a long time since David set foot on an Ajax-class destroyer. While the *Margaret Thatcher* was a Block-II vessel, different from his old command—the CSV *Yitzhak Rabin*—it still felt familiar. As he strode through the passageways, soldiers pressing to the sides to make way, the visuals brought back old memories. *Not so long ago. Four years.* When he first took command of the *Rabin*, it was like a dream come true. David got to run his ship his way, and he excelled in every facet of his assignments.

Then reality hit like a tsunami. In an engagement with a League of Sol battlegroup that included a Rand-class heavy cruiser, almost a quarter of the vessel's crew was killed. Out of the incident, David took command of the *Lion of Judah* and moved on from the loss. Being in a similar environment to the one on his old ship brought those feelings back to the forefront, especially with the message he'd already delivered to the *Thatcher's* commanding officer.

He exited the gravlift to deck one, marveling at how small everything was compared to the *Lion*. David pushed the nearest hatch on the left side open, revealing the conference room. Even it was tiny compared to the experimental carrier-battleship combination.

Lieutenant Colonel Savchenko stood and came to attention along with the rest of those present, including Dr. Hayworth, Merriweather, and officers David didn't recognize from the *Thatcher*'s compliment. "General on deck!"

"As you were," David said. "Colonel, care to introduce me to your personnel?"

"Of course, sir." Savchenko gestured to a shorter man to his right. "Major Kabar Masoud, my executive officer." An Egyptian flag was present under the CDF emblem on his uniform arm. "First Lieutenant Abigail Miller, my tactical action officer, and Captain Colton Ramos, chief engineering officer."

David made eye contact with each in turn. "Glad to meet you all. Let's get down to business." He dropped into the chair at the head of the table.

"I understand you intend for the *Thatcher* to engage the Vogtek force, defeat them, and rescue our people indirectly because the aliens have agreed to set them free if we win."

"That's correct, Colonel." David tilted his head toward Hayworth. "The doctor found a loophole in the myriad of laws these people have. A shame the single-combat clause was removed. I've no doubt a single Marine could've handled it."

Polite chuckles swept the room.

Miller leaned forward. Her arm had a patch of the flag of Houston, one of the American-settled worlds. "I've spent much time examining the sensor logs and deep scans we took of the Vogtek ships. They're equivalent in mass to something Border Enforcement would use back home. Fast and lightly armed, but ten of them will give us a run for our money."

Mercy 181

The observation matched David's. *What's that line on Houston? "Don't mess with Texas?"* "Agreed. I'd prefer to engage with the *Lion*, but the Vogtek made clear they understand her capabilities. And the *Thatcher* is the best ship in the fleet in terms of updated technology."

"And crew," Masoud interjected. He flashed a grin. "We have the Battle E for a reason."

David nodded as he smiled. "Indeed." Memories of the *Rabin* winning the same ribbon at the annual Valant Shield exercises flooded his mind. "As I explained to Colonel Savchenko this morning, my first CO billet was an Ajax-class, and I intend to temporarily take command of the *Thatcher* to deal with this threat."

Savchenko frowned before quickly wiping it away. "I'm confident in my team, General. They'll see you through."

"Thank you, Colonel. I'd like you to serve as temporary XO, and when this crisis has passed, everything will go back to the way it was." David again made eye contact with the other officers. "Savchenko is one of the best tin-can drivers I've seen in the CDF. This is by no means a reflection on him. I simply can't ask those under me to do something I'm unwilling to do myself. The entire crew will be given a choice to opt out of this mission, with no repercussions if they do."

Masoud leaned forward. "We're all here for the fleet, General. You can take that to the bank."

"After what I have to say next, you might not be." David had been kicking around his decision for hours, going back and forth over what to do. In the end, he knew what had to be done. "We're going to disable, not destroy, the Vogtek ships."

Hayworth blinked. "*What?*"

"None of the races seem to understand what mercy is.

Aside from *my* mistake in ordering that ore extraction, that's the primary reason we're here."

"How will not blowing them apart show mercy? Beyond the obvious," Savchenko asked. "And why does it matter to us?"

David laid his hands on the table. "Because we're here and are presented with a unique situation. As to how... under the rite we claimed, combat ends when one side either kills or defeats the other. The text is ambiguous as to what 'defeat' means. If we eliminate their ability to maneuver or fire weapons, I believe the chief arbiter will declare us the victors."

"Then what?" Masoud asked in disbelief.

"We get our people back and hope no one gets killed on either side, and perhaps these beings will see us be..." David bit his lip. "Merciful."

Hayworth crossed his arms. "You want to yet again interfere with the evolution of a nonhuman race. I told you the last time, General Cohen, it is not our place, and the consequences are far-ranging and messy."

"I want to get our people back, Doctor. And I *will* accomplish that by any means necessary. Even if I have to fly this ship by myself, with all systems on automatic."

"That won't be necessary, sir," Miller interjected. She had a barely perceptible drawl. "Can't let you go into combat without me on tactical. Besides, it's been a long time since your bridge-station rotations."

David allowed himself a grin. "Many, many years, Lieutenant."

"I want them back as much as you do, General," Hayworth said. His face turned red as he spoke. "But to try *again* to interject our values into their culture is unacceptable."

Mercy 183

"Why?" David glanced at the faces of each one of them. "We're not demanding they do something different. We're giving them an object lesson in the concept that there's another way of doing things."

Merriweather cleared her throat. "Perhaps the philosophical debate should be saved for a different day, sir... Doctor. There's a more significant matter here. How are we going to disable these Vogtek ships? Assuming we face the same ones we did at the planetoid, I'm pretty sure a few neutron-beam blasts at full strength would neutralize them. Their hull alloy is weak enough that our weapons would spear them from one end to the other."

She has a good point. CDF warships were designed to quickly win fights with overwhelming firepower. Subtle wasn't the idea behind any military vessel. "We'll need to lower the effectiveness of our weapons while increasing their ability to disable."

Miller spoke up. "That's simple for neutron beams. I can dial the power output back as low as we need. Less so for our missile armaments and mag cannons."

"All Coalition Hunter and Starbolt missiles carry the same fusion warhead. So do the mines this ship is equipped with," Hayworth interjected.

David's jaw dropped. *The doctor doesn't do weapons. Period.* "That's correct."

Hayworth licked his lips. "The fission ignitors in those fusion warheads produce electromagnetic pulses. Instead, I could alter the ignition sequence to turn them into fizzles with vast amounts of EMP generated."

Miller nodded. "We'd have to detonate practically on top of the Vogteks' hulls, thanks to space-vacuum effects... but I think that would work perfectly."

"Mag cannons already have EMP rounds for shield

disruption." David turned to Savchenko. "I'll have your magazines topped off with additional shells."

"At what point will you take the gloves off if this strategy doesn't work?"

"When the safety of the *Thatcher*'s crew is in question."

Masoud shook his head. "I intend no disrespect, General Cohen, but, sir... to pull off disabling ten hostile spaceships? That'd take a miracle. I don't see how it's fair to ask this crew to do the impossible."

"Strictly volunteer basis." David set his jaw.

"But *why*? We'd dust the floor with these guys with only our neutron beams at maximum yield."

"Because it would be morally and ethically wrong. We're in this place because of a bad call I made. I refuse to compound that error with one that sends hundreds, perhaps thousands of sentient beings to their deaths."

"You think they'd do the same if the roles were reversed?"

"No, I'm sure they wouldn't. That doesn't change that my plan is the right thing to do."

"Our lives and the well-being of this crew are more important than some aliens who will probably end up jailing half their population for jay-walking."

Savchenko started, "I think we're getting off track—"

"We're better than that." David pointed at Masoud. "I didn't honor our principles and got Hanson, Goldberg, and Al-Haddad into this mess. I'll get us out of it the *right* way. If that's not acceptable to you, *Major Masoud*, tell me now, and I'll relieve you."

Several people gulped audibly.

Savchenko leaned forward and put his hands on the table. "General, the Vogtek have particle-based energy weapons. My XO has a valid point. There's a good chance we'll take casualties."

"Which is why I intend to have force fields erected throughout the outer hull and pull all personnel within the secondary, inner hull."

"Uh, that would render us unable to repair battle damage, especially to the weapons," Ramos interjected.

"Yes, but it will also keep the crew safe as much as possible." David blew out a breath. "It is my intention to ensure no CDF personnel perish."

Merriweather glanced from person to person. "This is a very tall order."

"Yes, it is." David held up a hand. "I'm asking a lot from all of you, but it's no more than I ask of myself. We will find a way to accomplish the objective, disable the Vogtek ships, and get our people back."

"And if we fail?"

David turned back to Masoud. While he almost felt the anger radiating out of the man, it struck him as motivated by genuine concern for the *Thatcher*'s crew. *I'm taking one heck of a gamble. I know it, and so do they.* "Then we'll use the full power of our weapons and kill a great many Vogteks. But that is an outcome I hope to avoid with every fiber of my being."

Masoud remained quiet, seemingly placated.

"Doctor, I'd like you and Major Merriweather to assist in refitting the mines and missile warheads. We'll use Hunters, just to be sure."

Hayworth cleared his throat. "I'll do it, on two conditions. One... I will not enhance the destructive power of any weapon. Two, any modifications I make will have their schematics destroyed afterward." He glanced between David and Savchenko. "In case you're not aware, it is a principle of mine that I do not create lethal weapons, as I don't wish to be responsible for their unethical uses."

"You invented a reactor that powered a bunch of 'lethal weapons,' Doctor," Savchenko replied, his voice tight. "That's a mighty fine line you're walking."

"I refuse to become another Oppenheimer."

David had known Hayworth long enough to realize when he was painting a bright-red boundary. *And I respect it.* "That will be fine, Doctor. Anything else?"

The room was quiet.

"Very well. We have two days to get ready. I will return to the *Lion of Judah* and head back tomorrow morning to familiarize myself with the *Thatcher* before we begin. Dismissed."

Hayworth and Merriweather sprang up together and headed for the hatch before the *Thatcher*'s officers followed them out.

Savchenko remained behind. "Do you have a moment, sir?"

"Of course." David gestured to the nearest chair.

Sliding into it, Savchenko said, "I wish you'd run the business of trying to disable the Vogtek ships by me before making it public."

"Perhaps I should've. I'd been wrestling with it and finally came to a decision. I am immovable on this, however."

"Understood." Savchenko licked his lips. "I want your word, sir, that my crew will not be wasted on some hare-brained attempt to influence a bunch of aliens."

David stared at his eyes. "Colonel, I will never throw away the lives of *anyone* under my command. I realize this situation is highly unorthodox. But I believe it's how we have to do it. I hope I have your support."

"As a commissioned officer in the Coalition Defense

Mercy 187

Force, you may trust I will always do my duty and follow the chain of command, sir."

Not exactly a ringing endorsement of the plan there. "Excellent. In that case, I bid you good day and Godspeed." David stood and left the conference room as Savchenko came to attention.

David's nature was to second-guess major and life-altering decisions. During the walk through the destroyer back to the shuttle bay, he played what-if scenarios in his head. In the end, he remained confident he'd made the right choice. *I must trust in the soldiers in the fleet and in HaShem to see us through.* Though he had a lot of paperwork to catch up on and a briefing with Aibek, a spring came to his step because he knew what needed to be done.

———

AFTER WORKING for hours in his day cabin, explaining the plan to Aibek and working on new tactical maneuvers, David was not only physically exhausted but also mentally drained. The entire time he'd been going about the required tasks, his mind had churned. Rife with questions about what HaShem wanted him to do, David ended up at the shul after hours.

Prayers had already been concluded for the day, but David knew Rabbi Kravitz would still be hard at work. As he pushed open the hatch and put a small yarmulke on his head, light shone from the rabbi's office. *Some things never change.*

David rapped on the open door a few times before sticking his head in. "Hi, Rabbi. Got a few minutes?"

"Always." Kravitz gestured at an empty chair. Stacks of Torah commentaries and several tablet devices were strewn all over his desk, as was par for the course. "I know that look. Something troubles you, and if I had to guess, I'd say it was the situation with this new race."

"Guilty as charged." David chuckled as he slid into the nearest seat. "I feel like we've been through the wringer the last week. Though I'm sure none of that compares to what Ruth and Hanson are experiencing."

"Mining helium-3?"

"Heard about that, then?"

Kravitz nodded. "This race... They seem to have a singular focus on punishment. Perhaps justly, perhaps not. There's a rumor that Dr. Hayworth found a way around it, though. Yes?"

"He did." David grimaced. "Ship-to-ship combat of equal terms."

"Ah."

"This is going to sound nuts, but... I'm going through with it, and I aim to disable their ships rather than destroy them."

"Ships?"

"Ten of theirs versus one Ajax."

Kravitz's eyes widened. "*That* is an equal fight?"

"As you say, perhaps." David shrugged. "If we were using the overwhelming force and technological might we possess, we'd probably win handily."

"There's more to this."

Of course there is. David pondered how much of the situation was entirely of his construction. *Is it morally right to ask my people to risk their lives to make up for* my *mistake?* "The Vogteks don't seem to understand the concept of mercy. There is no such thing as context or even mitigating circumstances. You do the crime, you do the time or whatever punishment they apply. Now, I can get my head

Mercy 189

around the appeal of this. We both know that some planets, especially in neutral space back home, have lax law enforcement and even laxer laws. But that doesn't mean I want to send every petty criminal off to Lambert's Lament."

"So this is about more than getting our people back."

David licked his lips. "We seem to have positively impacted the Zeivlots and the Zavlots. What's to say we're not supposed to make one here?" *Am I just hoping that? It would be nice and tidy to put a bow on everything, as it's part of God's plan.*

"It is, of course, a possibility." Kravitz stared at him with hawklike intensity. "There must be a simpler way to execute it than fighting ten of their warships, however."

"Not and get any sort of lesson across. If I order a raid of their prison system, we'll get our people back, probably end up killing more than a few Vogteks, and end up at war. Perhaps operationally, that doesn't mean anything—it's not like they can mount an invasion of the Milky Way. But it counts for something morally."

"You'd risk lives either way."

"If we save one life, it is as if we saved the entire universe."

Kravitz narrowed his eyes. "While I respect that maxim and have repeated it to you on many occasions, be careful not to use it as camouflage."

"The helium-3 op."

"Yes. I know you well enough to know you've already realized it was wrong."

"It seemed like the best choice at the time." David shrugged. "Though the road to hell is paved with good intentions."

"Quite." Kravitz blew out a breath. "None of us is perfect,

and I probably would've made the same call with the available facts."

David turned his head. Guilt from his initial decision to mine the ore welled up. "If only I hadn't, none of this would've happened. You know, Rabbi, we judge ourselves by the intent of our actions. Which most of the time are noble. But these aliens, they—like every other species, including ours—judge by the *outcome* of an individual's actions."

"An interesting observation. But one that doesn't help you now."

"No, not really." David sighed. "I can't leave my people behind. I *won't*. Perhaps some good can still come out of this."

"It is not an easy task to go through this life living a faith such as ours." Kravitz gave David's hand a squeeze. "Trust me. I do not envy the path you must walk."

"Perhaps you could pray with me, Rabbi. HaShem's wisdom would be most welcome."

"Now, that sounds like the best thing you can do besides get some rest to cleanse your mind and soul." He bowed his head.

David joined him to pray and felt refreshed. Perhaps HaShem would bless his efforts and those of the crew. *Not because they're right but because He is merciful.*

24

THROUGHOUT DR. BENJAMIN HAYWORTH'S career, he had one guiding principle above all others: he didn't create weapons —not because he was against research into new and better ways of destroying things and killing people. His stance came from a desire not to go down in history as the man who'd invented the latest type of WMD and the realization that he couldn't control what happened to his creations once they left his lab.

And here I sit, working on a weapon. All around Hayworth, armory ratings carefully disassembled fusion mine casing. Like all Ajax-class destroyers, the *Margaret Thatcher* had a mine dispenser loaded with twenty-five of the devices. They weren't just any weapon, either. Each mine had a theoretical yield of fifty megatons of TNT. A handful of them could destroy even a heavy cruiser.

"Pass me the flow regulator," Hayworth barked at Merriweather as he cradled the fusion core, a compact sphere. The radiation-dampening alloy that coated the device made it safe to handle without a rad-suit.

"Yes, Doctor."

A few tweaks later, followed by uploading a new trigger program to the tiny computer embedded in the warhead, its yield was cut to barely a few dozen kilotons. *More of a fizzle than anything.* Yet the electromagnetic pulse generated by the unit would exceed fifty times what it had been a few minutes prior. *I suppose it's okay to make less lethal weapons.* Still, Hayworth felt unsettled about abandoning a long-held principle.

"May I have it back, please?"

Hayworth quickly complied. "How are you coming?"

"Three down. You?"

"Same." He pushed back from the work table and stretched his neck. "Once we get these done, it's on to the Hunter missiles."

Merriweather grinned. "You seem unusually energetic about a mundane task, Doctor."

"Sometimes, it feels good to be useful outside the lab." Hayworth picked up another core and ran a scanner over it.

She blinked rapidly. "You sounded like an engineer for a moment there."

Hayworth snorted. "Perish the thought, my dear."

An armory rating grabbed the finished core, cradling the thing like a newborn baby, and carted it away to a waiting mine housing.

"I've always been a man of science. You know this, Eliza. I detest war and find it to be one of the least useful things that humanity engages in." Hayworth shrugged. "But I also recognize there are times it is the only way. If a war can be avoided here with minimal loss of life, that is something I would like to see and am happy to help bring about."

"Well, I'm thankful for your help, as I'm sure General Cohen is." Merriweather flashed a smile.

Hayworth harrumphed. "He's more likely to attribute everything to God."

"That's not fair, and you know it." Her expression turned cross.

"I suppose you're right."

Merriweather slid a device into the auxiliary port on the core she was working on. "You know, there're a lot more atheists on the *Lion* than just you."

"And?"

"Why not try going to the secular humanist meeting?"

Hayworth smirked. "I don't care for any sort of church, even an atheist one."

"Now you're just being incorrigible."

"Which is different from my baseline behavior how exactly?"

Merriweather threw her head back and made a mock moaning sound.

"What's that line Cohen likes to use? Mission accomplished?" Hayworth chuckled. "We'll be done in no time."

"I hope we won't regret this."

Hayworth peered at her. "Why would we?"

"Because we're assuming the Vogteks will play by the rules they've set out in this archaic legal code of theirs."

"I trust they will. Their entire culture seems to be set up around laws and maintaining order. For them to deviate from it now would be surprising."

Merriweather sat back and wiped sweat from her brow. While the work wasn't particularly taxing physically, the ambient temperature in the aft magazine was considerably higher than on the rest of the ship. "That almost sounds like *faith*."

"If I were to place faith in anything, it would be that

bureaucrats and lawyers will eventually take over the known universe."

Several of the ratings laughed, as did Merriweather.

Hayworth finished the final core on his table. "I believe that concludes our work with the fusion mines. On to the forward missile room?" *The sooner I can get this over with, the better.*

"We're stopping by the mess first. I'm famished."

Food did sound good. *Perhaps this ship still has some actual vegetables and meat from back home.* Hayworth figured it was probably too much to ask, but one did have to live in hope.

———

DAVID SPENT a good bit of the last twenty-four hours before the trial by combat on the *Thatcher*, touring the ship, meeting the junior officers, and getting a feel for the differences between the Block-II Ajax-class and his old command. They were legion. While the *Rabin* had been crammed full of new tech, an upgraded reactor, and numerous systems designed to reduce reliance on human crew, the Block-II took that and kicked it up a notch. Reactor performance was twenty-five percent better, thanks to Saurian tech, while the weapons were stronger and more lethal. *I wonder how long before the Coalition can miniaturize the antimatter reactors enough that even a destroyer can carry one. Not that we'll have access to it four and a half million light-years away.*

The final stop on his tour was the small day cabin for the commanding officer on deck one. Walking toward it brought back so many memories of things he'd forgotten about the particular layout of the *Rabin* and small details. The ever-present emotions around the loss of so many of his crew were hard to keep suppressed. He'd made peace with it as best he knew how, but the truth was that kind of pain never completely went away. .

David pressed the buzzer.

"Come in!" Savchenko boomed from the other side.

He pushed the hatch open to find Savchenko sitting behind his desk. The knickknacks and a few shadowboxes of memorabilia from previous commands reminded David of how he kept his workspace.

Savchenko stood quickly. "Welcome, sir. What can I do for you?"

David gestured to one of the chairs. "Mind if we talk for a few?"

"Of course, sir."

"Tight crew you're running, Colonel." David dropped into the chair and flashed a smile. "I'm impressed."

"Thank you, sir. I aim for the *Thatcher* to be the best ship in the fleet."

"On the *Rabin*, I was the exact same way."

"But not the *Lion of Judah*? Or does it just default to the best in the fleet based on size and technology?" Savchenko grinned.

"Perhaps." David chuckled. "But you never forget your first command. There's something special about it. The *Rabin* was for me."

"Same here." He cleared his throat. "How can I help you, sir?"

"I wanted to make sure that your crew and you... are ready for tomorrow."

"As much as we can be."

"It seems obvious you still have doubts."

Savchenko put his hands on the desk. "Permission to speak freely, sir?"

"By all means."

"This mission is beyond risky. We should simply lay waste to the Vogteks, get our people, and leave. Maybe I'm looking at it wrong, but I couldn't care less about some alien society in a galaxy that, frankly, I hope we can get the hell out of any day now and never see again."

David snorted. "On that, we both agree. Sextans B isn't a vacation spot." His expression softened. "But we're here. And there's good that can come out of a bad situation."

Savchenko shrugged. "Don't beat yourself up, sir. You made the best decision with the information at hand. I would've done the exact same thing. The only difference was when we were facing off against the aliens, the *Thatcher* should've disabled one. I think the others would've headed for the hills."

"Perhaps. Perhaps not. Maybe you would've ended up taking out all four vessels and committing a crime, if not against our rules then certainly against our shared ethics."

"Your sense of right and wrong comes primarily from your religion, yes?" Savchenko asked.

David nodded. "That's a fair assessment. Orthodox Judaism is fairly strict as religious practice goes."

Savchenko gestured to his shoulder, where only the flag of the Terran Coalition sat. "I veer somewhere between atheist and attending church with my family once a year. I'm not a big believer in anything."

"That doesn't mean you don't have a code of conduct."

"Of course not, but I also value those wearing my uniform more."

"Our Christian friends would tell us that real character is loving those who hate us and doing good to those who do wrong against us."

Savchenko snorted. "I'm not much on that. My primary

Mercy 197

goal is to get my crew and me home alive."

"And I think there's a way to accomplish that goal, which is mine as well, while imparting something positive to the Vogteks and the other species in this system."

"Again, sir, I'd beg you... do not waste the lives of my soldiers."

David pursed his lips. "Never."

Before either man could speak further, the buzzer went off.

"Who is it?" Savchenko asked through the closed hatch.

"Colonel Amir, sir. I was told General Cohen was visiting you, and I have an update you both need to hear."

I wonder what Hassan's got up his sleeve. David turned. "Come!"

When the hatch swung open, Amir's broad-shouldered form filled the opening. He strode in and braced to attention. "*Assalamu alaikum.*" The traditional Arabic greeting meant "Peace be upon you."

"*Wa-alaikum as-salam.* Have a seat," David said as he patted the chair next to him. "Colonel Savchenko and I were just going over the final strategy for tomorrow."

Amir waved his tablet. "I've got something to run by you, sir. Lieutenant Kelsey put together a detailed report on the scanner systems employed by the aliens. Have a look at this." He held it out.

"What am I looking for?" David took the device and stared at it.

"Note the power signature, sir."

It took a few seconds of staring to realize what Amir was getting at. The Vogteks apparently used sensors that emitted radiation. A light bulb went on in his mind. "Didn't we use radiation-tracking warheads during the Second Saurian War, specifically to knock down their ability to track us?"

"Exactly, sir." Amir bobbed his head enthusiastically. "I took the liberty of checking. We have the schematics for RT-36As in our database, and the 3-D printers on the *Lion of Judah* can produce them. It would only be a matter of moving the high-explosive warheads from active munitions to the new shells."

"Those are designed to be fired by small craft, though. Valiant bombers, right?"

Amir grinned. "I also took the liberty of checking to see how many fighters we could fit into the *Thatcher's* shuttle bay. Six Phantoms and six Valiants can barely squeeze in."

Savchenko leaned forward. "You're sure about this?"

"Absolutely."

"Color me impressed. I think our chances of success just went up quite a bit, General. Still need to run this through my people and have the master chief double-check. You know the drill. Shuttle bay is considered deck force on an Ajax."

"Well, like someone I served with used to say, 'Now we're cooking with gas.' I think I will head back to the *Lion* and prepare for tomorrow, unless you two need me."

Savchenko shook his head. "No, sir. We're good here. All the updated nonlethal weapons are ready for action, even if I'd prefer something a bit more damaging in the tubes."

Still gonna get that barb in. Okay, Colonel, I read you loud and clear. David stood. "Then I will leave you gents to sort out turning the *Thatcher* into an escort carrier."

As David walked back toward the shuttle bay to fly back to the *Lion*, he pondered at length what they were able to do. While he'd had confidence in the plan before Amir's discovery, it was suddenly overwhelming. *We're going to pull this off, get Hanson, Ruth, and Al-Haddad back, and, I hope, have a positive impact on these people. HaShem willing.*

25

It had taken more than a bit of arm twisting to convince the Zeivlot command structure of the imperative to destroy the terrorist stronghold on the ground. Most had wanted to drop a fusion bomb on it and be done, but Calvin knew from experience such tactics didn't work. *If you want to kill the roaches, sometimes you've got to go in and stomp them to death.* Eventually, it went all the way up to the zupan herself, and Vog't had signed off on the operation.

A sea of human and alien faces stared back at Calvin. The balance of his Marines and hundreds of the best special operations soldiers in the Zeivlot military stood shoulder to shoulder. Months of training, working side by side, and learning how to execute together came down to one massive mission.

The wild card was a small team from Zavlot. Their premier had sent them as a token of goodwill. Calvin figured that David would appreciate it, but it was more of a risk than anything because they hadn't trained for the operation. Still, he'd made sure they had an active role. *Maybe*

*that diplomacy talk the general is always going on about is
finally sinking in.*

Nah. I'm just getting soft in my old age.

Calvin tapped the microphone. "Is this thing on?"

A wave of laughter pealed across those assembled.

"I'm not big on speeches, but considering what we're about to do, I thought a few words from the man leading the op might be worthwhile. Some of you have served with me for years, and many have undergone the rigorous training required to be called a Terran Coalition Marine. And some have only known us for a short time yet have trained an equally long time to serve in your armed forces. I have seen uncommon bravery shown by all, and it is an honor to lift my rifle next to yours."

Applause coupled with the unusual Zeivlot clicking and chanting met his words.

"Make no mistake. We're about to walk into hell itself. We are fighting a determined enemy who has no compunction against underhanded tactics, and to a man and woman, they will resist to the death. Which is fine by me because people who kill innocents and brag about it afterward deserve two rounds in the chest and one in the head."

Calvin held up his power-armor-gauntleted hand as more chants echoed. "We're going in hard. We have air support, regular army blocking forces to ensure no terrorist gets away, and enough collective firepower to reduce the mountain these thugs cower under to atoms. But none of that matters if *we* cannot defeat the enemy. So check your weapons, mount up in your assault transports, and move out!"

As he turned to walk away amid the deafening roar of five hundred highly motivated Marines and special opera-

Mercy 201

tors looking to put the hurt on the insurgents, one last thought popped into Calvin's mind. He spoke once more into the microphone. "Some wisdom from a Marine long since gone. If I charge, follow me. If I retreat, kill me. If I die, avenge me. Now, get out there and send these bastards straight to hell, where they belong! Dismissed!" By the time he was done, Calvin's voice boomed across the area with no need for amplification.

Those before him gave a guttural roar before melting away in groups toward the waiting rows of shuttles and Zeivlot VTOL troop carriers. A wave of emotion went through Calvin, as he knew some of the people he'd just addressed wouldn't survive the day. *Could be me, for all I know. Better set things right with God on my way to the drop zone.* He climbed down from the small podium and made his way to the command shuttle.

Menahem came up alongside him, matching his pace. "Not a bad speech for a Marine officer. But if you really want to see some motivation, have me give it next time."

"Yeah, you don't even cuss, Master Guns. Are you sure you're a real Marine?"

"See if you can keep up, old timer."

"Back at you."

Menahem put his hand on Calvin's shoulder. "You're doing the right thing here, Colonel. I'm proud to be mounting up beside you, and however this turns out, it's been an honor."

Calvin pursed his lips. "Don't go getting all soft on me, Master Guns." He smiled in a way that was filled with emotion. "I count my time with you and the rest of these Marines as the best part of my life. Now, enough of that talk. We're coming back alive, and these dumb bastard terrorists can die for their cause and go to whatever their version of hell is."

"Amen, sir."

———

On the joint-operations center floor, Susanna manned her usual post, monitoring ISR overwatch and merging sensor images in real time. Unlike most operations, a lot more people were in the JOC. She recognized top Zeivlot and Zavlot civilian leaders and enough brass that it would take her all day to polish it. *That's what Master Gunnery Sergeant Menahem would say.*

On her station and the large monitors displaying real-time data across the room, a 3-D satellite feed showed the task force heading to the terrorist command center. Advancing across four separate vectors, TCMC Marine assault shuttles supported by numerous Zeivlot rotary aircraft tracked relentlessly toward the enemy. The insurgents weren't toothless—they had antiair capabilities and used them primarily to engage the indigenous vehicles.

Blue dots disappeared as the incoming fire took its toll. But in revealing their launchers' positions, the terrorists opened them up to a withering counterattack. Loitering high above the battlefield, Marine AS-9V Hawker ground-support fighters laid waste to the launch sites. Secondary explosions reverberated through the mountainside.

Throughout it all, Susanna maintained her poise and focused on the task at hand. As the shuttle labeled One thundered through the sky, she focused on it and bowed her head. *Lord, please protect Colonel Demood and all those who fight today. Please help them return home safely, and watch over all who fight to stop this evil in Your name. Amen.* As Susanna opened her eyes and returned to her duties, it dawned on her that two years ago, the concept of ever harming another life, regardless of the reason, would've been anathema.

I am no longer a pacifist. The realization prompted some shock but was a long time in coming. Susanna had slowly walked back her aversion to the use of force, primarily from exposure to Ruth and the others she worked with daily in the CDF.

On Susanna's ISR overwatch feed, a few smudges appeared around the team's primary infil point. Though they were easily dismissed as errant pixels, she zoomed in on a hunch. Dozens of irregular fighters appeared as the image became clear. They had emerged from a mountain ridge to the southwest. After she checked other feeds, it became clear the enemy was preparing to do battle.

"ISR confirmed. Three hundred–plus combatants headed out of the tunnel complex," Susanna announced.

One of the Zeivlot generals blanched. "You are?"

"Private Susanna Nussbaum, sir. Intelligence analyst."

He nodded. "Your assessment, Private?"

"Hostiles were alerted by our approach vectors and are marshaling forces in preplanned positions. There are only a few decent places to land. They know the same things we do."

"Not bad for a human with little experience on our world, Private." He flashed a smile. "Alert the teams. We continue."

"Yes, sir." Susanna cued the tactical commlink for Calvin's command channel. "Home Plate to Eagle One. Come in."

"Read you five by five," Calvin replied. His voice echoed slightly amid a burst of static.

"Tangos inbound on your position, sir. Multiple

company-strength hostile units exfiltrating from the target."

"Dammit. Are they running?"

"Negative, sir. I think they're going to give you a fight."

"Well, that's just fine. It'll save me the trouble of having to hunt them down before I put a bullet through their Godforsaken heads." She could almost see Calvin's grin through the audio link.

Susanna turned red at the description. "Sir, you're on speaker with Zeivlot leadership."

"So? If they don't like something I'm saying, they're welcome to pick up a weapon and join the party."

To her immense relief, a wave of chuckles and guffaws swept the room. *Perhaps they have a sense of humor. Or it could be that no one cares what the colonel says as long as the terrorists are destroyed.*

"We're two mikes out from touchdown, Private. Keep the intel coming, and Godspeed."

"Godspeed to you, too, sir."

The commlink went dead with a click, and Susanna narrowed her eyes. It would take every bit of her training to keep the teams updated with life-saving intelligence. She would not fail.

―――――

BULLETS RIPPED through the air along with tracer rounds that lit up the sky. They made for an eerie display through the night-vision equipment in Calvin's helmet. Hundreds of insurgent fighters rushed toward what appeared to be prebuilt defensive positions, firing at incoming CDF and Zeivlot forces.

Mercy 205

Ballistic rounds pinged off Calvin's power armor, and he and the others dropped behind cover. At least the engagement was being fought in a wooded area, and they weren't above the tree line. "Contact front!"

"Contact left!" another Marine called out.

"Contact right!"

Damn, we've got 'em right where we want them—all around us. "Heavy weapons platoon, move forward. We'll cover you."

Calvin and the forty men with him gamely returned fire. A combination of Marines and Zeivlot special forces, all wearing power armor, they cut down terrorist after terrorist.

But for each one they killed, two more took his place. To Calvin's right, a Marine went down as dozens of the low-tech insurgent rounds hit the central armor plate. A few moments later, the squad command overlay showed a loss of vital signs.

"Corpsman! We need a corpsman over here!" Calvin thundered as he swapped magazines in his battle rifle, then he sprayed another sixty rounds of death downrange.

The cover was enough for the team's medic to crawl forward and crouch next to the wounded man. A few moments later, he shook his head. "Sorry, sir. Nothing I can do."

Menahem appeared at Calvin's side, clutching a Saurian plasma rifle. "Sorry, got hung up back there, sir. You called for fire support?"

"Light the mothers up, Master Guns."

"You got it, sir."

Saurian plasma rifles were some of the most fearsome weapons employed by a nearly peer opponent of the Terran Coalition. During the Second Saurian War, they had claimed countless Marines' lives. To call them rifles was a misnomer. The design included a backpack of charged power cells and plasma fuel and an attached barrel with a heavily reinforced alloy hose. It could melt bulkheads on a ship and burn through power armor with ease.

The *Lion of Judah* had a limited number of the devices on board, and Calvin had secured ten for his assistance force. He thanked God in heaven he'd decided to convince David of their necessity for the mission.

Menahem locked the firing mechanism into place and squeezed the trigger. The night lit up as dozens of pulses of superheated plasma erupted from the end of the barrel. The first few fell among the onrushing insurgents, and once he'd properly ranged them, Menahem swept the barrel from side to side.

The plasma rifle had been strongly considered for a blanket ban under the Canaan Convention on Human and Alien Rights for a reason. Something that could melt the strongest alloy was absolutely devastating to organic tissue. Zeivlots screamed in agony as the superheated liquid splashed on them.

Calvin turned his head, as the sight revolted even him. When he turned back, where hundreds of enemy fighters had been standing before, the ground was covered in pools of rapidly cooling plasma that set fire to any scrub brush nearby. Bodies littered the area as far as he could see, some missing limbs or worse. Those still alive and able to move fled as fast as their legs would carry them, while the teams shot down anyone still carrying a weapon.

"Passing checkpoint Epsilon," Calvin said over the commlink. "How copy?"

"Good copy, Colonel," Susanna replied. "All units

Mercy

moving forward. Heavy casualties among the insurgent forces."

"Let's finish this, Master Guns."

Menahem spun the plasma rifle down. "With pleasure, sir."

26

CALVIN PUT a three-round burst into the chest of a terrorist as he popped from cover and tried to fire on the Marine fire team. Most of the other enemies had retreated into the tunnel complex, and after a hard-fought battle, the combined TCMC and Zeivlot command gained a foothold into the enemy's lair.

The infrastructure built into the side of the mountain was impressive. A massive door that seemed to be a couple of meters deep was gimbaled on hinges the size of a human, while the tunnel could easily accommodate a main battle tank or two armored personnel carriers driving abreast.

More power-armored Marines rushed into position, and the amount of firepower aimed at the defenders became overwhelming. The terrorists didn't so much break as simply die where they stood, stitched from side to side with armor-piercing bullets from the TCMC battle rifles or melted by plasma blobs.

As Calvin surveyed the battlefield, Menahem trotted up. "Our units have pushed them back on all axes of approach, sir."

Mercy 209

"How are we doing on casualties, Master Guns?"

"Roughly five percent, sir."

Calvin growled. "Five percent too damn many."

"One is too many, sir."

"Amen to that." Calvin dropped the magazine from his rifle and slapped a new one in. "Any estimate on insurgents KIA?"

"Hard to tell, but I'd project in the thousands, sir. Keep in mind, though, we probably chewed up their cannon fodder. If whoever's running this outfit has half a brain, we're about to walk into hell itself."

"Well," Calvin replied as he adjusted his grip on the battle rifle, "what's that Cohen likes to say? If you're going through hell, keep going."

"Don't think that's a Cohen original, sir. The general is always quoting some leader from history."

"Yeah, it makes him sound smart." Calvin chuckled.

He turned on a thermal-imaging system in his helmet and used the suit's interface to release a group of sensor drones. The devices were no larger than insects and zoomed into the dark tunnel. Telemetry synched up almost immediately, identifying organic heat signatures, of which each was likely hostile.

"Target-rich environment," Menahem groused.

"Let's soften 'em up with tube-launched fragmentation grenades and close in." Calvin shrugged. "Not much to do here beyond a direct assault."

"Yes, sir. Though I could give our friends over there a plasma blast. Maybe wake them up a bit." Menahem hefted the muzzle.

"I'd like to avoid the overhead coming down on us, Master Guns."

Menahem chuckled. "Figured as much, sir."

Calvin clicked his commlink over to the all-units channel. "Listen up, ladies. We've done a decent job so far, but we're a long way from being finished. Our enemy is capable and ruthless and wants nothing more than to kill us all to achieve martyrdom. So we'll send these bastards off to whatever paradise they believe in while keeping ourselves alive. Fight hard. Fight well. And I'll see you once we've cleared the complex. Godspeed!"

"We're ready, sir," Menahem said as static squawked in the background.

"Light 'em up, Master Guns."

The heavy-weapons platoon raised grenade launchers and fired. Guided by the drones targeting information with pinpoint accuracy, multiple volleys of frags dropped among the defenders. The first group blew apart, sending shrapnel flying in every direction. The small devices would've had little effect against an armored enemy or anything approaching modern technology, but the ballistic shields the Zeivlot insurgents had access to did little to stop the wave of death.

Several more volleys followed, each inflicting horrific damage. The explosives weren't strong enough to damage the multilayered tunnel, but eighty percent of the terrorists were dead or maimed when it was over. A final round of pulse grenades detonated, disorienting the remainder.

"Charge! Double quick!" Calvin screamed as he rose from the scrub brush.

Two hundred other power-armored Marines and Zeivlots were at his heels, using the full motor assist of their suits.

Tracers and hardened alloy rounds that shredded any terrorist brave enough to return fire filled the air. Most were

Mercy

211

cut down, but a few tossed their rifles aside and held their hands out, palms down.

Calvin barely avoided shooting one such insurgent who appeared in his path. Instead, he clubbed the Zeivlot with his battle rifle, knocking him unconscious. Taking stock of the area around him, he was about to turn his attention to the newly updated map of the complex when a group of fifteen Zeivlots rushing forward from thirty meters away caught his eye. *Oh shit.*

"SVESTS! Incoming SVESTS! Aim for the head!"

Time seemed to slow as Marines engaged their high-resolution optics and aimed for the front of the hostile's neck to sever the brain stem from the rest of the body. Putting a standard CDF round through that junction of the nervous system would make the target unable to move or trigger their charges, preventing disaster.

Several onrushing hostiles fell as accurate fire from the Marines found them. The rest continued to charge as they screamed their battle cry. It reverberated off the smooth surface of the tunnel, making for the eeriest effect.

Calvin shouldered his rifle and put one would-be suicide bomber down before he realized the next one up was close enough to trigger his SVEST. As Calvin shifted his aim, the Zeivlot squeezed the detonator.

A thunderclap pealed through the tunnel, and a split second later, Calvin and several other Marines were slammed to the ground as the pressure wave hit them. Oodles of shrapnel pieces and ball bearings rained down on them.

It felt like somebody had repeatedly taken a sledge-hammer to Calvin's chest, bruising every rib. From the pain, he expected to cough up blood, but he didn't. *Damn. That packed a punch.* Pushing himself off the ground, Calvin saw that nothing moved beyond them, and it didn't seem like all of the explosive vests had gone off because of the number of intact Zeivlot bodies with blood pooling around them.

Moments later, Menahem knelt beside him. "Sir, you still with us?"

"It'll take more than a few pissant terrorists who want paradise to get rid of me, Master Guns." Calvin tried to laugh, but sharp pains shot through him. "Uh, yeah, maybe help me up here."

Menahem reached down with his servo-assisted armored gauntlet and hefted Calvin back to his feet. "No problem, sir. You're far too stubborn to kill with just one SVEST. We're lucky, though. I was sure they'd bring the overhead down."

Calvin glanced up to see scorch marks but no cracks. "Maybe there really is a God."

"Something like that, sir." Menahem gestured upward. "Scans indicate this structure is more than two thousand years old. Incredible that it's held up so well."

"I guess they don't build things like they used to, eh?" Calvin shook his head. "Just another example of how long these guys have been trying to wipe one another out, Master Guns. Take a head count. We're moving out."

"Yes, sir."

Time to finish this.

———

TEV'FIK UN'GOR HAD FOUGHT against the heretics of the Zeivlot government since he could hold a weapon, as had his father and grandfather before him. They'd longed for the day when judgment would sweep their land, and finally, the purifying fire of the Maker would engulf the evildoers.

He felt that once the interloping aliens had departed, the time was at hand.

And so it was, for a short time. But Un'gor realized that had been the calm before the reckoning. He couldn't figure out why the Maker hadn't aided them in their fight with the humans, but no matter what happened, *he* would die a martyr. Strapping on a vest loaded with enough explosives to bring down one of the passageways of the fallout shelters, he prayed that the Maker would lend His hand to smiting the enemy.

Others will take up the cause, until the blasphemers are destroyed.

He picked up his rifle and chambered a round. The end would soon be at hand. At the core of the final level of the redoubt, death awaited the humans. Un'gor would gladly deliver it.

———

THE ZEIVLOT TERRORISTS seemed to be determined to die, taking out as many Marines and commandos as possible. Every inch of ground was contested and paid for in blood. The farther they went into the complex, the narrower the passageways became. An ambush seemed to be around every corner, and Calvin lost more Marines than he'd expected.

They were down almost fifty power-armor suits by the time the strike force hit level eighteen, which was the last one, according to their schematics and sensor readings. Knowing that the remaining defenders would likely be heavily entrenched around the single elevator that serviced the floor, Calvin split his best Marines into two groups that crawled down maintenance shafts at either end of the complex.

As quietly as men in fifty-kilo armored suits could move, they crept out of the access hatch and spread out in a hallway. Calvin tried to take point, but Menahem held him back. "Colonel, we don't need you getting killed down here."

"Like we need any of us, Master Guns?"

Menahem shook his head. "I'll handle point. You back us up."

"Fine," Calvin replied as he checked his battle rifle. He knew his senior enlisted leader well enough to realize when he should listen to him. Taking the two o'clock position, Calvin patted Menahem on the shoulder. "Ready."

"Move out," Menahem said over the commlink.

The formation steadily pressed forward, and for twenty meters, they faced no resistance or saw another soul. Then two Zeivlots in ill-fitting fatigues rounded a corner. Their eyes bugged, and both raised ballistic rifles.

Calvin squeezed the trigger of his weapon and put a three-round burst into one of the Zeivlots. The man collapsed to the floor as blood flowed freely from his chest. Not to be outdone, Menahem fired nearly simultaneously and dropped the other terrorist.

Neither had silenced weapons, and the loud reports echoed down the passageway.

"Shit." Calvin blew out a breath as the sound of running feet came next. He cued his commlink. "Contact, corridor seven, subsection... Hell, I don't know. We're about to get it down here. Suggest we breach the gravlift and move forward."

"Acknowledged, Colonel," one of the Zeivlot commando team leaders replied.

A dozen enemy fighters burst onto the scene from an

intersection and poured fire into the Marines. Their fusillade was more accurate than most from the poorly trained terrorists and would've seriously harmed non-power-armored forces. Menahem took the brunt of it then switched his battle rifle to full auto and squeezed the trigger. Sixty rounds of standard-issue TCMC full-metal-jacket rounds blew down the hallway and into their foes.

Taking cover inside open doorways leading to empty rooms, the Marines stood their ground. Calvin picked off several hostiles, even while more showed up every minute. *They're making a last stand here.* He plucked a grenade from his belt. "Pulse, over!"

The small ball skidded to a halt at the feet of several insurgents before exploding in a bright flash.

The Marines leaned out of the doorways they'd taken cover in and peppered the enemy formation with rounds from their battle rifles. Calvin figured it was only a matter of time until the Zeivlots either gave up and ran or died.

A bullet slammed into the back of Calvin's armor, causing him to whirl around to see a small army of the poorly armed Zeivlots in their loose-fitting clothing or a combination of rough fatigues and tribal garments. *Oh damn. Where'd these idiots come from?* "Contact, rear!"

Several Marines turned and fired on the new set of enemies while being caught in a hellish crossfire of bullets. Terran Coalition power armor was impressive technology, but even against inferior weapons, it had limits. Dozens of rounds hitting the same plates weakened the alloy and caused ruptures between the armor joints.

"Demood to any friendly stations. We're getting our asses handed to us down here!" Calvin screamed as he slapped a new mag into his rifle. "Need immediate fire support!"

"We're pinned down at the level-eighteen lift exit, Colonel. Trying to push through."

"Try harder, or there won't be anyone to push to!"

On the life-signs monitor in Calvin's HUD, which showed his entire squad, several went critical as they took serious wounds from shrapnel and bullets. He felt for a grenade on his belt and came up empty. *Damn.* "Corpsman!" Calvin bellowed into the commlink before he fired a long burst down the passageway and crossed it, enduring several rounds into his armor. Kneeling beside a fallen young Marine, he interfaced with his suit. "Hang in there, son. Help's on the way."

Out of the corner of Calvin's eye, he saw Menahem heft the Saurian plasma weapon's muzzle and almost shouted at him to save the thing before he killed them all. *Nah. We're dead anyway. I'd rather go down on my feet.*

Menahem squeezed the integrated trigger and sent several globs of superheated plasma down the passageway. One hit a terrorist in the chest, went straight through, and cauterized the wound.

The man collapsed with a bloodcurdling scream as others fell from similar wounds. It took a few seconds for the reality of the situation to set in with the rest of the Zeivlot insurgents. The first one to run was shot in the back by another fighter, which steadied them all, until more plasma bolts fell, burning their compatriots and setting fire to the rubberized floor tiles. The main force turned and ran while the group that had caught the Marines from behind continued to fire.

We've got an opening. Calvin toggled his battle rifle to full auto. "Let the mothers have it, men!"

Seven weapons spoke as one, and hundreds of rounds slammed into the Zeivlots. Most of them were in the open,

Mercy 217

and the Coalition bullets cut them down like a scythe going through tall grass. As the Marines paused to reload, the rest of the terrorists fled, throwing their weapons down.

The guttural roar of another man attracted Calvin's attention. As he turned around, a Zeivlot came into focus. He rushed as fast as he could toward the Marines, screaming. Calvin dropped his battle rifle and drew his sidearm in a single fluid motion. He squeezed the trigger and put three rounds into the Zeivlot's center mass.

As the terrorist lay dying, he yelled and tried to press a trigger in his hand.

Calvin realized too late that the remaining hostile had a suicide vest on. *Well, shit.* Though he adjusted his aim toward the Zeivlot's head and squeezed the trigger, the insurgent's finger succeeded in activating the trigger. At the short distance, and with the beating their armor had already taken, Calvin figured there wasn't too much chance of survival.

A second passed, followed by another and another. It seemed like the squad collectively let out a breath into their commlink mics as Menahem knelt next to the unmoving Zeivlot. After a moment, he laughed softly, then it became uproarious.

"What the *hell* is so funny, Master Guns?"

Menahem gingerly disconnected the trigger from the device and held it up. A dark burn mark showed on the end of it. "Thing shorted out. Probably from all the sweat this guy was generating. To continue our conversation from earlier, sir, this ranks up there as proof God exists. Maybe you should quit asking about that."

Calvin snorted. "Yeah. Something like that, Master Guns." He let out a chuckle, surprised that after so many near-death experiences, another one had passed. "Now, it's time to help our partner forces and finish these bastards off."

"Amen to that," a Marine in the back called out as the fire-suppressing sprinkler system came to life, showering them all.

"Stop yakking," Calvin replied as he slapped a new magazine into his rifle. "And let's roll."

27

ANOTHER NIGHT WITHOUT SLEEP. David stared into the void, sipping a cup of decaf coffee, as it was the only thing he could find. The chronometer mounted in the officers' mess read twenty-three hundred hours, and almost everyone was either asleep or on the third watch. He wondered what the next day would bring. *One thing is for sure—either there will be a minor miracle, or this will go down as the dumbest thing I've ever done.*

Between sips, David admired the beauty of space. Both stars of the Jinvaas Confederation were visible, one a dim white dwarf, the other an orange main-sequence star. He found it surprising that four separate forms of intelligent life existed within the confines of the solar system. *Such is HaShem's handiwork.*

A rustling behind David's back caused him to turn.

Bo'hai stood there in a pink dress. "Am I disturbing you?"

He shook his head. "No. Just preparing for tomorrow."

"What's coming bothers you?"

"Is it that obvious?" David forced a grin.

"From your facial expression and body language, yes." Bo'hai sat in the next chair and glanced into the void. "I like to come here when it's quiet and see the wonders of the universe. But tonight, I was hoping to run into you."

David raised an eyebrow. "Oh?"

"There is talk everywhere that you will personally lead the fight tomorrow. You must have a great deal on your mind."

He stared into Bo'hai's eyes. *Something makes her easy to talk to.* It almost reminded him of Sheila. "Ah, yes, the *Lion*'s RUMINT engine is running at full speed."

She tilted her head. "RUMINT? I don't believe I've heard this word."

"It's an acronym for rumor intelligence, which is a play on our two main types of intelligence-gathering techniques... SIGINT and HUMINT. The use of electronic signals intercepts and human assets."

Bo'hai giggled. "I had never heard so many acronyms and made-up words until I came aboard your ship."

"Humans, especially those of us in the government or the military, are *especially* good at creating acronyms." David took another sip of the decaf coffee. "It was simple to fight the League of Sol. They invaded us and were clearly an evil force bent on interstellar domination, and there were no moral qualms about it."

"But this is different?"

"Yes. Because I'm going into battle to fix something *I* did wrong. And I sorely wish there were another way."

Bo'hai was silent for a few moments. She put her hands on her lap. "The Maker sees our hearts and knows our intention. He is faithful and just and will forgive us if we only ask."

"Blot out my transgressions, wash me thoroughly from

Mercy   221

my iniquity, and cleanse me from my sin." In response to her questioning expression, he continued, "It's a passage from the Psalms. One of the holy books of Judaism."

"Ah. I see. And how will you deal with this guilt you feel?"

Her observations are so astute. "Are you *sure* you're not a psychologist?"

"Quite."

Nothing wrong with explaining it to her. "As an Orthodox Jew, I look to the Torah and the Mitzvot to define how I live my life. I also ask God to guide me and protect all those involved."

"May I ask you a question?"

"Of course."

"I have been studying human religion and culture. Specifically, I looked up information on Judaism because I was fascinated by what you believe and how it aligns with our beliefs. One of my observations is you do not seem to resemble the images I saw of other... Is it, ah, Orthodox Judaism?"

"Well, I'm not a Haredi. That's a type of ultra-orthodox Jew. But depending on what you looked up in the library computer, you probably saw images of men in black frock coats and hats and wearing long beards and curled side-locks, yes?"

She nodded.

"To serve in the Coalition Defense Force, I must maintain basic grooming standards. No beards or curled side-locks. The idea in the military is that we are all the same. We look the same. The uniforms are exactly the same. It reinforces the idea that the CDF has one mission and one fight, and each individual soldier is interchangeable with the next man or woman."

"So where does that leave your religious beliefs?"

David shrugged. "Some might say I'm a bad Jew." He cracked a grin. "There's an old joke among my people. The only thing two Jews can agree on is what a third should give to charity."

Bo'hai chuckled politely. "We have similar debates." Her smile was replaced by a frown. "Sadly, they don't seem to end the same way on Zeivlot."

"It took humanity a long time to quit fighting one another over slight differences. An excessively long time." He sat his coffee mug, which was emblazoned with the CDF logo, down. "Would you believe that I wanted to be a rabbi at one point?"

She tilted her head. "Is that a religious leader?"

"Yes. It translates to *teacher* in English."

"Why didn't you?"

"Because there was a civilization-defining war between my people and the League of Sol. My father was killed in its opening battle, and by the time I came of age, all citizens were required to serve in the military for four years. When I reported for basic training, I'd already decided to complete my duty and go study the Torah afterward."

Bo'hai stared at him with rapt attention. "Something changed, though?"

"I..." David licked his lips. "I learned that I was *good* at being a soldier. In time, I accepted as my calling that I'm to protect others."

"To me, that seems noble."

"Most in our society would agree. But something even those of us who've served, which is most of the Coalition at this point, don't fully understand is how killing someone affects you." David glanced at his hands. "And I have killed many people. I make peace with it by telling myself it's a war

Mercy 223

and that even the Torah specifically disallows punishment for combat deaths. What I'm trying to say is that the tens of thousands of Leaguers I've seen off... from a moral perspective, I did no wrong."

She put her hand on top of his. "Yet it still affects you deeply."

David felt as if a bolt of lightning had shot through his body at her touch. His instinct was to yank his arm back, but he didn't. "Yes. When I look down at my hands, all I see is blood. Before we arrived here, after the war was over..." He bit his lip. "It seemed as if perhaps, *finally*, there would be no more killing."

"Don't all the lives you've saved balance it out? My planet would be burned to a crisp if it weren't for your actions." Bo'hai gestured toward the window. "The same goes for Zavlot. Perhaps the species in this system will learn something from how you and your fellow humans conduct yourselves."

"I appreciate your optimism. Sometimes I share it. But generally not on the eve of battle."

"You underestimate how much you alter those around you. Those who serve under you revere you as an almost-divine entity capable of winning any battle."

If she only knew. "Whatever I am, it's not that. I can and do make plenty of mistakes. Like this one." David sighed. "Tomorrow, I must be perfect in every aspect. The *Thatcher*'s crew has to be perfect too. Zero errors."

"Will worrying get you any closer to that goal?"

David shook his head. "No."

"But it will keep you up all night, deny rest, and cloud your judgment."

"I'm starting to think you're lying about not being a psychologist."

"Perhaps I am just attuned to emotional cues." Bo'hai took her hand off his and adjusted her hair.

David still found it odd that purple was a natural hair color for the Zeivlots. Also strange was how it used to be a streak but had turned solid over the last month. *But why not? If there are six-limbed reptilians that ritually eat other species back in the Sagittarius Arm, a race with purple hair pales in comparison.* "A mother, perhaps?"

"Not yet." Bo'hai grimaced slightly. "It is something I desire very much. To be a mother and raise many children."

"Be fruitful and multiply in the land the Lord your God has given you," David replied with a grin. "It's something of a maxim with Jews. If I may ask, why haven't you?"

She shrugged. "I haven't met the right mate yet. Much like you, we mate for life."

"Whoever told you humans mate for life?"

"I thought I read that in your religious texts."

David chuckled. "Oh, it's an ideal some... perhaps many... of us aspire to. But in practice, there are lots of ways a marriage can fall apart."

"Have you been married?"

"No. Not yet." David pursed his lips. "I haven't met the right woman yet. Or I should say that I haven't met a woman willing to put up with me."

Bo'hai tilted her head. "Put up with you?"

"Being married to a soldier isn't easy. We're gone for long periods, and leave can be maddeningly short. It's hard all across the board. Especially in wartime, with a career officer who asks for combat assignments."

"Was your cause not noble? From what I've read, you fought a war for survival against an enemy that would erase everything your people collectively believed."

Memories of the last time he'd seen Angie and their

Mercy 225

breakup flooded into David's mind. Even though he'd mostly put it behind him, it still hurt. When he was four and a half million light-years from home, though, it was simple to set such things aside. "Sometimes, that's not enough. I had an opportunity to retire from the CDF after the end of the war. Instead, I chose to keep going."

"Why?" Bo'hai's eyes were filled with warmth.

"Because... Because it's what I do. Being a soldier is what I'm good at, and why God gave me these skills, I'll never know. But He did. So I stayed in to help win the peace." Emotion crept up in David as he struggled to keep it at bay. "Someone I respect a great deal once told me that a life given in service of your country was a life well spent."

"I agree. And if you'd not remained in your military, my people would likely be gone."

"Going to keep going back to that, aren't you?"

Bo'hai giggled in a way that made her seem younger than she was. "Well, it's a rather important point to me."

David inclined his head with a smile. "I suppose that does make sense. Now, I'd better get some rack time. Oh dark thirty comes early."

"I understand. You should try not to worry about tomorrow. What will happen will happen. Do your best, and give the rest to the Maker."

"We have a similar saying." David stood. "And Rabbi Kravitz has preached on that very topic in the shul. Recently too."

"Then why not follow it?"

"Because I'm stubborn." David forced a wry grin.

Bo'hai touched his arm again. "Then I will pray for you."

"Thank you." As he turned to go, David paused. "I appreciate the company." Before he could say, "Ms. Bo'hai," he caught himself. "Salena."

"And I yours. May you rest well."

"Amen to that."

Even though he was exhausted, David parsed the conversation during the walk back to his stateroom. It had felt good to talk to someone, and Bo'hai seemed to naturally fill that role. Since she wasn't in his chain of command or a uniformed member of the CDF, he could let his guard down slightly. *Then there was that touching bit.* As the gravlift whisked David to the deck his stateroom was on, he wondered if there was something more at work. *Maybe she likes me.* That made him smile.

The grin quickly disappeared. *I don't have time for any romantic feelings until the Lion makes it home. Then... maybe. But Bo'hai won't want to go to our galaxy and leave her world behind. Nor would I ask her to.*

With his mind made up to focus solely on the task at hand, David pushed the hatch open for his cabin and got ready for bed.

28

In the lead-up to every battle was a moment when a switch was flipped in David's brain. Before it, questions about the mission, his tactics, and what they were doing were at the forefront. Afterward, nothing remained except the calm, calculated logic of how to fight.

He'd awakened at oh four thirty hours, completed his morning rituals, attended prayers in the shul, and finally executed a temporary change of command aboard the *Thatcher*.

David sat in the CO's chair on the bridge, which was about the same size as the *Rabin*'s command center, though it had several notable technology improvements. The biggest was a revamp of the seating arrangements to have the XO's chair next to the CO's on a raised platform in the center of the room. He glanced at Savchenko. "How's it going, Colonel?"

"Peachy." He flashed a grin. "Precombat butterflies."

"I get them too," David replied quietly. "Thirty minutes to engagement." Knowing the precise time when combat was to begin was different too. *How many times did the* Rabin *get only a moment's notice? Too many to count. Such is the nature of war.*

"Should probably go to condition one. Give everyone time to settle."

David nodded. "Agreed." He cleared his throat and toggled the intercom built into his chair to 1MC. "Attention, all hands. This is General Cohen. General quarters. General quarters. All hands man your battle stations. Set condition one throughout the ship. This is not a drill. I say again, this is not a drill."

The bridge lights dimmed and turned blue, while the alert klaxon shrilled a few times. It would sound throughout the ship for five minutes.

"Conn, TAO. Condition one set throughout the ship, sir," Miller reported.

"Raise shields. Charge the energy weapons capacitor."

"Aye, aye, sir."

David cast a glance over his shoulder at Taylor, who was manning the communication system. Fury exuded from every pore in the lieutenant's body. *Yet another sign there will be real consequences from these events.* But David's mind had no room for such rumination. It would be dealt with after the battle.

He decided it was time to say something to the crew and keyed the intercom once more for 1MC. "Attention, all hands. This is General Cohen again. As we prepare for battle, I want to thank everyone who volunteered for this assignment. It is an honor to serve with you and to lead you. I realize that combat with the aim of destroying no enemy vessels is unusual. But I also believe it is the right thing for us to do. I wish us all good luck and Godspeed. Cohen out."

Time counted down, and David wondered how good a sensor system the Vogtek vessels had. *Will they figure out what we're up to, or will it be a surprise?* Five minutes before H hour, he whispered a short Hebrew prayer. "Adonai, if it is Your will, please spare the lives of my crew and those on the vessels we will fight. Give me the wisdom to do what is right in Your eyes. Amen."

"I didn't catch that," Savchenko interjected. "Hebrew, right?"

David nodded. "I pray before every combat."

"For victory?"

"No." David shook his head. "Never. I only ask HaShem to save my crew's lives. Today, I petitioned Him to spare the Vogteks too."

"Conn, Communications. Incoming message from the Vogtek fleet. Text only. Reads... The hour of judgment is at hand. Commence the examination."

Before David could reply, Miller interrupted. "Conn, TAO. Subspace wake bearing three-five-five, negative declination eight degrees." She paused. "New contacts on the same bearing, ten Vogtek patrol vessels."

"Designate them as Master One through Ten."

"Aye, aye, sir."

One of the enhanced features of the Block-II Ajax class was a better realized tactical display. Turning to his left, David observed the enemy's formation on the holotank. The ten ships roughly bunched around one another. *I doubt they have much in the way of training for a fleet fight.* He still wished he had more information about how the Vogteks fought. The words of Sun Tzu roared into his mind. *"If you know the enemy and know yourself, you need not fear the result of a hundred battles." Of course, since I don't know my enemy that well, I'll suffer a defeat for every victory. I don't like fifty-fifty odds.*

"They're on a direct intercept course," Savchenko said.

Jolted out of his thoughts, David turned toward him. "I noticed that too. They've got guts. I'll give them that. Navigation, come to heading zero-three-five, positive declination five degrees. All ahead flank."

Savchenko narrowed his eyes. "Going to cut their T?"

David nodded. "If they give us the opportunity, why not take it?" He flashed a grin. The maneuver would allow the *Thatcher* to bring her entire weapons complement to bear while limiting return fire to whatever the Vogteks had on their forward arc. *Ten ships' worth of it, anyway.*

"Agreed."

"TAO, firing point procedures..." David double-checked the plot. "Master Seven, neutron beams, fore, and aft magnetic cannons."

"Firing solution set, sir."

"Confirm neutron-beams power at ten percent and EMP rounds in all magnetic cannons."

"Confirmed, sir."

Staring at the plot, David waited until both weapons systems were in range. "Match bearings, shoot, neutron beams and magnetic cannons."

Blue spears of energy raced away from the *Thatcher* at the speed of light and lit up the shields of the Vogtek patrol ship. Orange energy discharges raked over the vessel's hull as the deflectors did their job of dispersing the directed energy beams—momentarily anyway. The destroyer's three mag-cannon turrets loosed two-hundred-fifty-millimeter shells at extreme speeds, the tactical computer and Miller expertly placing them in the enemy's path. All six EMP warheads struck home, causing complete shield failure before several exploded across the hull.

"Conn, TAO. Master Seven slowing. She's falling behind the formation, sir. Reading fusion core shutdown."

Mercy 231

Savchenko glanced up from his chair-mounted display. "One of those EMPs fried its primary power relay. That thing isn't going anywhere."

"Well, that was simpler than I—"

The bridge rocked beneath him. Through the windows, the shields lit up in a pale blue as half a dozen orange energy discharges battered the ship. Going back to the tactical plot, David dialed up a deep-scan image. It showed six emitters on the forward arc of each Vogtek vessel. *That's a good bit of firepower.* "TAO, what are they shooting at us?"

"Thermal-charged particle beams, sir. Decently powerful too." Miller rocked in her harness after another bombardment. "Seems to have a lower range than ours. Forward and port shields down thirty percent cohesion."

David glanced at Savchenko. "Push the reactor to one hundred ten percent standard output. Redirect all additional power to the engines. Nav, angle us away from the hostiles. We'll gain distance and reengage."

"Engineering advises not to exceed reactor safety tolerance, sir," Savchenko replied quietly.

"Acknowledged. Now, instruct Captain Ramos to do so."

"Aye, aye, sir."

I pray to God the overengineering of the original Ajax reactor made into Block II. David cued up the Grim Reapers squadron channel on his chair's intercom. "Cohen to Amir."

"Amir here. I read you loud and clear, sir," he replied. A burst of static followed.

"Launch all craft, and engage the enemy."

"Aye, aye, sir."

David turned to Savchenko. "Open the shuttle bay doors." *HaShem, watch over them. This must be the craziest thing I've ever tried.*

LIEUTENANT COLONEL HASSAN AMIR loved pawing the vacuum. He also enjoyed hotdogging his Phantom space-superiority fighter and causing mayhem on the battlefield. However, trying to launch thirteen combat spacecraft from the shuttle bay of an Ajax-class destroyer had to be the nuttiest thing he'd ever tried. *If I'm being honest with myself, at least.* He double-checked the preflight checklist's final steps before adjusting his helmet one last time. "Reaper One to flight bay. We are ready to depart."

Someone with an unfamiliar voice responded, "Understood, Reaper One. Shuttle bay doors opening momentarily."

"Getting out of this hangar without killing ourselves will be the feat of the century," Major Kamari Nguyen said over the commlink. She commanded the Blacksnakes squadron and had the highest kill count for capital ships of any pilot on the *Lion*.

Amir still felt uneasy about the abbreviated resupply and maintenance team aboard the *Thatcher*. *Back on the* Lion, *we'd have six times the number of personnel from every aviation rating department.* He reminded himself that all they'd done was fly from one vessel to the other, and only once aboard the *Thatcher* had the crew chiefs removed safety features from their weapons and made the fighters combat ready.

Ahead of him, the space doors opened. They'd looked large and imposing when taken in from outside his craft but suddenly appeared small. *It must be an optical illusion.*

"Reaper One, this is flight. You're clear to depart."

"Acknowledged." Amir tightened his grip on his flight stick while punching his throttle to half power. The

Mercy 233

Phantom shot forward into the void. "All craft, follow me out on the prearranged launch sequence."

After what seemed like only a few seconds, orange energy discharges streaked by Amir's cockpit canopy. He rolled away and accelerated to max thrust while tracking their origin back to one of the Vogtek ships. *Didn't take them long to engage us.* "Reaper One to all craft. Watch for incoming point defense. Break into elements, and maneuver aggressively."

"Ah, they wouldn't make it easy on us, now, would they," Nguyen replied.

"Reaper One, this is *Thatcher* actual. Come in. Over."

Amir would recognize the voice of David Cohen anywhere, even on a half-garbled commlink in the middle of a warzone. "Go ahead, sir."

"I'm designating Master One, Six, and Five as your primary targets. Disable them while we deal with the others."

"Yes, sir."

"Good hunting, and Godspeed, Colonel."

"*Inshallah.*" Amir clicked his commlink back to the command frequency. "Reaper One to all craft. Form up on my wing, and prepare to engage." A chorus of affirmative replies echoed as he aimed his Phantom toward the nearest Vogtek warship. *God willing, we will defeat the enemy.*

29

David gripped the armrests of his chair as the ship bucked wildly. Everywhere they turned, a group of Vogtek vessels waited. He had to begrudgingly admit that after disabling one of them, the hostiles started behaving in a far more cohesive manner. Three trios of warships nipped at the *Thatcher*'s heels, boxing her in. As he worked over the data, another wave of orange energy beams splattered against their shields.

"Conn, TAO. Port shields at failure point."

While he could see that from the status display, Miller's report made it clear that David had to change the battle-field. "Navigation, roll one hundred eighty degrees, and present our starboard deflector arc to the enemy. TAO, firing point procedures, neutron beams, and magnetic cannons, Master... Three."

"Aye, aye, sir," Miller and the navigator chorused.

The *Thatcher*'s artificial gravity allowed for extreme vectoring with no impact on the crew, so David was free to rotate the ship as much as he wanted, though there was a

Mercy 235

slight increase in g-force as the roll occurred. "Match bearings, shoot, neutron beams and magnetic cannons."

Another series of EMP rounds and blue energy spears rocketed out of the *Thatcher* and slammed into the targeted Vogtek vessel. The critical factor was they'd learned—quickly—how to make a few mag-cannon shells miss by rapid-fire maneuvers.

"Conn, TAO. Master Three still combat capable, sir."

David searched the tactical plot, trying to find anything he could use to make a difference. *I can't play their game. I've got to play mine.*

Then he saw it. "Navigation, come to heading one-one-eight, negative declination twenty-three."

"Aye, aye, sir."

He leaned toward Savchenko. "Can we push the reactor to one hundred twenty percent?"

"Why, sir?" Savchenko's face blanched.

"Because for what I have in mind, we need to go faster, and the rough math in my head says one twenty gets us there."

"Even if we can, we'd need an entire safety standdown to inspect the torus afterward. Along with microscans of all coolant and output lines."

"Immaterial. All that matters is whether it will hold for the next five minutes."

Savchenko shrugged. "It ought to. I personally inspected the inside of the reactor chamber before it was brought online. It's just as overengineered as the previous version."

That's what I needed to know. "Here goes nothing." David tapped his integrated control panel. "Direct engineering to boost reactor to one hundred twenty percent output. Navigation, pour it all into the engines when you get that power. Bleed everything we can."

"Aye, aye, sir," the navigator replied.

"I hope to hell you know what you're doing, General," Savchenko grumbled.

The *Thatcher* suddenly burst forward with additional speed. The effect was highly noticeable, as her artificial gravity and inertia-damping systems struggled to keep up. David was pressed back into the contours of the CO's chair, and moving his hand was difficult.

"We're up to one point eight Gs, heading to two Gs, sir," the navigator called out. "Two point five."

On the tactical plot, the destroyer gained distance on the Vogtek vessels. Incoming fire slackened and became markedly less accurate before petering out.

Savchenko let out a sigh. "We should back off the reactor output now and let the shields recharge."

"Negative," David replied. "We need as much distance as possible between us and our pursuers."

"*Why?*"

"Because I've got a surprise in store for them, but we need to be out of sight of their sensors for a few seconds." David manipulated his controls once more. "TAO, firing point procedures, aft mine dispenser. Load eight EMP charges."

"Any particular discharge pattern, sir?"

"Negative. It'll be a snap shot."

Savchenko grinned as he seemed to get what David had planned. "You've got a brass set, General. Time this wrong, and we're the ones dead in the water."

"Hey, you're the one telling me how crackerjack your crew is. Now's the time for 'em to put up or shut up, as Demood would say."

"Touché." Savchenko snickered.

The *Thatcher* raced on while the Vogtek ships continued

their chase pattern. David watched the plot like a hawk, calculating the exact timing for his next maneuver.

As they entered the weak gravitational pull of the planetoid, he made his move. "Navigation, high-speed turn, come to heading zero-nine-zero, neutral declination."

"Aye, aye, sir."

As the g-forces increased with the turn, David was pressed all the more into his chair. He counted off six seconds until the planetoid masked them from the onrushing enemy. "TAO, snap shot, aft mine dispenser, eight EMP charges."

"Charges deployed. Spreading out. All away."

David blew out a breath. *This is going to be close.*

On the tactical plot, the nearest trio of Vogtek ships seemed to have taken the bait and charged pell-mell around the six-hundred-kilometer-wide planetoid—right into the path of the reworked mines. All at once, the void came alive with eight flashes of light that seemed to radiate in all directions. David held his breath, hoping they'd gotten the desired effect.

"Conn, TAO. Master Three, Six, and Nine are disabled, sir. They're drifting in space, and I'm reading their reactors have SCRAMed."

"Yes!" David pumped his fist. "XO, power the reactor down to one hundred five percent. Navigation, reduce speed, and prepare to come about. Communications, get me Colonel Amir."

"Strike while the iron is hot?" Savchenko asked.

David nodded. "Now's our chance. They're off balance, and we've got an opportunity to strike a knockout blow here."

"From your lips to God's ears, sir."

THE AMOUNT of incoming point defense fire had slackened to the point that Amir no longer had to regularly jink his Phantom, which was fine by him, as they were headed toward the farthest group of three Vogtek vessels. "Reaper One to all craft. Break into elements to engage hostiles. Two bombers per contact, as designated."

A smattering of acknowledgments came back over the commlink. The six fighters and six bombers settled into loose formations of two each, tracking the Vogtek ships separately.

Amir would've preferred to erase the vessels from the void, which would've been easy enough with Terran Coalition antiship missiles. Instead, they were going to try the untested antiradiation warheads and hope they knocked out the alien sensor arrays. *Inshallah. If God wills it, indeed.*

Orange streaks of energy converged closer and closer on Amir's fighter and those of his fellows, leading to increasingly violent maneuvers to avoid being hit. He toggled his missile selector to dual fire and lined up on one of the offending PD turrets. "Reaper One to Two. Engage my target. Maximum range launch."

"Wilco, sir."

The lock-on tone sounded, and Amir pressed the launch button. Two LT-47F Vulture LIDAR-tracking missiles roared toward the closest Vogtek vessel. His targeting reticle turned green, and he sent a barrage of neutron-cannon bolts into its deflectors. His wingman joined in the fusillade.

Behind his fighter, the two lumbering bombers got into range. Both loosed multiple EMP-generating warheads before breaking formation to gain distance and observe the kinetic results.

Mercy 239

Simultaneously, the small missiles Amir had fired along with two from his wingman slammed into the offending point defense emplacement, which continued to flash its defiance in the form of a directed energy assault on his Phantom. At least one got through the locally weakened deflectors and slammed into the turret. A brief burst of flame later, it ceased attacking.

Not a moment too soon, Amir observed. His forward shields had taken repeated hits and were close to collapse.

"Blacksnake Two, Magnum, magnum, magnum."

The antiradiation warheads tracked toward the enemy ship as the EMP-charge-tipped missiles exploded against its deflectors. While such tactics wouldn't work against CDF standard shield generators or even Leaguers, the Vogteks were sufficiently behind in technology that the EMP virtually collapsed their defensive screens.

Meanwhile, the RT-36A Hornet missiles relentlessly tracked the sensor arrays mounted amidships on Master Two. With the enemy's deflectors collapsed, they smacked into the hull at the exact point where the masts extruded from the vessel's interior. Immediately, the weapons fire emanating from the Vogtek ship slackened. Point defense became wildly inaccurate and its course erratic.

Amir grinned. "Reaper One to all craft. Master Two neutralized. We showed you how to do it. Now lather, rinse, repeat. Bombers, reengage Master Two with antiship missiles, and disable their engines with EMP charges."

"Wilco, sir," Nguyen replied.

Perhaps victory is within our grasp. Inshallah.

30

DAVID STARED at the tactical plot. As the third and final member of the Vogtek trio tumbled into the void, mostly disabled from the bombers' successful strike, the remaining three ships pressed the *Thatcher* sorely.

"Conn, TAO. Starboard shields failed, sir," Miller said. A series of energy-weapon impacts that jostled the bridge crew underscored her report.

"Evacuate all remaining personnel from the outer hull," David barked.

"We'll lose the ability to reload our VRLS."

David glanced at Savchenko. "I realize that, but I refuse to let anyone die on this ship."

Savchenko gritted his teeth. "Then take the gloves off, sir. We're getting shot to pieces by these aliens, and we're fighting with one arm tied behind our backs. Lieutenant Miller can finish this in five minutes if you'll let her turn the neutron beams up to normal combat power."

"Not yet." David was growing exasperated and ensured his voice was quiet enough not to carry. "Until the last

Mercy 241

possible second, we try to accomplish this without bloodshed. We're most of the way there."

"Yes, sir," Savchenko ground out.

"Navigation, adjusting heading sixty degrees to port."

"Aye, aye, sir."

A few moments later, the shaking stopped as the alien beams fell on the still-energized aft shielding. David blew out a breath and studied the plot. He doubted the same tricks would work again, as the aliens showed a surprising capability to adjust their tactics on the fly. "Navigation, begin a series of high-energy turns. Evasive pattern alpha six."

Savchenko raised an eyebrow. "Another trick?"

"No, hoping to shake one of them loose."

"Conn, TAO. Magnetic-cannon reload complete, sir."

"Excellent, Lieutenant. Firing point procedures, Master Nine, aft neutron beams and magnetic cannons." David leaned forward. He was targeting the nearest flanking member of the trio.

"Firing solutions set, sir."

"Match bearings, shoot, aft neutron beams and magnetic cannons."

Weapons fire crisscrossed the void as the Vogtek energy beams struck the *Thatcher's* aft shields while return fire bracketed the hostile vessel. Blue and orange spears of light were interspersed with brief explosions from the EMP shells as they hammered the enemy's deflectors.

David watched the tactical plot, happy to see their strike had done some damage. *But our deflectors are losing cohesion to the point of being dangerous.* "Communications, get me Colonel Amir again."

"Aye, aye, sir," Taylor replied.

Amir's voice crackled over the speaker in the CO's chair. "I read you, *Margaret Thatcher*."

"Nice shooting out there, old friend."

"Thank you, sir."

"I need one more miracle out of your bag of tricks. Tactical net says the bombers are almost Winchester."

"Correct. We've only got a couple of antiship missiles left."

"Think you could distract the Vogteks point defense fire for a few minutes?"

A pause followed. "Yes, sir. We can strafe them with our neutron cannons if nothing else."

"Excellent. Good hunting, and Godspeed."

"*Fi Amanillah*, sir." The Arabic phrase wished for the safety of God upon them.

You, too, Hassan.

As the commlink cut off with a click, he turned to the tactical plot. Another wave of hostile energy-weapons fire smacked the *Thatcher*'s shields, jostling the bridge crew. *They're persistent. I'll give them that.* "TAO, firing point procedures, VRLS. Master One, Nine, and Ten. Four missiles each."

"Firing solutions set, sir." Miller turned. "Sir, that's our entire complement."

"Well aware, Lieutenant. We only get one shot at this, so we'll swing for the fences."

Miller raised an eyebrow as she swiveled back to her console. "Aye, aye, sir."

"Make tubes one through twelve ready in all respects, and open outer doors."

"All tubes ready to launch, sir. Outer doors are open."

David gulped. "Communications, order Colonel Amir to begin his attack run."

Mercy

243

THE VOID WAS alive with streaks of orange energy as the Vogtek point defense emplacements gunned for Amir and his fellow pilots. Most of it missed, but the sheer volume of incoming fire had its own quality. Their objective was simple: get enough hits to attract the enemy's attention. Beyond that, the flight of six Valiants didn't have enough antiship missiles to make a real difference.

Amir rocked his Phantom from side to side, throwing off the enemy sensors, before going into a corkscrew and pulling out in time to put a burst of neutron-cannon bolts into the side of a Vogtek cruiser. "Reaper One to all craft. Put some distance between the aliens and us, then take another shot."

"Wilco."

Out of the corner of his eye, Amir saw a neutron beam from the *Thatcher* smack the closest vessel's shields, which failed at the last moment. He confirmed that the port shield quadrant for Master Ten was offline before whipping his Phantom around. "Reaper One to all craft. New orders. Target Master Ten's point defense turrets, and engage."

"Ah, got a death wish, Colonel?" Nguyen asked cheerfully.

"Not today, *inshallah*."

Amir pulled a one-hundred-eighty-degree Immelmann and pushed his inertial dampers to the limit. Coming out of the turn, he adjusted his fighter until it settled on a direct course with a point defense turret. The moment the lock-on tone sounded, Amir pressed the missile launch button. "Reaper One, fox three."

A Vulture LIDAR-tracking warhead fell away from Amir's Phantom, and its gel-fuel engine ignited. As it raced into the void, he cranked his craft away to avoid accurate return fire. Around him, other Phantoms and Valiants did the same. Multiple PD turrets on the Vogtek cruiser went down within thirty seconds, though it wasn't without cost. One of the lumbering bombers took so many hits that the pilot had to eject.

Still, Amir was pleased with the results. They'd inflicted more damage than he thought was possible. As he banked his fighter away for another pass, he hoped it would be enough.

31

"CONN, TAO. Master Ten has lost most of its point defense coverage, sir."

David gave a fierce grin as he glanced at Savchenko. *And that's the opening we needed.* "Match bearings, shoot, tubes one through twelve."

The *Thatcher* shuddered for several moments as the warheads leaped out of their launching tubes, one after the other every half a second. After the rumbling subsided, Miller turned. "All units fired electronically, sir."

"Transfer control to the AI, and continue to prosecute the targets, Lieutenant. Firing pattern at your discretion."

Miller nodded and bent back over her console.

The Hunter missiles streaked through the void, deftly avoiding Vogtek point defense fire. The smart warheads, with their shackled-AI-driven targeting and maneuvering systems, corkscrewed into the sides of all three ships, hitting their weakest deflectors and overloading them. The follow-up strikes by more Hunters along with judicious use of the *Thatcher's* still-function neutron beams left the Vogtek cruisers floating in space.

"Conn, TAO. Master One, Nine, and Ten have ceased thrust and appear to be disabled, sir."

David let his head hit the headrest. "Acknowledged. Nice shooting, Lieutenant."

"Thank you, sir."

Savchenko set his jaw. "I think I may have underestimated your tactics, General. Please accept my apologies." His voice was very low and likely didn't carry beyond the platform.

"Thank you, Colonel. But we're not out of this yet. Not until there's a formal surrender from our Vogtek friends." David blew out a breath and turned his gaze to the tactical plot. It showed ten unmoving red icons. "TAO, lower our shields to allow the generators to recharge. XO, damage report."

"Port engine pod is offline. Main power conduit and enough secondaries are out from the reactor as to prevent thrust from being generated. Most of our neutron-beam emitters are affected by the same conduit failure. Forward ventral mag-cannon turrets disabled. And half our armor plating is gone." Savchenko forced a smile. "All things considered, the other guys look worse."

"I'll second that. Casualties?"

Savchenko sobered. "Two reported so far. No fatalities."

HaShem, please watch over my crew, and if it is Your will, heal them of their injuries.

"Sir, we're also low on EMP rounds for the mag cannons. Less than ten percent stores remaining in both fore and aft magazines," Miller interjected.

"Let's get the missile tubes reloaded just in case, Lieutenant. Away all weapons-loading parties."

"Aye, aye, sir."

David turned toward Taylor. "Communications, send a

Mercy 247

wideband-frequency demand for surrender to all hostile contacts. Time for us to end this."

"With pleasure, sir," Taylor replied. He still had an edge to his voice, but it seemed like it might be starting to fade.

All that remained was waiting for the inevitable. When the Vogteks formally gave up, David and the *Lion* could ride in and retrieve their people, and that would be the end of it. *How we'll get the* Thatcher *patched up is beyond me, but once the space installations at Zeivlot and Zavlot are online, it'll be easier to perform repairs.* All in all, he was feeling quite pleased with the outcome.

———

GRETWIM STARED in shock at the smoking ruins of his cruiser's control center. Alloy panels hung from the overhead at odd angles while severed wires crackled and sparked. That the alien ship had defeated not one but *ten* of their very best procurators was inconceivable. Such a stain on his honor was unbearable.

"Are our engines still functional?" Gretwim asked a crewman manning the damage-control substation.

"Yes, Procurator. Our technician just restored power to them, but weapons are still down."

Most senior officers were incapacitated, and it fell to Gretwim to decide how justice would be served. For as long as he could remember, he'd wanted to be a procurator and enforce the law. Justice, above all else, was his credo. And the aliens had made a mockery of it. Gretwim seethed as he considered his options. It wouldn't do to allow criminals to triumph.

"Attention, all enforcers and custodians. You are directed to the nearest ejection pod. I repeat, proceed to the nearest ejection pod." Gretwim turned back to the damage-control station. "Redirect all power to the engines. I will claim justice." After all, the human ship was heavily damaged too. He felt the distance was close enough that he could destroy them, even if it meant taking his own life.

"They will grant you entry to the order of Advocates for this, Procurator."

Gretwim offered a grim smile. "As long as justice is served, *that* is enough. Now go. See that all behind the control room make it to a pod."

The young Vogtek stood and saluted with two hands. "It will be done!"

As Gretwim adjusted his controls to allow him full navigation of the cruiser, he computed an intercept vector for the human vessel. *You* will *know justice this day.*

———

DAVID WAS STILL SHOCKED they were still alive and in one piece. But all in all, the engagement had been a success. *If getting my most combat-capable destroyer shot to bits can be counted as a success.*

Savchenko continued to handle the reports rolling in to the bridge.

"Any casualties reported so far?"

Shaking his head, Savchenko replied, "A few injuries, two serious, but no fatalities, sir."

"Thank HaShem for that. Deploy damage control to the outer hull. We'll give it a few minutes then contact the chief arbiter and see about putting an end to this."

"Aye, aye, sir." Savchenko turned around. "Master Chief, away all deck-force teams. Focus efforts on the forward weapons, and reload our VRLS."

Mercy 249

Before he could reply, Miller cut in. "Conn, TAO. Aspect change, Master Two. Sir, she's regained propulsion and is headed toward us at maximum sublight."

Though David's eyes went to the tactical plot, he knew precisely what the Vogtek commander would do. The bright-red dot advancing toward them only confirmed it. "Navigation, evasive maneuvers. Communications, tell Amir to use anything he's got left on Master Two."

"What are you seeing?" Savchenko asked.

David drew a line with his finger from the hostile warship to the *Thatcher* on the tactical plot.

"My God, he's going to ram us."

"Precisely. But not if we have anything to say about it."

32

WHILE THE *THATCHER* gamely tried to dodge the incoming Vogtek vessel, the damaged thrusters and limited engine thrust allowed the enemy to steadily close the distance. David considered overriding the safety protocols, but after gambling with the reactor and getting favorable results from several difficult calls throughout the engagement, he erred on the side of caution.

The ship rocked from repeated energy blasts, and David grabbed his armrests to steady himself. "TAO, what's working on the aft quarter?"

"One neutron beam emitter and the mag-cannon turret, sir."

"Any mines left?"

Miller turned around and shook her head. "Negative, sir."

"Nav, keep them guessing." David turned to Savchenko. "Any bright ideas?"

"Double-load the aft mag cannon with high-explosive rounds, power up the neutron beams to full power, and give them a broadside. That ought to be enough to take those bastards out."

David pursed his lips. "TAO, take that working neutron beam up to half power."

"Aye, aye, sir."

"Firing point procedures, Master Two. Aft neutron beam and mag cannons."

Miller cleared her throat. "Firing solutions set, sir."

"Match bearings, shoot, all weapons."

The blue beam shot out of the *Thatcher* at the speed of light while twin EMP shells slammed into the Vogtek vessel. Its shields crackled orange while energy discharges radiated into the void. At the same time, return fire raked over the Ajax-class destroyer, slicing into her armor and exposing the inner hull to the vacuum.

Savchenko touched David's arm. "Hull breach, aft quarter, deck ten, section eight on the port side." As he spoke, the ship rocked again. "Make that sections seven and eight."

David's eyes went to the ship-status screen on his viewer, and it told a scary tale. Aft deflectors were under ten percent power and barely stopping any of the incoming fire. Worse, the back of the *Thatcher* had limited armor. As with any destroyer, her defense lay in speed, not layers of heavy alloys. *I'm going to have to make a difficult choice soon. Otherwise, the ship will be shot out from under us.*

"General, I get what you were trying to do. We outperformed even my best estimates here." Savchenko's voice barely rose over a whisper. "But you have to resort to lethal force. If you don't, my crew won't survive. That is *not* an acceptable outcome."

HaShem, forgive me. Knowing that his decisions were about to cause him to do something he knew he would regret the rest of his life was sobering. David briefly considered ordering the crew to escape pods and continuing the fight himself. But that was wishful thinking. *We're not going to win with our forward mag cannons out, our missile tubes empty, and half our neutron-beam relays wrecked.*

"TAO, increase power output on all neutron-beam emitters to maximum yield, and double-load the aft mag-cannon turret with high-explosive shells." The Saurians had a unique technology that allowed them to put two shells into a barrel and fire both simultaneously. They'd shared it once Chief Minister Obe Sherazi had signed on to the Canaan Alliance three and a half years prior.

"Thank you, sir," Savchenko said under his breath.

"Aye, aye, sir, reload commencing." Miller glanced back. "Targeting pattern, sir?"

"We'll go for their vitals. Reactor and engines."

Another barrage smacked the *Thatcher* and pitched David forward. Feedback through the power system caused a short in one of the consoles behind the CO's and XO's chairs and blew smoke from a screen and a computer unit. Damage-control teams quickly deployed fire-suppressant foam before it could get out of hand.

"That last hit took out most of our starboard engines. We're down to thirty percent thrust."

David glanced at Savchenko. "Nurse what you can, and tell engineering to reroute whatever they can to the thrusters. We'll use them for extra speed if nothing else."

"Aye, aye, sir."

"Navigation, come to heading two-seven-zero. Maintain zero-declination trajectory. TAO, firing point procedures, Master Two, all available neutron beams and aft magnetic cannons."

"Firing solutions set, sir."

Mercy   253

"We'll let them close a bit more then take them by surprise."

Savchenko nodded. "Sound strategy, sir."

———

AMIR WAS beyond impressed with the nonlethal tactics David and the *Thatcher*'s crew had employed so far. Had it been up to him, they would've eliminated the Vogtek vessels with extreme prejudice. The whole thing reminded him of working with the Little Sisters of Divine Recompense back on Monrovia.

Yet it seemed the jig was finally up. With the *Thatcher* heavily damaged, Amir watched on his taclink as her weapons powered up to full strength. *If he goes through with this, it will haunt him for a decade. But what other choices are there?*

"Reaper One to all craft. Stores check."

"Reaper Five, Winchester."

"Blacksnake Three, Winchester."

"Blacksnake Six, one Javelin. All other stores expended."

Between the ten fighters and bombers still combat capable, there was one antiradiation warhead, a few Vultures, and the one Javelin left. *They will have to be enough.* Amir configured a series of waypoints via his squadron-level tactical network before engaging the commlink. "Reaper One to all combat-capable craft. Break left to new heading two-three-eight, positive declination seventeen. Our objective is the aft quarter of Master Two."

"Sir, we're virtually out of ordnance," one of the pilots interjected.

"I'm well aware of that, Lieutenant," Amir replied. "Our combined strength should be enough to degrade the enemy's deflectors so that our single EMP warhead can get through."

"That sounds like a suicide run."

"It's a long shot but the only option remaining to us. Form up into finger-four formations."

"Reaper Six to Reaper One. Requesting permission to join the formation, sir."

Six was one of the Phantoms heavily damaged by point defense fire. Amir shook his head. "Negative, Reaper Six. Stay clear of the combat area. I'm not losing anyone today, Inshallah."

"Acknowledged, sir."

It took a few minutes, even with the Phantoms' superior speeds, to adjust their course enough to avoid sustained PD fire from the Vogtek vessel. Luckily or perhaps by design, the enemy ship didn't seem to notice them closing in. *Or maybe they don't care.* Amir didn't like that idea because an enemy with no concern for whether they died was prone to unpredictable moves. *And those tend to be deadly.*

After twisting and turning, Amir's fighter and four others slid into a firing position behind Master Two. His targeting reticle turned green, and he squeezed the integrated firing trigger in the flight stick. Blue bolts of concentrated neutron energy raced from the five craft and lit up the Vogtek vessel's shields like a Christmas tree. All at once, the enemy seemed to recognize their danger, and return fire found the flight of Phantoms.

Amir's forward shield dropped from three separate hits before he rolled away, briefly avoiding the incoming. "Break, and reacquire," he barked into the commlink, trying to follow his own orders. Two PD turrets covered the aft quarter, and he selected the one that seemed to have the most accuracy as the primary target for his flight.

Mercy

"Reaper One to all fighters. Anyone who's got a Vulture, now's the time." Amir waited until the lock-on tone buzzed. "Reaper One, fox three." The LIDAR-tracking warhead separated from his Phantom, and its gel-fuel motor engaged, blazing away in the void.

Two more missiles launched from other craft in the formation as they all tried to keep up the barrage of neutron-cannon bolts. While insignificant alone, five Phantoms' worth of energy weapons affected the less-advanced Vogtek shield technology. To his immense relief, Amir's scanner showed a hole open in the enemy's aft deflector.

One of the warheads slammed into the still-powered defensive screen and exploded, taking the next Vulture with it. But the third weaved in and out of Vogtek point defense fire and somehow threaded the needle. The resulting detonation turned the offending turret into molten alloy, silencing it forever.

Amir grinned. *Allu Ackbar.* "Blacksnake flight, you are clear to engage. Use your energy weapons to enhance the gap in their deflectors."

"Wilco, Reaper One," Nguyen replied. The enthusiasm in her voice was unmistakable.

Four Valiants swept through the void and flew behind their smaller brethren before adding their neutron cannons to the mix. The incoming fire was simply too much for the Vogtek vessel to handle, and its aft point defense was heavily degraded by the loss of half their turrets.

"I've got a clean shot. Blacksnake Six, fox four."

The Javelin raced away from the heavy bomber, accelerating. What seemed like only a few moments later, it slammed into the outer hull of the enemy cruiser and blew apart in a blinding flash of pure-white light.

Amir held his breath, hoping the EMP effect worked as

256　　　　　　　　　DANIEL GIBBS

intended. The result was quickly evident as Master Two slowed, and a haze of blue energy crackled around its engines. They went out one by one, and the Vogtek ship began to drift.

"Blacksnake Six, scratch one hostile capital ship."

Wild cheers broke out across the commlink as the pilots congratulated one another.

Amir let out a breath. *I think we dodged one today, thanks be to Allah.* On his tactical screen, the *Thatcher* gracefully moved aside and held her fire. *David doesn't have to kill anyone, which was his wish.* It felt good to help his old friend right a wrong. *We can only hope now that these aliens uphold their end of the bargain.*

———

DAVID RECALLED an old master chief he'd served with a decade ago who used to say, "It's better to be lucky than good." At that moment, he felt luckier than anything. *Perhaps that was HaShem stepping in for us.* Emotion welled up in him, and he bit his lip before blowing out a breath. "TAO, can you confirm Master Two is disabled?"

Miller turned. "Their entire engine compartment got blasted by the EMP, sir. They're not going anywhere until that reactor is restarted."

Which, if their fusion reactors work anything like ours, will take hours. If not yard time. David allowed himself a smile. "Nice work, Lieutenant." His gaze swept the room. "That goes for everyone here. I don't know if we executed this without causing casualties on the other side, but we did our best. Thank you all for a phenomenal effort."

"Conn, Communications. I've got an inbound tight-beam transmission from Master Two, sir."

Mercy

"On my monitor, Mr. Taylor."

David turned his eyes upward in time to see an image of what he assumed was the alien vessel's bridge appear. While foreign in design, it was clearly a smoking wreck. Alloy pilings had fallen from the overhead, while injured Vogteks milled about in the background, tending to one another.

"This is Adjudicator Gretwim." One of his four arms was hanging limply, and a light-pink liquid dripped from a wound on it. "You have disabled my vessel, human, along with those of all my brothers and sisters."

"There is no need for us to continue this fight, Adjudicator." David chose his words carefully. *This being was willing to kill himself and his crew to take us out. I must tread lightly.*

"It is fortunate for you that you destroyed my engines. Otherwise, I would *never* stop in my quest for justice."

David set his jaw. "Do you require assistance?"

Gretwim narrowed his eyes and moved his three working hands together. "Have you not done enough, human? It is only by a miracle of the just that we do not have fatalities. Repair vessels are on the way. In the meanwhile, I am forced to concede the battlefield to you."

"We will retire, in that case."

The feed abruptly cut out.

Savchenko snickered. "I guess they're not happy we kicked their rear ends back to Vogtek or whatever they call their planet."

"Probably not," David replied.

"Conn, Communications," Taylor interjected. "Sitrep request coming in from Colonel Aibek, sir."

For a moment, David considered a standard reply, then his lips curled into a grin. "Transmit the picture of a broom, Lieutenant."

"Clean sweep?" Savchenko asked.

"I think we've earned it."

"No argument from me, sir."

David swiveled around. "Lieutenant, get the Jinvaas ruling council on the vidlink. It's time for us to get our people home."

For the first time in what seemed like an eternity, Taylor smiled. "With pleasure, sir."

Minutes passed, and everything started to return to normal on the *Thatcher's* bridge. As the adrenaline passed, David took stock of the situation. He prayed silently, asking HaShem to spare the lives of all involved.

33

WHILE RUTH, Hanson, and Al-Haddad had known almost immediately they were to be released after the *Thatcher* vanquished the Vogtek procurator force, it seemed to take some time for that to come to fruition. She was also *quite* sure that the alien custodians took great pleasure in the invasive searches they performed during outprocessing.

None of it mattered. Ruth had endured far worse, and for all their antics, the Vogteks had nothing on League of Sol political commissars.

She blew out a breath and glanced at Hanson. "How are you holding up?"

"Oh, stiff upper lip and all that. But between you, me, and the fencepost... it's good to be getting out of here."

The antiseptic white walls of the waiting room gleamed. Ruth thought it was probably some kind of alloy-and-polymer mixture. The reflective nature of the area was off-putting and disorienting. *I'd bet it's designed for prisoners, so we'd have a difficult time planning escapes.*

"No talking!" a custodian boomed over an unseen speaker.

Ruth rolled her eyes but forced down the snarky retort that came to her lips.

Time seemed to lose its meaning as the wait dragged on. Eventually, after what felt like hours, a portal opened at the far end of the transfer area. Several Vogtek guards in different uniforms from those of the custodians came in along with David, Aibek, and a small group of Marines.

Hanson was the first one on his feet, followed by Ruth and Al-Haddad. They all came to attention.

"As you were," David said as he strode over and shook everyone's hands. "I'm sorry this took so long."

"Just glad to be getting out, sir." Ruth replied.

"The limited news we heard after the combat was no one died," Hanson interjected. "I overheard custodians... the guards... talking about it."

David pursed his lips. "I hope that's the case, Major. We took great pains to avoid casualties on either side, though several crewmen from the *Thatcher* remain in the *Lion*'s medical bay."

Ruth grinned. "Too bad I wasn't on the bridge for that one, sir. I miss the *Rabin* sometimes."

"I do too." David glanced around. "You're all free to go, and I have a shuttle waiting beyond the hatch. Who's ready?"

Al-Haddad took a step forward. "Let's get out of here, sir. And I hope we never return."

"Amen," Hanson replied.

David gestured toward the portal that lay beyond. "By all means, ladies and gentlemen."

As they made their way out, Ruth took special consideration to march, like she was back in basic training—not too fast, not too slow, with her hands clasped behind her back. *This place didn't beat me. Nor will any walls or jailers* ever *defeat*

Mercy 261

me. The moment she got through the doorway, the size of the asteroid installation came into focus.

The largest shuttle pad Ruth had ever seen lay before her with a series of giant airlocks built into the dome's ceiling. *They could send a dozen Marine transport-sized cargo craft through here.* Her eyes darted from left to right, and the enormity of the structure came into focus. *This place must house tens of thousands of prisoners, if not hundreds of thousands.* Domes, connecting tubes, and security towers stretched as far as Ruth could see. *I suppose that's one way to keep your population in line.*

Ruth took the final few steps into the shuttle, followed by Al-Haddad, with Hanson taking up the rear. She realized he was symbolically the last man off the pad. *Good on him. He's becoming more of a leader and less of an engineer.* It was a change from the uber-nerd reactor guy she'd met back on the *Rabin. We've* all *changed so much.*

"Strap in," David said as he slid into one of the seats and pulled his harness down. Once they had, he pulled up his handcomm. "We're ready back here. Let's get the heck out of here, Warrant."

"Aye, aye, sir."

The thrusters fired, boosting the craft and momentarily increasing the g-forces. Ruth realized the only thing she cared about was seeing Robert Taylor, hugging him, and being in his arms. The thought almost brought tears to her eyes, but she still had standards. One of them was to *never* show emotion publicly. *Yes, we've all changed.*

———

How much of a difference three days make. David looked a bit worse for wear, sporting a bruise on the left side of his face.

He could've had Dr. Tural use a dermal regenerator on it but wanted a reminder of the battle for the forthcoming conversation.

While the Jinvaas Confederation ruling council had indicated they wanted the *Lion of Judah* and her battlegroup to leave the system immediately, they'd agreed to speak with David one more time after repeated requests.

So David was back in the secure conference area belowdecks. The holoprojector came to life with an image of the Fradwig, Vogtek, and Otyran council members along with the chief arbiter.

Opaltis, the Otyran chairman, spoke. "General Cohen. I do not understand why it was so vital that you talk with us. Your ship won, even though it was unjust combat. We have allowed you to retrieve your crewmen. Why do you still pester us? Leave. Humans are not welcome."

David pursed his lips. "Mr. Chairman, I understand why you look at us with disdain. We... I... screwed up. But I'd like you to consider our actions afterward. We honored your laws and adhered to your system, and while we might have used a legal anachronism to free our people, did a single Vogtek die?"

"What does that have to do with it?" Opaltis snapped.

"In my holy book, it says that the Lord our God is a merciful God. He will not forsake us, destroy us, or forget the covenant he swore unto our fathers. It also says repeatedly that HaShem is gracious and merciful, slow to anger, and great in forgiveness. The Lord is good to all, and His mercies cover all His works and creations. I had the power to destroy the ten cruisers you sent against our vessel. Instead, I chose to honor the word of God and show mercy. We fought you with our weapons powered to ten percent and magnetic cannons set to EMP only. Even at great cost to

Mercy 263

our ship, which is so damaged that it won't be much use without yard time. I did what I thought was right."

"*We should be happy you didn't kill our procurators?*" the chairman thundered. "You broke the law in the first place!"

The Fradwig councilor held up a hand and spoke in the familiar computer-generated voice. "Wait. These beings could've destroyed us with ease. I have studied the sensor reports and the battle logs. Instead, they chose to risk their lives to save ours. This concept is astonishing to me."

"Because it makes no sense," Opaltis snapped. "If you break the law, you deserve punishment."

"These humans have demonstrated another way," the Fradwig replied. "We could learn from this. General, do you have writings that explain more of this concept?"

David nodded. "We do."

The Vogtek chief arbiter, who was wearing his ceremonial robes, leaned forward. "Do you mean to say that you specifically attempted to avoid any loss of life by our procurators while exposing your own people to our fire?"

"Yes," David replied. "That is precisely what we did."

"I would know more of this," the chief arbiter said as he rubbed his four hands together. "We should seek to understand these concepts."

"There is still the matter of their breaking our laws." The chairman's fur seemed to stand on end. "Don't you remember *that* minor detail?"

"Perhaps the totality of the humans' actions is worth considering," the Vogtek councilor said. "I, too, would hear more of their philosophy."

"Two to one?" Opaltis fumed.

"What is the harm of it?" the chief arbiter asked. "I have served the cause of justice my entire life. And never before have I seen someone live out ideals that put them at a disadvantage and were against their rational self-interest. Many have suggested such, but they always turn out to be fakes. These humans, clearly, are not."

Opaltis stroked his chin fur. "I don't like this. But... if the leader of our tribunals and two-thirds of the council agree, I have no choice but to follow." His eyes blazed defiance, even through the holoprojector. "Make no mistake, General Cohen. I still oppose continued contact with your species."

David spread his hands out on the table. "Perhaps in time, we can come to find common ground."

"Per the rules of the trial by combat, it is the responsibility of the loser to make good on equipment losses to the winner," the chief arbiter interjected. "I believe the human vessel sustained significant damage. Perhaps we could offer them repairs."

Well, that's a mighty excellent solution to our problem. "We would be grateful if you allowed us to use your zero-G shipyard to effect hull repairs. And I would be happy to compensate you in any reasonable manner."

"What about access to your FTL technology, which seems vastly superior to ours?" Opaltis asked with a wry grin.

"I'm afraid it's our policy not to share *that* tech, Mr. Chairman. The Terran Coalition especially frowns on giving higher-level technology to species which haven't discovered the Lawrence drive because we find that artificially accelerating a species leads to catastrophic and unforeseen problems."

Opaltis nodded. "Perhaps the first sensible thing you've said, General. We will repair the hull of your vessel without charge. That is what the law demands, and we obey the law."

David inclined his head. "Then I am in your debt. Thank you."

The Fradwig councilor spoke up. "It is my fervent wish that in time, our five species may yet become friends."

"That is my hope as well, councilor." *Might as well press my luck.* "There is the small matter of fueling our ships, however. Perhaps we could work out an agreement to trade helium-3 for some of our medical technology."

"We will consider it in due time, General, and in good faith."

Something about the interaction shifted as the conversation carried forward. David could feel it, like a dark cloud had lifted. "Thank you, Mr. Chairman."

"If there is nothing else, we have other matters of state to attend to," Opaltis replied.

"Of course. Thank you for speaking with me, and I wish you all Godspeed."

"May the Creator reveal His justice to you, General."

The holoprojector switched off, and David let out a sigh. It had gone better than he had any right to expect, and the possibility of gaining helium-3 was an added bonus. *Still, let this remind me not to allow hubris to infiltrate my thought process. There're still two members of my crew down in the medical bay.* The severe injuries suffered by the *Thatcher*'s crewmen weighed on David. He offered a prayer in Hebrew, asking God to watch over them and heal them swiftly. *And now I must attend to my duties.* He stood and got back to work.

34

THE AFTEREFFECTS of the successful raid by the TCMC and Zeivlot military on the primary terrorist compound reverberated around the planet for days, which turned into a week as civilians celebrated in the streets. It felt like a well-earned victory to Calvin, and he knew the rest of them believed the same. But there was still work to do.

Calvin sat in a classified briefing room not unlike those he'd been in on Canaan. Numerous Zeivlot military officers and government officials crowded the table while he, Susanna, and Master Gunnery Sergeant Menahem were relegated to the chairs along the wall. That suited him just fine. *Listening to talking heads blabbering on doesn't appeal to me anyway. Let General Cohen do that, since he's got stars.*

"Do we have an accurate count of how many fighters were killed?" Zupan Vog't asked from the other end of the room.

"At least four thousand, Zupan."

She nodded. "Captured?"

"Fewer than a thousand. We're still processing the

detainees. Most proclaim innocence, but with the help of our human friends, the truth will be illuminated."

Calvin's ears perked up. *I wonder what he's talking about.* "Ah, I don't follow."

War Leader Ceren turned toward him. "We made use of those intelligence feeds and used artificial intelligence to compare the stories given to us by those we captured. The AI is exceptional at finding falsehoods and connecting events to people."

A sense of having overstepped swept through Calvin, but he pushed it aside. "Glad to hear it. What happens next?"

Ceren flashed a smirk before turning back toward Vog't. "Military tribunals will begin meeting in three cycles. The most obviously guilty terrorists will be tried and executed quickly. We feel it should be swift, sure, and just. Those with blood on their hands deserve no mercy."

Calvin nodded. Beside him, Menahem did the same.

"And the others? Those whose guilt is not easily established or who do not have blood on their hands?"

"They will be shunted to the regular legal system," Ceren replied with distaste. "We will endeavor to ensure that as few as possible end up going this route."

"You will go where the truth leads you," Vog't replied. "Swift, sure, and *just.*" Her eyes went to another minister. "Best estimates for reprisal attacks?"

"Limited, Zupan. We disrupted several cells that acted rashly. Others have surely gone to ground, but we will eradicate them in time."

The demeanor of the Zeivlot government had changed. Previously, they were scared of the terrorists and their sympathizers. *Now, they know they've won.* It provided a significant change in how the civilians looked at the issue. *On some level, that realization disgusts me. You never give in to douchebags who strap bombs to their chests.*

Vog't pursed her lips. "This is an excellent day for our people. One that I believe both Zeivlot and Zavlot will remember as perhaps the beginning of the end of religious terrorism and strife on our worlds. And we have the Terran Coalition to thank once again." She motioned to her protective service detail members. "The remainder of this briefing is classified at the highest levels, ladies and gentlemen. All those lacking code word IVAR clearance or higher, please leave. Our human guests may remain, as their input will be valuable."

I wonder what she's up to now. Calvin had never quite trusted Vog't. While David had respect for her, and so did he, he would never fully trust an alien leader with her own agenda. *After all, her primary goal is to take care of Zeivlot.*

Numerous civilians and military officers exited as quickly as possible. When the door finally closed, less than fifteen people were left, including Calvin, Susannah, and Menahem.

Ceren cleared his throat. "The feed is ready, Madam Zupan.

Since there were now so many openings at the main table, Calvin stood and sat in one of the chairs. The others followed him.

"What feed?" he asked.

Vog't turned her head. "While your victory on the battlefield was impressive, Colonel Demood, your intelligence staff and my own people showed me that the true culprits behind the mass unrest on our world weren't a few thousand men willing to kill themselves for the cause. No... it is those with large amounts of currency who fund them."

Mercy

"My algorithm bore fruit?" Susanna asked.

Calvin grimaced and made a mental note to remind her that enlisted personnel didn't speak to a head of state without being addressed. *Can't blame her for being excited, though.*

"It did." Vog't gestured to a screen that had descended from the ceiling. An image appeared on it, and the lights dimmed.

At first, Calvin wasn't sure what they were watching, but as the camera panned around, it became clear the feed was coming from a drone flying over the estate of someone quite wealthy. A vast mansion with outbuildings, a garage with eight bays, and a driveway that was kilometers long came into view.

The tranquil scene didn't last long. Half a dozen hovercraft roared into view, followed by what seemed like an entire division of armored personnel carriers. They surrounded the mansion, and Zeivlot commandos poured out.

Moving in precise formations, they quickly cleared the compound's exterior, taking whatever private-security force was there by surprise. A few suit-clad guards tried to resist and were quickly cut down. The rest threw down their weapons and surrendered without a fight. The image briefly went staticky, and a few minutes later, a well-dressed man was trundled out the front door.

"That is Re'za Hikmetia. You probably don't recognize him," Vog't said as she turned back to Susanna. "But he is what we found at the end of the chain. You see, Mr. Hikmetia is one of the richest business owners on Zeivlot. He has virtually unlimited wealth. While I have no objection to the accumulation of riches, I *do* have an issue with funding massive terrorist networks."

"Does that mean we won?" Calvin affixed her with a hard stare. "No more money... no more insurgents, right?"

"Perhaps." Vog't smiled coldly. "But I believe in harsher measures. Many others, from all walks of life, have backed extremism for decades. If we learned nothing else from your General Cohen, it's that it's high time for us to purge hate from our society. This vine sprouts up and takes over everything. All we have to do is cut the roots, and it will wither and die. You cut the head off, and in the next cycle, we'll finish the job. Please understand I couldn't have human warriors execute this mission. It had to be us."

Calvin nodded. "I do. There are some things an alien power can't do without causing more problems. How many more are you going to round up?"

"Anyone for whom we have evidence of monetarily supporting the terrorists. It doesn't matter who they are. Members of our government are being arrested as we speak, including an individual who was just in this room."

Wow. That's intense. Calvin admired her attitude and approach. "Then?"

Vog't turned her palms outward. "Then we put our trust in the Maker and the idea that without hatred flooding mass media, our attitudes as a society will change in time. It won't happen overnight, but this is a solid first step."

"What else can we do to help, Zupan?"

She shook her head. "Nothing, for now. I suspect there will be some... How do you humans put it? Mop-up operations?"

"Yeah." Calvin chuckled. "We're good at those."

"Then until we meet again, I wish you peace from the Maker, Colonel."

When Vog't stood, so did everyone else.

Calvin watched her and the rest of the Zeivlots leave

Mercy 271

before turning to Menahem and Susanna. "Well, not bad for a month's work."

"General Cohen is going to kill us. Or at least bust us down a few ranks and PT you until you're back in shape."

Calvin gave him a withering stare. "I will challenge *any* CDF puke to a twenty-kilometer hike any day of the week. That includes the general."

"What about me?" Susanna asked brightly.

"You're an honorary Marine for the time being."

Menahem guffawed and shook his head. "You going to tell her, or am I?"

"Oh, I'll do it." Calvin took a small case out of his pants pocket. "We decided you've earned this." He held it out to Susanna.

She took the tiny black velvet box and snapped the top open before letting out a gasp. "But..." Tears formed in Susanna's eyes.

"Hey now, none of that emotional stuff," Calvin said with a faux drill instructor's rasp. "You've earned those stripes, Corporal. Keep it up, and you'll pin on Sergeant before we get back to Canaan. Now stand at attention."

Susanna squared her shoulders and adopted a rigid posture as Calvin expertly removed her rank insignia and attached the new one.

"At ease, Corporal."

"Thank you, sir." She relaxed to a parade rest stance.

"Now, let's head back to the base and see about properly wetting your stripes down."

"Um." Susanna blinked a few times. "Sir, I don't drink alcohol. I've never had a drop."

Calvin turned around. "What? I guess you've yet to get drunk, either."

"No, sir."

272   DANIEL GIBBS

"You want to start? I mean, Marines are known for our parties."

Calvin and Menahem snickered.

She turned a bright shade of red. "Um. No, sir."

Calvin knew that she'd been a devout Amish Christian prior to joining the CDF and decided he wouldn't push it or rib her further. *Getting soft in my old age.* "Well, how about this—you join us and drink water or whatever nonalcoholic beverage you want, and everyone else will wet down your stripes."

"I would be honored, sir."

"That's the spirit, Corporal." Calvin turned back toward the door. "Now, let's get out of here before somebody hears us talking about booze and arrests me for having an illegal moonshine still behind the barracks."

To the laughter of the others, he walked out. For the first time in a while, Calvin felt good about himself and the mission. It had cost too much, and there were too many Marines in the ground far from home. *But that's what we signed up for.* And putting unquestionably evil people down before they could kill innocents was a cause he would always take on. *No matter where. Even in some messed-up galaxy four million light-years from home.*

─────

WHILE LIFE ON A WARSHIP, especially one so far from home, occasionally felt like prison, it was nothing like the real thing, Ruth realized as hot water washed over her body. She'd taken a Hollywood shower and used five minutes of water. *But I finally feel clean.* The sonic showers provided by the Vogteks left her feeling grimier than she had in her life.

Mercy 273

And that counts my resistance days. Sometimes, it truly was the little things that mattered most.

Once she'd gotten dressed, Ruth pushed open the bathroom door to find Taylor in their stateroom. His presence shocked her, as she hadn't heard him come in. "Hey."

"Hey yourself. We haven't had much time, so I got out of watch standing today." He flashed a grin at her.

Ruth tried to return it, but her heart wasn't in the gesture. Instead, she sat down on the couch next to him. "I'm sorry. I'm not quite myself yet."

"Why would you be?" Taylor took her into his arms. "I can't imagine being in an alien prison, nor what it was like."

Part of her wanted to push him away, to insist she was strong and could handle it herself. But the warmth and love that radiated from him silenced that portion of her mind, and instead, she gave in to the embrace. "It put even those awful anktar things into perspective."

"They're an acquired taste."

All at once, Ruth gave in to her emotions. What started as a few tears and a sniffle turned into a torrent of loud, wrenching sobs. She clung to Taylor with all her might, as he did to her.

"It's okay, baby. You're safe now."

After a few minutes, she was able to get control of herself and used her shirtsleeve to wipe her eyes. "I heard you demanded to be assigned to the *Thatcher*."

Taylor tilted his head. "I would've preferred to lead a Marine unit to blow the door off that Vogtek holding facility and rescue you, but running comms during the fight seemed like a decent-enough option."

Even through the tears and pain, Ruth found his Boy Scout–like charm endearing. "No one's fought for me before," she whispered.

"You're worth it."

"Thanks." Ruth had never felt as if another person valued her like he did. She'd existed solely as a loner, intent on erasing one more ship's worth of Leaguers from the cosmos. It felt good to know she wasn't alone anymore. That prompted her to lean in and kiss him.

They sat on the small couch for a few minutes, neither saying anything, before Taylor patted her leg. "We should go eat. I heard about a traditional Jewish meal being prepared for you this evening in the officers' mess on deck three."

"Ah. You just heard about it?"

Taylor grinned. "I'm the communications officer. I... *hear* things."

Ruth laughed and blinked a few times, clearing the last of the tears from her eyes. "Oh, I'm sure you do." She stood. "Yeah, I guess I can toss on my service khakis."

"So, uh, I was thinking," Taylor said as he followed her into their bedroom.

"That's a dangerous phrase."

He snickered. "Maybe we could think about getting married on the ship."

"What?" Ruth whirled around. "Seriously?"

"You don't like that idea?"

"I mean, you have a vast family. I figured they'd all get invites. That, and we'd have to rent a sports arena to house them."

"Very funny." Taylor scrunched his nose. "Of course I'd like them to attend, but..."

"But?"

"I want to spend the rest of my life with you, and I want us to do it the right way." He wrapped his arms around her. "And I think my folks will understand when we get back. I'm sure they'll throw a big party."

Mercy 275

Ruth let her head rest on his chest. "I suppose we could talk to the chaplain. Would you be okay with the Christian chaplain, Major Estrada?"

"You wouldn't want us to have Rabbi Kravitz perform the ceremony?"

"He can't. I'm no longer a practicing Jew, and neither are you." She smiled at him.

"Oh. I figured you would want some cultural things included, like breaking the glass."

Color me impressed he looked that up. "There's no reason we can't. It's our wedding." A shiver went through her. *I can't believe I just said that.* "Better question... Where am I getting a dress?"

"I take it our dress uniforms are out."

Ruth whirled around and rolled her eyes. "*You* had better show up in one, but while I may not be the epitome of a feminine woman, this is one day in my life I *will* be."

"No complaints here."

"Oh, so you don't think I'm feminine enough?"

Taylor turned bright red. "Uh, er, no, of course you are, dear."

She giggled before playfully pinching him. "Good save." *And I could probably do a better job at that. If we weren't four million light-years from the nearest women's clothing store.*

"Who's telling the general?"

"I'm the highest-ranking, so I'll do it," Ruth replied. "And I've known him longer, so maybe he won't be as shocked if it comes from me."

"You think he'd say no?"

"If we were in the Milky Way? Of course. But here... the rules are different, as you've pointed out. I think it'll be fine."

Taylor smiled at her before kissing the top of her head.

In that moment, Ruth knew that they would be okay, no

matter what else happened around them. The feeling made her heart sing.

35

The *Lion*'s medical bay was always quieter than the rest of the ship. Something about the area seemed to dull noises and encourage silence. That was especially true after the end of the first watch. David strode through the double hatch to be greeted by the charge nurse, who came to attention.

"General, sir." Her posture was ramrod straight.

"Is Dr. Tural available?" David asked.

"Yes, sir. Should I escort you?"

David shook his head. "His general direction is fine. I need some exercise anyway."

She pointed down the passageway. "We only have two patients right now. He's making rounds."

"Thank you, Lieutenant."

He set off down the corridor, passing several empty treatment rooms. Only a few medical personnel were on duty, and a light shone through one of the doors. David pushed it open to find Dr. Tural standing between two enlisted soldiers lying in beds. Both stiffened as he entered the room.

"As you were," David said, feeling it was wrong for them to show him respect when *he* was the reason for their being in the bio beds.

"General," Dr. Tural said, "I would've greeted you if I'd known you were coming down."

David shook his head. "Informal visit. I wanted to thank Private Levine and Corporal Gonzales for their bravery and make sure they were on the mend."

"Yes, most wounds are healing well, as we were just discussing, but Corporal Gonzales's arm could not be saved. It would've represented a lifelong impairment, so we amputated it this morning."

Gonzales pulled his arm from under a blanket and waved the stump in a comical and gut-wrenching display. "Doc tells me I get a cyborg replacement."

David forced himself to laugh and flashed back to another young soldier, Doris Hunter, who'd once occupied the same medical bay. Though she'd lost three limbs. "I see. And from there, a flash-cloned replacement?"

Dr. Tural smiled. "Yes, I've already begun the process. In six months, Gonzales will be as good as new. Until then, he'll get a substitute robotic arm next week. The surgical site needs to heal for a few days before we can properly graft the circuit inputs into his nerves."

Unlike other races in the Sagittarius Arm, the Terran Coalition outlawed enhancing a human or alien body with any mechanical or neurological device that would blend man and machine. The only exceptions were for medical interventions, and they were limited to what was needed to restore full use of the damaged limb or function. While the Saurians had similar beliefs, many of the minor races and neutral human worlds had far more allowance for improvement than the Coalition.

"I'm glad to hear it." David stuck a hand into his pocket and pulled out a small velvet case. "Gents, we're a long way from the facilities that make ribbons and medals, but I felt your heroism demanded proper recognition and respect."

Levine tried to interject. "Sir, it—"

David held up his hand. "'I was just doing my job' is the refrain of the CDF, and it's the same thing I've said when being handed a citation too. But in this case, you weren't *just* doing your job. You were cleaning up my mess. And I apologize to both of you for the pain you're enduring."

Gonzales and Levine exchanged uncomfortable glances.

"Sir, I... Look, I wish my arm were still attached, and I don't look forward to the recovery. But, sir, I signed up for this. The run you took at the Vogteks was a volunteer assignment. There's nothing to apologize for. It's an honor to serve with you, and I believe you and the rest of our officers will do their best to get us home."

"What Gonzales said, sir." Levine chuckled.

David tried to smile but felt emotion welling up. Determined not to show it, he clenched his jaw. "Thank you. Well, I'll leave you to the healing hands of Dr. Tural. Good day, gentlemen."

"Ah, I am but a humble servant of Allah. He alone works through my hands to bring peace. I was wrapping up, General. Please, I'll walk out with you."

After a final goodbye, David strode out of the room and back into the passageway.

Once he'd closed the door, Dr. Tural gestured toward the front of the medical bay and shook his head. "I sense you are taking a great deal of guilt on yourself, sir."

David nodded. "Yes. It is incredible how a single lapse in judgment can cause all this chaos. Not to mention a reminder that I'm quite fallible."

"We all need that from time to time." Dr. Tural smiled and put his hand on David's shoulder. "Don't take all of this on yourself. I was in the room when the decision was made, and these aliens were beyond unreasonable. Perhaps you should consider talking to someone."

"A counselor, you mean."

He nodded. "Yes, or a close friend. Rabbi Kravitz... or me, if you feel comfortable. Don't hold these emotions in."

"If we were in the Sagittarius Arm, I'd call an old friend who also treated me for several years. But she isn't here, and I don't want to start rumors that the fleet's commanding officer needs mental help."

"You know that's not how others look at it, sir." Dr. Tural frowned. "Keeping up with your mind is just as important as keeping up with the body."

"For now, it'll have to be Rabbi Kravitz. Perhaps Miss Bo'hai."

"The Zeivlot linguist?" Dr. Tural asked in surprise.

"We've become friends. She has this odd way of listening to what I have to say."

They stopped in front of the double hatch leading back to the rest of the ship.

"It only matters that you process things, sir. How you do it and with whom... is for you to decide."

"Make sure Levine and Gonzales get the care they need. Regardless of what it is, we'll get the raw materials."

"God willing, they will make a complete recovery."

David inclined his head. "Thank you, Doctor. Godspeed."

"Godspeed to you, too, sir."

Walking through the corridor toward the gravlift, David still felt a weight on his soul. It felt similar to how it had after they'd lost members of the crew, Marines, and pilots

Mercy 281

during their intervention at Zeivlot and Zavlot. *Some of this is simply the cost of being in command. As for the rest... I should visit the shul more often. More importantly, I need to ask HaShem for wisdom. If He grants it, I can make better decisions and not put the fleet in danger.* Sometimes, David wished he would have yet another personal experience with God, even though the first had terrified him.

The doors swooshed open, revealing the empty lift. *Not today, apparently.*

———

REPAIRS on the *Margaret Thatcher* continued apace, and David found the time to do a few things he felt needed attention, such as have one-on-one conversations with Hanson, Ruth, and Al-Haddad to apologize privately. Hanson had been first, followed by Al-Haddad. For whatever reason, Ruth had been scheduled last.

The entry buzzer on David's day cabin went off, and he glanced up from his paperwork to see the appointed time had arrived. "Come!"

A moment later, the hatch swung open, and Ruth stepped through. She came to attention before his desk. "Captain Goldberg reports as ordered, sir."

"At ease. Have a seat," David replied as he gestured toward the side chairs. "And drop the ranks."

Ruth slid into the closest one to the desk and tilted her head. "I take it something is on your mind, sir."

David sucked in a breath. "I owe you an apology for sending the shuttle in to mine the helium-3. It was the wrong decision, and it could've gotten a lot of people killed. You guys went through hell, and that's on me. Please forgive me."

"There's nothing to forgive, sir. I would probably have made the same call. The only difference between us is I would've lit the Vogteks up." She shrugged. "And regretted it later."

"I've done a lot of soul-searching."

"That's kind of your thing, sir." Ruth grinned. "It all worked out. My mother used to say that the poor get their ice in the winter, and the rich get their ice in the summer. Everything evens out in the end. No one died—how you pulled that off is beyond me—and the *Thatcher* is fixed up almost as good as new. I heard through RUMINT that the aliens have been examining our religious texts and talking with the chaplains too."

"Yes, they wanted to understand the concept of mercy." David steepled his fingers. "We'll see if it sticks. I think the object lesson got through to them, at least partially."

"It's difficult to change how you view the universe and wide-ranging cultural norms."

"Maybe Colonel Demood is having an easier time of it."

Ruth snorted. "We both know that's unlikely."

"We live in hope."

They both laughed before Ruth turned serious. "This will sound nuts, sir, but I feel like we're supposed to be in this galaxy, doing these things we stumble into. Obviously, I can't back that up with anything besides my emotions, but... look at the Zeivlots and the Zavlots. They were on a horrible path."

"Dr. Hayworth would say we're just trying to impose our beliefs on others and interfering with the evolution of alien species."

"What do *you* say, sir?"

"That there's a fine line between meddling in affairs we have no business in and trying to guide people to a better way of looking at themselves and the universe. I'm trying to navigate it as best I can and get us home."

Ruth nodded. "We're all muddling through." She paused before meeting his eyes. "I have something I need to ask."

"What's on your mind?"

"It's about Robert and me, sir. We... Ah, well... We'd like to get married before returning home."

David blinked. He knew they shared quarters but hadn't thought much of it outside the obvious. A decent number of crewmembers were, the last time he heard the statistic from Master Chief Tinetariro. "A wedding... on the *Lion of Judah*?"

Ruth's cheeks turned bright red. "I know, sir. It seems somewhat ridiculous when you say it out loud."

"Well, if we were anywhere besides a different galaxy, four and a half million light-years from home, yes." David flashed a smile. "But since we are, if that's what you two want, we'll make it happen. Gotta be a cargo bay we can clear out. Maybe get a Marine shuttle to use as your honeymoon ride."

"Uh, sure, sir. I was thinking more something small."

David spread his hands out on the desk. "That works too. I'll make sure the chief mess steward saves enough flour to bake a cake. Lieutenant Taylor is a good man, you know. He was ready to lead a commando team himself to bust you out of prison."

"I know." Ruth's face was in danger of turning permanently red.

"Well, I'm sure we'll be able to work out all the details in the coming weeks... months?"

Ruth grinned. "No date set yet. That's next. And don't worry, sir. We won't be trying to have a baby on a warship."

"Depending on how long we're stuck out here, we might

have to examine becoming a generational vessel," David replied. *There are many possibilities.*

"Let's avoid thinking about that for now."

David chuckled. "Agreed. Thank you for coming down."

Ruth stood. "I found it interesting, sir, that you used the reasoning that God has mercy on all of us. The law demands incredible strictness. I mean, there is that small matter of being unable to tear toilet paper on the Sabbath."

"And I still have my tissue dispenser." Since the motion of tearing was considered work, it could not be performed on the Sabbath. However, pulling a piece of already-cut tissue from a holder was ruled by the rabbinate not to be an act of work. "I've always felt that God demonstrated mercy constantly throughout His actions, as recorded in the Tanakh."

"It seemed to me like you were using a Christian argument with the Vogteks, arguing for doing good to others when they wronged you."

"While I will certainly concede that Jesus preached mercy... so does the Tanakh. Look at King David. He was a man who, while being described as having a heart devoted to HaShem, also conspired to get a man killed so that he could take his wife. Among many other things that don't exactly highlight moral Jewish behavior under the law."

"That's a good point, sir."

David peered at her. "Your conversion has stuck, hasn't it?"

"Yes, it has. To my surprise, I actually feel like I have a relationship with God now." Ruth shrugged. "I'm still a work in progress."

"We all are." David stood and crossed the few steps to be next to her. "It's been a long, brutal road the last twenty-five years."

Mercy   285

"Not that the one we're on now isn't just as hard."

David extended his hand, but Ruth sidestepped it and hugged him instead. He awkwardly allowed the embrace and gave her a squeeze.

Ruth moved back after dropping her arms. "We're going to get home, sir."

"Count on it." David grinned. "Now, I'd better get back to filling out my after-action reports. I believe you have a watch to stand."

"Yes, sir."

As she walked through the hatch, David returned to his desk. He wondered what General MacIntosh would think of the situation, if someday he read the reports. *I wager he'd give me a good dressing down then make some snarky comment about all the universe needs is a race of legalistic trial lawyers descending on it.* With a chuckle, he got back to work, glad to soon be heading out into the cosmos once more.

36

CSV *Lion of Judah*
Jinvaas System
6 June 2464

As the *Lion of Judah* and the rest of the fleet returned to normal, the weekly department and science briefing resumed. David had looked forward to it for most of the day, even though he usually detested meetings. Though the situation had ended in a way that could be considered positive, he still felt apprehensive. *It was a far closer thing than it should've been, and that's on me.*

David exchanged salutes with the Marine sentries in the command-deck passageway as he exited his day cabin. He pushed open the hatch to the conference room to reveal a sea of people, including the senior officers, Dr. Hayworth, Amir, Major Merriweather, and Dr. Tural.

"General on deck!" Master Chief Tinetariro barked as she came to attention.

Mercy 287

"As you were." David gave them a moment to sit back down before he slid into his seat at the head of the table. "Well. I think I speak for all of us when I thank HaShem and the crew of the CSV *Margaret Thatcher* for the return of Major Hanson, Captain Goldberg, and Chief Warrant Officer Al-Haddad."

"The Prophet smiled on our efforts," Aibek rumbled. "And the Iron Lady did not turn."

Ruth chuckled. "Didn't realize you were up on old earth politicians, Colonel."

"I make a study of the names you humans give your warships. Saurians only name them after warriors who won a battle or acted heroically during victorious combat." He raised an eye scale. "Humans seem to name space vessels after anything that strikes their fancy. Politicians, warriors, places... it is difficult to understand the convention."

David grinned and shook his head. "That's humanity for you. Each block of us has its own ideas on how to do things. The Saratoga-class fleet carriers, for instance. Americans built them, and they're all named after former presidents of either the United States on Earth or the US colonies within the Terran Coalition. Hey, it keeps us on our toes."

"Well, I'm glad to be back to our crappy Zeivlot vegetables and what passes for meat," Hanson interjected. "Vogtek food was so awful that I looked forward to combat rations."

"Forget the food. The poetry was worse." Ruth made a face.

"Poetry?" David asked. *I wonder what alien poetry sounds like.*

"Well, sir, I'm not a huge poetry fan. More into blowing things up," she replied. "But they piped this stuff over our translation units every night for an hour. It was awful. I

288 DANIEL GIBBS

wanted to smash the earpieces, but the custodians promised to punish us if we didn't listen."

While her tone was light, David couldn't help but feel a pang of guilt. He pushed it down and focused on the tasks ahead. "How are the *Thatcher*'s repairs coming?"

Hanson leaned forward. "Completed this morning, sir. She's ready to get underway and has resumed formation with us."

David nodded. "Outstanding. We're going to end up with another passenger. An Otyran scientist. In exchange for taking him aboard and allowing him to participate in the exchange program we worked out with the Zeivlots and the Zavlots, we'll get all the helium-3 we need."

"Sir, as I'm ultimately responsible for security on the *Lion*, I need to remind you that all races in this system have a reason to want exposure to our vessel. They need better FTL technology," Tinetariro interjected.

"Oh, I realize that, Master Chief. But we need friends out here." David grinned. "Make sure the masters-at-arms are on their toes. No one who isn't cleared gets inside the engineering spaces. Period."

"Yes, sir."

Hayworth cleared his throat. "One of the more intelligent things to be said recently in this room."

"Thank you, Doctor."

"I mean it as a compliment, General." A rare smile creased Hayworth's lips. "If I keep saying it enough, perhaps my noninterference beliefs will imbed themselves."

"We did try to change this alliance of species's outlook on justice and mercy, Doctor."

"Yes, quite." Hayworth harrumphed. "At least you didn't hand them Lawrence drive schematics."

Give me some credit, Doctor. David only flashed a grin.

"I think we made a difference," Ruth said as she placed her hands on the table. "And even though my experience in the Vogtek prison wasn't pleasant, if that's what it took to introduce some better ideas to a society... so be it."

"Oh, we're now the arbiters of what's better?"

Ruth narrowed her eyes and stared back at Hayworth. "Doctor, locking somebody up for twenty years for stealing a protein bar isn't just. You know that."

He shrugged. "By my standards and yours. How this society handles itself isn't any of our business." Hayworth wagged his finger. "If there's one charge about the Terran Coalition that is negative and has weight, it's that we impose our views on others."

"There's no imposition here. We simply offered an object lesson in a better way. It's not like we're soft in the crime department," David replied.

"Compared to the Vogteks, the *League* is soft on crime," Aibek interjected.

A wave of laughter followed.

"Absolutely right, XO." *I'm glad he's back to his joking self.* "The council has promised us the first helium-3 shipment before we head out. They also offered shore leave, which I declined for obvious reasons."

Tinetariro made a face. "Half of this bunch would end up in lockup."

David again had to suppress laughter. *It's probably too soon.* The jovial mood contrasted with the two injured soldiers still being treated for severe wounds in the medical bay. *But that's my burden to bear, not theirs.* "Where are we with the artifact research, Doctor?"

Hayworth eyed him and Hanson. "Once the force field was bolstered, I continued my experiments. Partial power got through to the device, and we were able to retrieve a set of coordinates from it. I believe they are the location of the precursor race's home world."

Many people's jaws dropped.

"Burying the lede there, Doctor."

"I try not to brag," Hayworth replied, grinning. "But my ego doesn't write checks it can't cash."

Another round of chuckles swept the room.

First Lieutenant Shelly Hammond, the *Lion's* navigator, interjected, "How far away from our present position, Doctor?"

"With proper cooldown between jumps, roughly two weeks."

"That's a bit of a journey but well worth it." David stroked his chin. Sextans B, compared to the Milky Way, was a compact galaxy. Otherwise, the journey could've been out of reach.

"Perhaps we can avoid interfering with any more alien species for a while." Hayworth's tone was gruff, but at least his expression seemed amused. "At some point, our luck is going to run out. I'm surprised it hasn't already."

"That's because luck has nothing to do with it, Doctor," Tinetariro replied. "The reason is clear... the *Lion of Judah* is doing God's work." Her deep English accent seemed to come out more.

"Ah, yes, I prefer to stick to provable answers. That one doesn't qualify."

David acted before any further debate could break out. *Not what we need today.* "So, the *Thatcher's* good to go, the rest of the battlegroup is shipshape, and we're ready to move out tomorrow morning for a journey that will, I hope, give us some answers. That about sum it up?"

Heads nodded around the table.

"Good. Then let's get back to work, and give thanks to

Mercy 291

HaShem, Jesus, Allah, or the random chance of the universe, because we shouldn't be where we are right now." David flashed a smile as he stood. "Dismissed."

The sea of uniformed soldiers filed out along with Hayworth in his white lab coat. In some ways, it was the doctor's uniform, David reflected.

Once the conference room had cleared, he returned to his day cabin and busied himself with his remaining paperwork. *I can't escape filling out CDF forms, even four and a half million light-years from home.* He supposed since no one would be checking, there was no need to do the various after-action reports, write-ups, and documentation, but staying in a routine was comforting.

Hours later, after he'd visited the shul for evening prayers, David ended up in his favorite officers' mess, enjoying a quiet late dinner. In the middle of chewing a bite of food, he glanced up to see Bo'hai and her purple hair, standing with a tray.

"May I join you?"

David quickly swallowed. "Um, sure."

She put her food on the table and sat. "Another long day?"

"They're all long." David flashed a grin and took a drink of water. "You?"

"My life is so different now. I used to teach, you know. That was my profession. Advanced linguistics. I'd never signed up for something more than a few hours from home before I joined the Life Search team... and now, here I am. Exploring the stars and translating languages from species with six limbs." She chuckled. "If I stop to think about it, I'm instantly overwhelmed."

"I feel the same way about how we ended up here."

She took a bite of a vegetable medley and munched

happily. "Mmm. Your spices are so different from ours. I like them."

David couldn't help but smile. "Food is a universal thing, isn't it? All species have to eat something to stay alive, and it's typically at the heart of most cultures."

"It is amazing that you were able to resolve the situation without loss of life on either side," Bo'hai said between bites. "I am impressed."

"The credit goes to the officers and crew of the *Margaret Thatcher* and Dr. Hayworth."

Bo'hai shook her head. "You... What's the human expression? Sell yourself empty?"

"Short." David chuckled then took another sip of water.

"You inspire them, General. Even if you don't realize it."

David pursed his lips. "I'm the one who got us *into* this mess in the first place. So I appreciate what you're trying to do, but the fact is I screwed up. And it's enough to remind me that even a small, seemingly insignificant misstep from the Mitzvot can result in disaster."

"'He that covers his sins shall not prosper. But whoever confesses and forsakes them shall have mercy.'"

"Proverbs... chapter twenty-eight, verse thirteen, if I remember right," David replied. "You're reading the Tanakh."

She nodded. "Yes. I rather like it."

"Why?"

Bo'hai shrugged. "I wanted to compare human beliefs to ours. Starting with Judaism made sense because you were the one who orchestrated stopping the destruction of our worlds."

"Trust in the Lord with all your heart, and lean not into your own understanding. In all thy ways, acknowledge Him, and He shall direct your path."

Mercy 293

"That is also from Proverbs. Our holy text has a similar sentiment: 'All concern and worry should be given to the Maker. He will guide our path.'"

David let out a sigh. "I could do a much better job trusting in HaShem. It is one of my biggest failings as a Jew. More often, first, I focus on myself and what I feel like I can do."

"Is tomorrow not a new day?"

"Of course."

"Then resolve to make a change." Bo'hai smiled.

David appreciated how easy it was to talk to her. *It's comforting to be able to discuss some of these burdens.* "Why don't you drop by the shul sometime during a service if you're interested in learning more about Jewish customs."

Bo'hai tilted her head. "I would be allowed in?"

"Of course. Remember to cover your hair, and if it's an Orthodox service, the women must sit separately from the men."

She nodded. "I will sometime. Perhaps I will see you there."

"It's entirely possible." David took the final bite of his food and felt content. They'd survived, gotten the fuel the fleet needed, and perhaps done something positive along the way. *Even though I screwed up. Yes, maybe the master chief is right. We're out here doing God's work. The best explanation I've got so far anyway. Tomorrow is a new day with infinite possibilities,* as Bo'hai said. *"This is the day the Lord has made. Let us rejoice and be glad in it."*

EPILOGUE

CDF Shipyard Complex
Churchill – Sagittarius Arm
10 June, 2464

VIRTUALLY EVERY NIGHT, Kenneth Lowe left his office by seventeen thirty hours for a shuttle ride down to the surface. He'd been dating Catherine Owens for months, and while they didn't live together, nor had he asked her to marry him, Kenneth felt it was essential to stick to a schedule conducive to family life.

But not tonight. Instead of a thirty-minute hop down to Churchill, Kenneth sat in his office, speaking with Dr. Peter Saunders. A member of the Coalition Scientific Union, Saunders had some unique theories about faster-than-light travel, which was why Kenneth had recruited the scientist to review the CDF's official findings around the disappearance of the *Lion of Judah.*

Saunders also had a less-than-stellar reputation in the Coalition.

Kenneth leaned back, appraising the man. "So, thanks for taking the time to meet with me this evening."

"It's not every day you get a personal invitation from the CEO of Stridescliff Shipboard Integrators." Saunders smirked. "Then again, work's hard to come by these days. What exactly is it you need? Covert weapons research or something?"

Kenneth shook his head. "No. I have a particular research division focused on the *Lion of Judah* and the circumstances of her loss."

"You read my paper."

"Yes. Unique theories, to say the least."

Saunders narrowed his eyes. "Is this an officially sanctioned program? Or are you doing it off the books?"

An interesting question. Kenneth licked his lips, trying to find the best way to respond. "Perhaps a bit of both. I'm receiving some funding from the highest reaches of the CDF, but it's... quiet."

"Ah, the plot thickens! And you want me because I think the ship survived."

Kenneth nodded. "Yes, you're one of the few published researchers I could find who support that theory."

"There is no way I could've been at the top of your list."

Right again. Kenneth had already talked to everyone else. They'd all refused to work for SSI or on a program to find the *Lion*. *Probably think it's career suicide.* "Well, you know how these things go. Next man up and all."

"No sane individual would touch this with a ten-meter pole." Saunders snickered. "But I'm not sane, or at least, I'm nuts enough to consider it. My career is already trash since my last paper on time travel."

"You mentioned something about the negative energy interacting with a Lawrence drive."

Saunders tilted his head. "I did. There were traces of negative energy in the publicly released science report. I suspect there's a lot more in the scanner logs from PASCORE. Which are classified, but I bet you have access to them." A smile spread across his lips. "Don't you, Mr. Lowe?"

"It's possible." Kenneth tried to portray his best poker face.

"Mm-hm." Saunders steepled his fingers. "What would my role be again?"

"Chief researcher. I want to figure out definitively whether the *Lion* survived."

"I believe she did. With the basic calculations of possible energy output from the publicly released findings, it's likely the wormhole generated had a destination of five to ten million light-years from here."

Kenneth's jaw dropped. "*What?*"

"It's a simple calculation of the output of the vessel's reactor and Lawrence drive coupled with the trace amounts of negative energy. The potential is incredible. You're talking, at a minimum, a type-two civilization on the Kardashev scale."

"I'm sorry, but what's that?" *This high-end science stuff is a bit over my head. I fix ships for a living.*

"It's a measure of how much energy a civilization can harness. Type two is equivalent to a star, while type three could theoretically use the entire power output of a galaxy."

Kenneth blinked. "That's pretty insane."

"Basic science, Mr. Lowe."

"I take it you believe it's not a natural phenomenon?"

Saunders shook his head. "Almost assuredly not. You

have to realize, though, that a race capable of this sort of technology is so far ahead of us..." He shrugged. "It'd be like your showing up on ancient earth with a particle-beam weapon. They'd think you were either a god or performing magic."

"There are no known races like what you describe in this galaxy. That we're aware of, anyway."

"The key word there is *aware*. Our knowledge of the galaxy is limited. The war with the League diverted most of our exploration resources. The truth is we don't know what else is out there." Saunders leaned forward. "If you could get me the PASCORE data or, even better, a scan set going back a few years, I could look for traces of this signature. It's possible we could find evidence of a highly advanced race. Or even that they used to exist here and died out."

"I could probably obtain access to classified xenoarchaeological data."

Saunders grinned. "There you go, thinking like a conspiracy theorist."

Kenneth raised an eyebrow. "I don't think so."

"When you investigate oddball theories as long as I do, you get some oddball beliefs. Ask me sometime how humanoids managed to pop up all over the galaxy."

This guy is probably nuts. But he seems intelligent and has references that aren't horrible and a willingness to take some risks. Exactly what I need. "Is there anything in your background that would preclude you from passing a CDF security-clearance investigation?"

"As long as my paper on time travel doesn't disqualify me, no. It's not like I go around promoting the overthrow of the government."

"Excellent. I'll work out your compensation-package

details and get an offer over." Kenneth stood. "Thank you for coming in."

Saunders stood as well. "I'm looking forward to this assignment. Finally, something fun to do in the lab."

"Discretion will be paramount in this position, Dr. Saunders."

"As in I can't talk about it?"

"No. I'm under strict orders by the Joint Chiefs of Staff to keep it all under wraps." Kenneth extended his hand.

Saunders shook it warmly. "I'll keep that in mind. Good day, Mr. Lowe."

As the scientist walked out, Kenneth returned to his seat. *I sure hope this works out. In more ways than one.* He felt as if he owed David and the entire crew of the *Lion* a debt. While they'd saved the Terran Coalition repeatedly, it felt more profound than that to him. *Which is probably why General MacIntosh picked me for this assignment.* He glanced at the chronometer on the wall. *Nineteen hundred hours. Time for me to head home.* The thought of a call to Catherine during the shuttle ride brought a smile to his face.

The Lost Warship: Book 3 – Valor:
General David Cohen is faced with an impossible choice,
when a malevolent force impervious to CDF weaponry
comes to light: Break every oath he holds dear or witness
the complete annihilation of all life in the universe.
Now available on Amazon!
Tap HERE to read NOW!

THE END

ALSO AVAILABLE FROM DANIEL GIBBS

Battlegroup Z

Book 1 - Weapons Free

Book 2 - Hostile Spike

Book 3 - Sol Strike

Book 4 - Bandits Engaged

Book 5 - Iron Hand

Book 6 - Final Flight

Echoes of War

Book 1 - Fight the Good Fight

Book 2 - Strong and Courageous

Book 3 - So Fight I

Book 4 - Gates of Hell

Book 5 - Keep the Faith

Book 6 - Run the Gauntlet

Book 7 - Finish the Fight

The Lost Warship

Book 1 - Adrift

Book 2 - Mercy

Book 3 - Valor

Book 4 - Justice (Coming in 2023)

Book 5 - Resolve (Coming in 2023)

Book 6 - Faith (Coming in 2023)

Breach of Faith

(With Gary T. Stevens)

Book 1 - Breach of Peace

Book 2 - Breach of Faith

Book 3 - Breach of Duty

Book 4 - Breach of Trust

Book 5 - Spacer's Luck

Book 6 - Fortune's Favor

Book 7 - The Iron Dice

Deception Fleet

(With Steve Rzasa)

Book 1 - Victory's Wake

Book 2 - Cold Conflict

Book 3 - Hazards Near

Book 4 - Liberty's Price

Book 5 - Ecliptic Flight

Book 6 - Collision Vector

Courage, Commitment, Faith: Tales from the Coalition Defense Force

(Anthology Series)

Volume One

ACKNOWLEDGMENTS

Here we are, with yet another novel. This marks thirty-one.

I continue to be astounded, humbled, and downright gobsmacked over reader reaction to my universe, and how the words continue to flow.

Thank you all for your support - and especially those who assist me in preparing these novels for publication.

To those who have helped along the way - thank you from the bottom of my heart. You know who you are.

To the servicemen and women of the US military, especially the US Navy and Marine Corps, that I have had the honor of working with for the past 15 years, thank you for your service. Because of you, I can write these novels and say anything I want. All too often, we collectively take this for granted.

Finally, it is fitting (and always will be) to thank God for the ability to write these novels, and bring the universe of the Terran Diaspora to life.

And, but certainly not least - a special thanks to all of my Kickstarter Backers for The Lost Warship, and especially:

Brian Clairmont

Avi Beidani
Lonnie Bristol
Alexander Roth
Christopher Hayes
Lewis Brande
Oridon

Thank you all - and we'll do it again soon!

Godspeed,

Daniel Gibbs

Printed in Great Britain
by Amazon